Aloha Cowboy

An Island Cowboy Novel

Aloha Cowboy

LEXI POST

NY TIMES & USA TODAY BESTSELLING AUTHOR

Aloha Cowboy
Island Cowboy Series Book 1

By Lexi Post

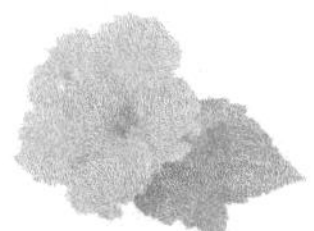

Sometimes being a Pennington can be a disadvantage.

Cordell Pennington considers himself a simple cowboy and he doesn't want to be in Hawaii. He doesn't even want to be on vacation, until he meets Leah Pennington, the manager of The Puanani Resort. What intrigues him is not that they have the same last name or that they are both from Arizona. It's her habit of vacillating between a professional façade and her personal self that has him taking notice.

Leah's breathless moment at seeing a cowboy at the reception desk is as much caused by concern as excitement. Upon meeting Cord, she is happy to help him enjoy his stay, as long as it stays professional. But their constant proximity, thanks to her job, and Cord's kindness, is taking a toll on her willpower, until she not only finds herself falling for him, but even reveals her reason for never returning to Arizona.

As Cord's vacation draws to a close, he's determined to convince Leah they could have a future together despite the miles that separate them. But when his own secret is revealed, the ocean between them is the least of his troubles.

For updates, sneak peeks, and special prizes, sign up to receive the latest news from Lexi
http://bit.ly/LexiUpdate

Acknowledgments

For Bob Fabich, Sr., my favorite vacation partner. And for my sister Paige Wood, who is also fun to vacation with. I'm so lucky!

A huge thank you to Kumu Carolyn Derrico for all her expertise on Hawaii. I now hear the beautiful language in my head thanks to her, plus I understand so much more about those wonderful islands and warm people.

Thank you to my steadfast friend and critique partner, Marie Patrick, for her willingness to both listen to the story as I come up with ideas and read it as I write it.

Lastly, thank you to Pamela Todd, Lisa Fishback and KC Crocker for reviewing this story one last time. They are *hoalohas* I couldn't do without.

Author's Note

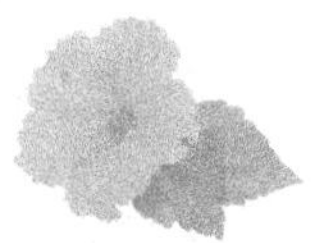

Aloha Cowboy was inspired by Bret Harte's short story, "Found at Blazing Star" published in 1882. In Harte's story, after a particularly rainy night, a gold miner by the name of Cassius Beard discovers a plain gold band in the mud with an inscription inside that reads, *May to Cass.* Being as superstitious as the next miner, he believes it's meant for him since it has his nickname "Cass" engraved on it, so he drops it into his pocket, hiding it. He keeps his secret of the ring safe, afraid of ridicule from the others, but he tells a few other miners who are his friends.

About six months later he's panning in the bush and finds himself on the road to Red Chief when a young woman by the name of Ms. Porter, riding by on her horse, calls him to see what she's discovered —a dead body. Cass lifts the head and they realize the man was shot. Ms. Porter fetches the coroner and as he inspects the body, Ms. Porter find's Cass's ring, which the coroner keeps as part of the investigation. Ms. Porter eventually charms the magistrate into giving the ring back to Cass.

Months later, an ad in the local newspaper requests whoever found the ring to come to Red Chief to receive a thousand-dollar reward. Cass meets the woman who placed the ad and agrees to show her where he found "her" ring and where the dead man had lain. She asks to be alone and while Cass is waiting, Ms. Porter finds him and tells him the woman is a fraud. They are too late to find the woman, but they discover what she was after, the stolen Wells Fargo treasure from a robbery over a year earlier, the dead man being one of the robbers. Cass, thanks to Ms. Porter is heralded as a hero.

But what if the found object was another person with the same last name in the least likely of places? Would that mean they belonged together, or would one lose his treasure as well? How could he possibly get it back with no Ms. Porter to help?

Chapter One

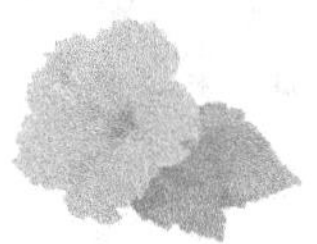

Leah Pennington picked up her pace at the sound of a guest's raised voice in the open-air lobby of the Puanani Resort.

Who was at the front desk today? Oh, no, it was Ulu. He was probably making his interest in the male guest far too clear. Stepping around the corner, she sucked in her breath.

Aloha cowboy. Emotions swirled within her, from excitement at seeing the back of a broad-shouldered cowboy who reminded her of home, to fear he might be someone she knew.

Gathering her professional persona like a shield, she continued toward the front desk and glanced at the man next to the cowboy, his black hair tied back in a short ponytail. Two such muscular men visiting Momi would be hot news and all over this side of the island by tomorrow morning. With only fifty thousand residents, the presence of handsome tourists spread fast. Giving Ulu a quick reprimand with her gaze, she stepped behind the counter to face the guests with a confident smile.

She held her smile by force of habit, barely stopping her eyes from widening in surprise. The two men, around her age, couldn't look more opposite. The cowboy's deep green eyes were crinkled at the corners as if he found something amusing. His nose was straight, his lips a pale mauve and his chin hard. As he doffed his hat at her appearance, he revealed very short brown hair, which though shaved close above his ears was thick about his head. In his white shirt with western pockets and sleeves rolled up to his elbows, along with his new blue jeans, his appearance sent a pang of homesickness tugging at her heart.

The other man, just as tall and broad, had bright blue eyes shadowed by his dark lowered brows. His nose was slender, though also straight, his lips fuller and his cheek bones were far more prominent. The darkness of his hair was accented by his tight black t-shirt and blue jeans. He was the first to address her.

"*Mademoiselle*, there's been a mistake. I sincerely hope you can rectify it." The irritated tone was no surprise since he'd been dealing with Ulu, who continued to gaze at the men as if they were his own personal eye-candy.

What was a surprise was the guest's accent. He used a French word, but he didn't sound like any guest they'd had from France. "I'm sure we can take care of everything." She moved her gaze to Ulu and raised her brow. "Let me see what we have."

Ulu pouted before reluctantly turning away and disappearing into the small office behind the counter. She had no doubt he would be glued to the two-way window at one end to further ogle their guests.

She stood in front of the reservation screen and quickly read it through. Pennington? Her heart leapt again. Everyone in Arizona knew that name, the very same as her own. She wanted to ask if he was one of *the* Penningtons, but since she hated people asking her that, she kept her question to herself. She looked directly at the cowboy. "Mr. Pennington, I see you have the honeymoon suite."

He grinned sheepishly. "Yes, my sister, Hailey, booked the room. She sent me to scout your resort as a possible place for her to hold her wedding."

She smiled more warmly at that exciting news. "Oh, she would love it here. I'll be happy to show you what we can do for her." A wedding at the Puanani would be good for their precipitous bottom line. Auntie would be thrilled if they could make it happen.

"Let me see what the problem might be." She looked over the reservation, but there was only one name. Understanding dawned. Ulu thought the two men were gay, which was right up his alley. She hoped he hadn't ruined their chance to impress the men. He was too forward since his last break up. She'd have to talk to Auntie about his behavior…again.

Just to make sure, she looked at the dark-haired gentleman. "I'm guessing you two are not together?"

"Yes."

"No." The cowboy raised an eyebrow at his friend.

She cocked her head. "I think I'm confused."

Mr. Pennington smiled at her, showing perfect white teeth. She wasn't sure if the yearning in her belly was for home or him. She blinked quickly to clear her head.

The cowboy looked at her name tag before speaking. "Leah, we are together in that we're friends and traveling together, but we expected there to be two rooms."

"Oh, then perhaps there are." She bent her head and prepared to type. "What's the other name?"

"Philippe du Bourbon," the other man replied. As his deep voice with the accent hit her, she bit her lip to keep from chuckling.

Bourbon? Really? She keyed in the name and came up with no reservation. Shoot, not good. She quickly moved through a few more screens, finally finding what she needed—an open room, sort of.

She lifted her head and smiled at Mr. Pennington before moving her gaze to Mr. du Bourbon. "The reservation was only for one room, but there's no problem. I have another I can give you. How long are you staying?" Her gaze drifted back toward the cowboy, probably because he kept his sense of humor, and it was easier looking at a smile than a frown.

He replied for them. "I'm here for a couple weeks, but Phil will be staying longer, right?"

Phil nodded. "At least a month. Is your free room available that long?"

She nodded. "It is, but I'm afraid it's in another building. However, we are a very small resort, only twenty rooms, so it won't be hard to find each other."

"Is there a chance you have a normal room for me in that building? Maybe something less expensive?" The cowboy, who was quite tall, looked toward the computer as if he could see what was listed there. "I don't know what my sister was thinking."

She shook her head. She didn't want him to know that the room she'd found for his friend had been on tentative hold for a personal friend of hers and was the only one left.

"Not at the moment, but I might in a few days if you want to move."

"Yes. I don't mind moving."

She moved her fingers over the keyboard, making adjustments. She wasn't surprised he wanted a less expensive room. Some of her old friends back home were cowboys and they didn't exactly make a ton of money. Then again, neither did she. It also meant he'd answered her question. He was definitely not one of the original families who settled in Arizona. *Those* Penningtons were ridiculously rich.

When the computer gave her the confirmation screen, she smiled. "All set. Let me get you your keys and a map of the property. We're small, but we have a lot to offer."

She looked down to pull a couple maps from the shelf below when a hand touched her shoulder. She ducked beneath it and turned to face whoever was behind her. "Oh, Auntie." She turned toward their new guests. "Gentlemen, this is Auntie Loke, one of the owners of The Puanani."

The older woman grinned widely, her gaze quickly taking in the eye-candy in front of her. "It's a pleasure to have you."

Leah handed each man a map. "Auntie, Mr. Pennington's sister has sent him to investigate the Puanani as a possible place for her wedding."

Auntie's gaze turned calculating. She was a shrewd business woman and hadn't kept the boutique hotel going by missing opportunities. "Pennington? Are you from Arizona?"

The cowboy nodded. "Yes, ma'am."

"Then you must know Leah."

Oh shoot. Leah sucked in her breath.

"I'm sorry ma'am. The state has millions of people in it. I'm afraid I just met Leah."

Auntie shook her head. "I thought with the same last names that maybe you were related. Oh well, you know each other now."

The cowboy's gaze snapped to hers. "You're a Pennington as well?"

"Yes. And no, I'm not one of *the* Penningtons."

He laughed. "I see you get that question a lot, too. People seem to think there's only one Pennington family in the whole state."

She nodded before she pulled out two room cards and swiped them through the machine to activate each for the appropriate room.

Auntie scanned the area. "Where's Ulu? He has the front desk today."

Before she could say anything, the man bopped out of the office.

"I'm right here, and I'll be happy to show you the way to your room." He gave Phil a wink.

Leah groaned silently as their guest stiffened.

"Nonsense, you man the desk. That's your job." Auntie swiped up the small folder with the room number and key inside and sauntered out from behind the check-in desk. "I will show…" She glanced back.

Leah supplied the name. "Mr. du Bourbon."

Auntie raised her brows before she gave the man a warm smile. "Is that French?"

The man loosened up for the first time since Leah had

seen him. He nodded politely and held his arm out for Auntie. "It is. I am Phillipe, but my friends call me Phil."

As her boss escorted Phil away, she finished inserting the honeymoon suite key into the folder. "Here you go, Mr. Pennington." She held out the folder.

"Please, call me Cord. Let's leave the whole Pennington business behind us." He winked.

Her heart fluttered in her chest just like it had when she was in high school. How dumb was that? She was a grown woman who'd grown up among cowboys. It had to be the reminder of home that caused her breath to catch.

Ulu started to walk past her. "I'd be happy to show you where your room is, Cord."

She stepped back, cutting off his escape from behind the desk. "You heard Auntie."

Ulu pouted as his shoulders fell. "You take all the fun out of my job."

Cord laughed.

She gave him a relieved smile, thrilled he didn't mind Ulu's forwardness. "The suite is at the other end of the property. Would you like me to call a staff member to bring your bag for you?"

He shook his head. "No, just you to lead the way."

She gave him a quick nod before moving out from behind the counter. "It's this way." She opened her arm toward the archway that led to the pool courtyard at the center of the property.

Cord threw his duffle bag over his shoulder, the muscles in his forearm moving in stark relief as he settled it on his back before he donned his hat and gave her a nod.

She turned to focus on their direction, her belly tightening at how even more attractive he was with his hat on. No wonder Ulu was practically salivating. She didn't have to wonder if Cord followed because the sound of his cowboy boots on the tile was loud enough for the guests by the pool to look.

As she led him around the flower-shaped pool toward the Hibiscus building, Deidre Snyder in a polka-dot designer bikini, white sun hat and dark glasses rose from her lounge chair and blatantly watched them walk by.

Leah wanted to smack her. It figured Deidre would be staying here right now. At least she was in a building on the near side of the grounds. The woman preferred the Executive Suite because it had an adjoining room that allowed her to spread out, as she put it, and it was on the second floor, which gave the best view, according to her.

Finally, Leah and Cord reached the shaded walkway between buildings at the other end of the pool, and she halted to explain where they were headed. Cord must not have expected her to stop because when she turned, he grabbed her arm as he walked into her.

At the contact she flinched, and quickly stepped away, breaking his hold.

"I'm sorry." He scanned her as if looking for a wound or something. "Are you okay?"

"I'm fine." She brushed it off without explanation. "Your suite is at the farthest point from the lobby. Are you sure you don't want me to get a staff member for your bag?"

His brows lowered, clearly affronted. "Leah, a saddle weighs more than my clothes."

"Of course. I apologize. We don't get many stateside

cowboys here." She turned and headed down a set of flat stones placed strategically to form a pathway over the sandy ground. "In fact, you're the first since I've been here."

He didn't respond until they reached the area of heavy bushes where the path split. "I was hoping to visit a ranch while I'm here. Are there any nearby that wouldn't mind a visit from a 'stateside cowboy'?"

She turned to the left and led him along the path before stopping in front of the honeymoon cottage. *Remain professional. Don't let him see that he rattles you in more ways than one.* "The Pono Ranch isn't too far. I'd be happy to make arrangements for you." She held out her hand for the folder she'd given him. "Once you see this room, you may not want to switch."

He looked over her head at the small building. "If it's that nice, then Hailey will probably love it, which means I won't. My sister and I have opposite tastes." He held out the folder, and she pulled it from him, taking the key out to open the door.

Usually, the bellmen did this. She'd shown guests to a room before, just never the honeymoon suite. As she stepped inside, it suddenly occurred to her how it would look to a cowboy who was not on his honeymoon. The whole suite screamed "love nest" and she became acutely aware of the man behind her.

Cord stepped in as Leah moved aside. Well shit. Wasn't this just the perfect place for a couple of newlyweds. It was one large room with a mini fridge beneath a tiny counter where a microwave and coffeemaker sat. It also boasted a table for two, a loveseat, and a huge four-poster bed with gauzy white draping over the top.

Even worse was the hot tub he could see outside on the patio with the ocean view. Trying to ignore the obvious purpose of the room, he looked to the painting on the wall closest to him, but that didn't help. It wasn't erotic by any means, but the suggestion of sex was blatant in the woman's face as her lover kissed her bare shoulder from behind, his hands clasping the silk wrap against her, revealing the hard nubs of her nipples pushing out the material.

"There's a closet over here with a safe, and through the door over there is the toilet." Leah pointed across from the bed where a glass enclosed shower was located in full view of most of the room. Next to it was a sink set against the wall, the only "private" area being the commode.

He moved his gaze to Leah to get his mind off the room, but as she walked toward the sliding glass door, he couldn't help staring at her ass as her hips swayed in her tight white sleeveless dress that barely reached her knees.

It was the very reason he'd almost knocked her down when she'd stopped, and now, imagining her wearing a thong beneath the large purple flowers printed on the dress didn't help his concentration at all. In fact, his jeans began to feel tight.

She opened the sliding door to reveal a huge, secluded patio surround by a half-wall of concrete. Flowering bushes surrounded the patio, giving it privacy on both sides almost all the way out to the beach. There the water lapped at the yellow sand, while floral scents filled the patio with a sweetness that wasn't overpowering, but definitely noticeable.

The secluded area was mostly in shade except at the

farthest end where Leah stood. The sun there made her straight, shoulder-length brown hair shine with deep red slivers of color that were hidden in normal light. The purple flower behind her right ear paled in comparison.

He dropped his duffle bag on the large bed and followed her outside, closing the door to keep the room cool.

Leah turned around and leaned against a gate nestled between the bushes. "As you can see, it has everything a newly-married couple would want, plus it comes with a private butler that can be called upon to arrange any service from massages to a midnight snack to a private sunset cruise."

"I'm more likely to request a pizza for breakfast and a ride to the ranch."

She laughed, the sound as enticing as her voice. "We can make those arrangements, and don't worry, I'll be sure not to assign Ulu to the duty."

Her confidence was attractive, as were her dark brown eyes. So much so that it took him a second to process what she said. "Are you the manager here?"

Her head came up a little higher, her pride in her position obvious. "I am. Graduated from Arizona State, top honors in the hospitality program."

He gave a soft whistle. "That program has a great reputation. No wonder you landed a sweet position here in the Hawaiian Islands."

Her smile faltered as pain flashed in her eyes before she turned and opened the gate. "This walkway will lead you down to the ocean. If you're an early riser, you can catch spectacular sunrises here."

What was that? He'd only been with Leah for less than a

half-hour, but he noticed a difference in her voice when she spoke as the manager of The Puanani and when she was just herself. His curiosity about Leah from Arizona grew.

She closed the gate and faced him again. "We have a restaurant just off the lobby. It's very casual, so shorts and flip-flops are fine. If you want recommendations for more formal eateries, there's a list in the local magazines inside."

"Except for a visit to a ranch and a thorough run-down of wedding possibilities, I was instructed to relax, so casual suits me fine."

Leah cocked her head. "Instructed?"

He thought back to the last dinner he had with Hellion and his folks. "Yes. My father told me in no uncertain terms that I had to take a vacation after running the ranch for a month while he was out of…um, out of town. My sister insisted I come here to check it out for her wedding."

"Does she have many places she's looking at? Obviously, she's looking for a resort venue."

He scanned the patio again, noticing the double lounge on the other side of the hot tub. This had Hailey written all over it, but her mind worked in mysterious ways, and he couldn't pretend to be sure what she'd like. He shrugged. "I think it's three or four. I try to stay away from the wedding talks. They make my head spin."

Leah laughed. "Oh, I understand that. We've had many a bride here and some have been absolutely delightful and others true monsters, but both were anxious about a million details. Having been knee deep in those plans, I know when I get married it will be very simple."

She was a woman after his own tastes. Was she seeing

someone? A quick glance at her hand showed no ring. Now that he looked, she had no jewelry of any kind. That was unusual. Before he thought about what he was saying, the words were out. "Will you be planning your own wedding soon?"

Her eyes widened in a look of shock. "Me? Hardly. I haven't had time for a relationship." She opened her mouth to continue, but shut it quickly, a slight blush rising to her cheeks.

Before she spoke again, he knew what tone of voice she would use.

Sure enough, Leah "the hotel manager," walked toward him. "I'll let you settle in. If you like, tomorrow I can show you what we can do for your sister, or if you wish, we can wait a couple days, so you can relax first."

He opened the sliding door for her, and she ducked back inside. Even as he stepped in, his awareness of her rose. Whoever designed the bungalow knew what they were doing. "No, I'd rather get it over with."

She stopped halfway through the room. "Will your friend be joining us?"

"I doubt it. He's from a completely different culture. He thinks once a man proposes, he shouldn't have to do anything except show up at the appointed time. We can count him out."

Was it his imagination or did her smile widen? "Great, then I'll come by tomorrow morning. The time change will be most noticeable when you wake up in the middle of the night, so you'll probably be up early Hawaii time. Try to stay awake as late as you can tonight. I'll stop by around eight when I get in and treat you to breakfast."

Eight? He was up at five every morning. So the time change would make it, what, five hours earlier? Did they have

Daylight Savings Time? When did that start? He'd figure it out later. She would know better than he would. "Sounds good."

She gave him a quick, professional nod and headed for the door.

He stepped in front of her quickly and opened it for her.

"Thank you." She took the two steps down and started up the path.

That's when he noticed a much bigger building farther inland from the honeymoon suite. It was the same color as the rest of the resort, but didn't look like more rooms. Maybe it was where they held the weddings.

As Leah turned to take the right, heading back to the resort, she smiled at him then disappeared behind the bushes.

He walked back inside the cottage and scanned the large room again. From the fragrant flowers blooming on the dresser and bookcase to the plush robes hanging on a hook next to the glass shower, the room was the perfect love nest. Hailey would love it.

"Hellion, we're definitely even after this." Doubtful his little sister would catch his sentiments from across the Pacific Ocean, he strode to his duffle bag where he'd dropped it on the bed and began to unpack. He pulled out a pile of shorts and bathing suits.

Then he dug to the bottom and lifted out a couple pairs of jeans. With any luck, over the next two weeks, he'd have a chance to wear them. Opening the drawer in the dresser, he dropped his clothes inside. He returned to his bag and pulled out his flip-flops.

When his parents had come back from a month-long trip

to Spain and suggested he take a couple of weeks vacation after running the ranch for them, he'd shrugged it off. They weren't happy with his reaction, but when Hailey joined them, telling him it was time he flew to Hawaii and checked out The Puanani for her upcoming wedding, he couldn't refuse… though he wanted to.

He wasn't good at vacationing. Usually, he grew bored and left early. At least Hailey's request-demand gave him something constructive to do. He glanced down at his flip-flops. Why waste daylight time unpacking when he could get started right away?

Decision made, he quickly stripped and donned a pair of swim-shorts, the beach and ocean his first destination. Digging into his duffle, he pulled out the sunscreen his mother insisted he use. He slathered his ghost-white legs then rubbed some on the tips of his ears just in case. He'd burnt his ears when he was eleven and still remembered the pain. After that he'd always worn a Stetson.

He grinned as he grabbed a towel from the pile next to the door. Funny that he remembered the pain but not the girl he'd been trying to impress. Walking outside, he took a deep breath, the floral scent stronger than in the room, but cut with the salt of the slight ocean breeze.

He walked to the end of the concrete path then kicked off his flip-flops and continued in bare feet. He'd heard Hawaii had black sand beaches, but this one was a warm orange-gold color. Though the color wasn't exact, it reminded him more of Sedona than the beaches in the Caribbean where he'd gone to college.

The resort beach here was clearly defined by the lava rock showing at the far end and the veritable jungle almost down to the water on his end. In between was sand, empty lounge chairs, and two wall-less shelters with floral curtains swaying in the breeze.

Now why was the beach empty? Was it safe to go in the water? Being born and bred in Arizona, he didn't know much about Hawaii, but he knew enough about the Caribbean ocean to be cautious. He should have done some research before he left. Scanning the area for posted warning signs, he didn't find any, so he moved toward the water.

"Cord!"

At the yell, he stepped back and looked toward the far end of the beach. He relaxed as Phil strode toward him. "I thought you'd be out at the pool, checking out the women."

Phil was the epitome of a lady's man, yet so respectful that none of his conquests seemed to mind the shortness of their relationships. Cord had no idea how his friend managed that, nor did he want to.

Phil shrugged. "I'll get there. First, I want a good long swim after being cooped up in that air-tank." He rolled his shoulders. "I want to be refreshed before contending with the ladies' flirtations."

His friend's description of the airplane they flew in was hardly fair, but since Phil was used to his private jet, the commercial airline didn't quite meet his expectations, even if they had flown first class.

"Did you check if there are sharks, sea urchins, or jelly fish in these waters?"

Phil raised one eye brow. "That never stopped you from swimming in St. Croix."

No, it hadn't, but back in college he'd thought himself

invincible. That was ten years ago and he was bit wiser now. "Even there, we had our classmates from the island letting us know where to swim and where not to. I'm cautious in uncharted territory."

"I guess that learnin' we got on island was good." Phil's smirk was a dead giveaway he was just messing with him.

Cord shook his head, ignoring him.

"But to put your mind at ease, Loke said the reef out here keeps the bigger sharks away."

"Loke?" Cord approached the water. Despite being a desert cowboy, after going to school in the US Virgin Islands, the scent and sound of the sea made him feel younger.

Phil strode up next to him. "Yes. From what I've gathered, all older women are Auntie, but the owner of this little oasis asked me to call her Loke, which is Hawaiian for Rose. She assured me the swimming was excellent. In fact, she never swims in the pool."

That was all he needed to hear. Striding out to his thighs, he plunged into the small waves and struck out toward the reef. The buoyancy of the water was different than he remembered in St. Croix, but it had been years.

He hadn't reached the reef yet when Phil overtook him. He didn't even try to compete. Phil was the prince of a small island nation in the Caribbean. The man could swim before he could walk.

Reaching the reef, he treaded water as he watched larger waves crash on the other side, minimizing their impact as they rolled into the waters in front of the resort. He turned to look back toward his suite. To the right were four two-story buildings in a row parallel to the ocean. He could just make out a fifth one in-land.

He didn't know where else Hellion was looking at for getting married, but he had to admit, for only family and friends, this was a great spot. He completely understood her desire to marry away from Arizona. Any resort there that hosted her wedding would be crawling with press, even helicopters. After all, she was the first Pennington in their generation to marry and that was news.

Having already completed a sprint, Phil swam up to him and turned to look at the resort. "What are you looking at? There are no women on the beach."

Cord chuckled. "I know that. I was trying to look at it from my sister's perspective."

"Ah, you're working already. I should have known. Are you sure you don't want to run my personal guard for me?"

He shook his head. "No thanks. I'm sure there's all types of politics involved in that. Remember, I'm the simple rancher. You're the royalty."

Phil's brows lowered. "Not here. I have no personal guard with me to keep the media away."

"Right. So this trip you're just Phil, a rich man from the Caribbean."

"*Oui.* And you are a lowly cowboy with barely two dollars to rub together."

"Let's not make it that poor. I'm here to scope out the place for my sister's wedding."

Phil gave him a shrewd look. "And if that entails spending time with *mademoiselle* manager then that just makes the job easier."

He shrugged. "Who am I to argue with that?"

Phil laughed. "Who, indeed?" He scanned the resort for a moment. "I can tell you, from a woman's perspective, this place is the perfect spot to have a private, intimate wedding with just the right number of exotic nuances to make it special."

Cord lowered his brow. "How would you know what a woman's perspective would be? You don't even have a sister."

"Ah, *mon ami*, but I know women." Phil nodded sagely before striking out with his arms to continue his swim.

He couldn't argue with that. He and Phil had always been opposites, except for having wealth, yet in school they had become fast friends. For him, he'd appreciated Phil's knowledge of island life, even if St Croix wasn't his home island. For Phil, Cord was sure that his friend liked having someone who wasn't embroiled in politics and island shenanigans.

Cord struck out for shore again. Phil had once told him that he was honest to a fault, but it had been meant as the highest compliment. It was true, which is why it was so hard for him to hide the fact that he came from a wealthy family.

His older brother Greyson and his sister Hailey didn't have a problem flaunting the family money, but they were far more sophisticated than he was. He was convinced that while they inherited his mother's genes, he and his younger brother were all his dad.

As he reached the shallows, he peered through the water before putting his feet down. There may not be sharks in the area, but sea urchins could go anywhere and just because they weren't in the waters when Auntie Loke swam last, didn't mean they hadn't reached the Puanani resort this afternoon.

Stepping out of the water, he grabbed up his towel. He

should have suggested that Leah show him around today. Wiping his arms and chest, he watched the walkways from each building as if she'd appear suddenly. Was it his interest in accomplishing his mission or his interest in Leah that had him anxious for the tour?

Definitely both. He wanted to learn more about her, though why he wasn't sure. It wasn't as if they could have a relationship in two weeks. He wasn't like Phil. Was she?

Chapter Two

Leah checked her hair one last time in her office mirror, securing the purple flower with a clip, before heading down the hall toward the front desk. Nani was working today, so Leah wouldn't have to worry about Ulu hitting on their newest guests.

As she entered the open-air lobby, she stopped. Every piece of wicker furniture was filled with local women from Olino, the land division the resort was located in. Momi, like all the Hawaiian Islands in the mid-nineteenth century, had been divided into pie slices of land running from the highest elevation down to the ocean. Within them, everyone knew almost everyone.

She recognized many of the women camped out in the lobby and knew for a fact they were all single. Obviously, they'd heard of the Puanani's newest guests. Well, shoot. She hoped Cord and Phil weren't looking for a *private* vacation.

"They all paid the day fee." Nani's soft-spoken words easily reached across the eight feet of space separating them. "They even have *me* anxious to see our new guests."

Leah stepped up to the desk. "Auntie will be pleased, but I'm not sure about our guests, especially Deidre."

Nani grimaced. "I'd forgotten *she* was here."

Leah leaned her head closer and whispered. "Wishful thinking?"

Nani smiled, her white teeth contrasting brightly against her beautiful dark skin. The bold flowers on the white background pattern of her dress not only showed off her lithe figure, but her long ebony hair as well. "Absolutely." Her light laugh filled the space between them but didn't carry far.

Leah always counted on Nani when discretion was required, whereas Ulu was good for making people feel welcome in a big warm way. Overall, she'd been happy with those she'd helped Auntie hire and felt bad that they had to contend with the occasional "difficult" guest.

She glanced around to be sure no one approached, pleased that the locals had decided to spend the day. She just hoped they wouldn't be disappointed when at least one of the men they expected, didn't appear. She turned back to Nani, keeping her voice low. "I'm taking one of our new guests for breakfast and then going over our wedding package with him."

"He's engaged? Better not tell these ladies." Nani nodded toward the crowd in the lobby.

She shook her head. "No, he's here on behalf of his sister who's engaged."

"Oh, good. I'd hate to have this many disappointed women on my hands." Nani rolled her eyes at the thought.

"I'll bring him back forewarned. You may want to call Philippe du Bourbon's room and give him fair warning."

"And is he also available?"

Leah shrugged. "I didn't ask."

"Maybe I will." Nani winked.

Nani might ask, but she would never pursue a guest. It was against hotel policy. Besides, Nani rarely found a *haole* attractive. She preferred native men, but she might just make an exception for Phil. As grumpy as he was the other day, there was no doubt the man was attractive.

Leah couldn't help teasing. "I think even you won't be immune to Mr. du Bourbon."

Nani's eyebrows rose. "Really?"

She grinned. "You'll—" The sound of sandals hitting the tile floor hard had Leah turning around just in time to catch Deidre stalking toward them.

The woman, who'd been born with a silver spoon in her mouth and was happy to let everyone know it, frowned as she waved her arm toward the lobby. "What are all these natives doing in the lobby? Don't you have a no trespassing policy or something?"

Leah pasted on a professional smile. "The Puanani allows local people to enjoy our facilities for a daily fee."

Deidre's blue eyes glittered with irritation. "That's one rule you need to change immediately. Where's the owner?"

"She won't be in until this afternoon, but I don't think you'd want her to change the day-fee option. If she did, then neither Kawika or Io would be allowed to spend the day with you." Leah sincerely hoped that the loss of the two native men who liked to dote on Deidre would sway her away from her purpose.

Deidre looked out at the women in the lobby. "Why today? They look like a batch of seagulls ready to pounce on a bucket of fish."

Leah stifled her chuckle at the description and avoided

revealing the real reason the women had made the hotel their destination of choice. Deidre would never understand island life. "My guess is they have the day off and wanted to make the most of it. After all, we *are* the nicest resort in Olino. If we weren't, we wouldn't have such lovely guests such as yourself."

The woman sighed in resignation. "I suppose I can't fault them for having good taste." Deidre turned back toward the front desk. "I came in here to find out when Phil and his friend were planning to make an appearance. I rose early just to be sure I didn't miss them."

That Deidre had already managed to introduce herself to their new guests didn't surprise Leah. "I imagine they have been up and about already. With the time change and the fact it's the first full day of their vacation, they may have already left the property."

"I really don't see why it should affect people so much. I had no problem with the time change when I arrived."

Leah tightened her jaw to keep from replying. The day Deidre had arrived, she'd given strict orders that she not be disturbed after dinner, then she was up at three in the morning trying to get breakfast in bed, but none of the staff had arrived yet. The woman's memory was obviously selective.

"I guess there's no help for it. I might as well return to my room." Deidre looked over her shoulder at the women talking amongst themselves then turned back and leaned in closer. "As soon as either of you see Phil, I expect you to call me. Understood?"

Leah nodded as Nani assured the woman she would.

Pleased, Deidre smiled. "Good." Then without another

word, she sauntered past the ladies in the lobby as if they were beneath her notice.

What she didn't see were the giggles and eye-rolling that went on behind her back as she exited.

Nani's dark eyes twinkled with mirth. "Since I'm manning the front desk today, I doubt I'll see anyone."

"And since I'm about to leave the property, my chances of seeing Philippe are even lower than yours." Leah grinned.

Nani's eyes rounded. "You're leaving the property?"

"I don't think I have a choice. I need to sell this wedding package. If I bring him to our restaurant for breakfast, he'll be surrounded in no time."

"Ah, I see your point."

"Be sure to take a lunch when Auntie arrives. I don't want you to fall behind in your classes."

Nani's eyes lit with excitement. "I'm almost halfway done with my courses. By this weekend, I'll have enough for an Associate's degree."

"Excellent. If you have any questions, we can talk after your shift."

"Thank you, for telling me about the online hospitality degree." Nani reached across the counter to grasp her hand.

Immediately, Leah pulled her arm from it, masking her movement by stepping back. "Just remember that an Associate's is just the beginning."

"I know." Nani turned toward the lobby entrance as a couple entered followed by a local taxi driver. "Looks like the Randolphs are here. I better get to work."

"Me too." Leah walked away from the front desk and through the lobby, exiting near the laundry facilities instead of going by the pool. No need to push her luck. The last thing she needed was for a local to get curious and follow her.

At the end of the stone path, she arrived at cross path to Auntie's house. Before taking a left toward the honeymoon suite, she checked behind her to make sure she wasn't followed. With no one in sight, she headed directly for the little concrete love nest.

Her heart beat a little faster as she neared. She'd like to blame it on the possibility of a sale, but she wasn't that clueless. What she couldn't tell yet was if it was Cord himself that had her heart racing or if it was that he reminded her of home. She'd be the first to admit to homesickness if ever asked.

Still, Momi was a beautiful island with friendly people who had adopted her at once. She felt lucky every day that Auntie had taken a chance on a *haole* from the mainland, but it didn't stop her from missing Arizona. It wasn't better or worse than the island, it was just where she grew up, went to school, landed an awesome job and then—.

No, she wouldn't go there. She'd had no choice but to leave, and Momi was the next best thing to home. Besides, she paused as she reached the top step to the honeymoon suite, she had half a day planned with a cowboy from home. What more could she ask for?

Taking a deep breath to calm the excitement in her belly, she knocked. She waited, listening. Was he awake yet? The thought of him coming to the door, his hair a mess from a good night's sleep, a shadow beneath his chin while his green gaze took her in had her swallowing hard. She turned around, smoothing down her lavender sheath dress as she took another deep breath.

"I thought I heard someone knock." Cord stepped from the corner of the house to the front.

She sucked in her breath at the sight of him. He must have gone for a morning swim. His hair was a deep brown and soaking wet. Water droplets trailed over the short hairs on his chest, past his mounded pectorals and down his rib cage to soak into his wet board shorts. "You're up?" Her voice came out in a squeak.

Mortified, she brought her gaze to his face where his lips twitched. "Of course. I'm an early riser. Ranch life."

He said it like she'd know what he meant, and she did. "But the time change."

He shrugged, sending water off his shoulders to run over his biceps and down to his healthy forearms.

She cleared her throat. "I can come back."

He stepped in front of the steps as if to keep her from leaving. "No, please. If you don't mind waiting on the patio, I can be ready in ten."

She nodded quickly, afraid to try and speak. With him so close, she could not only see the moist scruff on his chin, but the movement of his Adam's Apple as he swallowed after speaking.

He stepped aside to let her pass. "I'll be right out." Then he jogged up the two steps and disappeared.

Quickly, she headed for the side of the house, her heart racing and her body tingling. He was even handsomer when wet. The urge to giggle had her shaking her head. Since when did she fall over a handsome man? Heck, she hadn't even had a serious relationship since she'd left Arizona.

And whose fault is that? She grimaced at the reminder of

how terribly she'd failed at dating since coming to the island. She'd had plenty of dates. They just never materialized past second dates except once. She always ruined it, and it had only become worse.

Stepping through the back gate, she walked toward the patio table which had two chairs. She pulled one out and sat.

Oh shoot. Cord had drawn back the drapes of the sliding glass doors, giving her a perfect view of his naked backside as he washed his hair in the shower.

She jumped up and strolled over to the hot tub and leaned against it, her back to the tempting view inside the suite. It didn't help. Despite staring at the crashing waves bleached by the sun as they broke out on the reef, all she could picture was Cord's white backside.

The line between tan back and white butt looked as if it had been drawn with a ruler, but the skin color did little to take away from how tight and muscular that cowboy was. She'd even glanced at his hard thighs before catching herself.

Thankfully, he'd been facing the spray. If she'd seen his front, she would've run for home, calling in sick for the next couple weeks. As it was, he'd inadvertently made it that much harder for her to remain professional. And here she was thinking she'd get to enjoy a taste of home for a couple weeks.

Hmm, tasting. The thought morphed into a whole new meaning in her head. She'd just have to get through today. Then she'd turn him over to Auntie. If she had to, she'd spell it out. Auntie would understand.

The sound of the slider opening gave her a split-second warning, and she pasted on her best professional smile before turning to face him. "Wow, I don't think that was even five minutes." She forced herself to keep eye contact, but even that was hard.

"Wearing shorts and flip-flops is a lot faster than jeans and cowboy boots. I forgot to account for the light clothing."

She chuckled. "I get that. Moving here was a bit of an adjustment for me. It's even more casual than home."

"Casual?" His gaze moved from her face to her chest and down her lavender floral dress to her low open-toe sandals. "You look dressed for an interview."

"Not exactly, but since I'm working, I need to be a bit more formal. Now, when I'm hanging out at the Cracked Coconut with my girlfriends, it's a whole other story."

"That I'd like to see." He winked.

She hid her blush by turning toward the patio exit. "Are you ready to try some local cuisine?"

He stepped around her to open the gate. "I went to the restaurant last night. It was crowded and a woman named Deidre demanded a lot of the wait staff. I felt sorry for them. I found a spot at the bar and ate there. It was very good."

She barely kept from grimacing. Though she couldn't control other guests, it still didn't look good for the resort. "Our chef is excellent, but I thought you might like to try a more laid-back place this morning, with no unruly guests to contend with." She stopped at the end of the concrete path where it disappeared into the beach sand. Standing on one foot, she balanced precariously as she pulled off one of her sandals.

"Here, let me help." He held out his arm for her to hold on to.

She stepped away quickly, her bare foot sinking into the

sand. "I'm fine. I do this all the time." Quickly, she lifted her other foot and yanked off her shoe. Ignoring the puzzled look on his face at her action, she pretended her behavior wasn't odd. "I thought we could walk along the water to Keoki's Bar on the beach."

He raised his brows. "A bar for breakfast?"

She grinned. "Oh, this isn't just any bar. George makes the best malasadas this side of the island. Just don't tell anyone. We like to keep the secret just among those in Olino."

"Malasadas? They don't contain crickets or anything, do they?"

She laughed. She couldn't help it. Her reaction to the word had been just as hesitant but in a completely different way. Men were definitely on another wave length than women. "I can assure you, there are no bugs of any kind in George's cooking. However, if you're afraid to try the local cuisine, we can always go to the resort's restaurant." Though how she'd explain all the women waiting for him or Phil to make an appearance, she had no idea.

He stood straighter, making what had to be a six-foot-three-inch frame even taller. "I'd be happy to try the local chow."

She bit the inside of her cheek to keep from laughing at how quickly he took up her challenge. "Trust me. You'll like it." She started to walk toward the water, and Cord fell into step next to her. "I also want you to see how easy it would be for the newlywedded couple to escape from the rest of their family and friends for a while."

"You mean outside of the honeymoon suite?"

She glanced at him to see the grimace she heard in his

voice matched the one on his face. "I know. It seems a little overboard for people like us who are single. Uh, I mean…I didn't mean to imply—"

"No implication at all. I *am* single. The ranch is my girlfriend at present. If my sister hadn't asked so, um, persuasively, I wouldn't be here right now."

Though he didn't seem to mind her blunder, she still felt her cheeks heat. His relationship status had nothing to do with getting his sister to book her wedding at the Puanani. Leah turned her head back to look where they were headed.

Though she could already smell the fried treat from where they were, she also sensed Cord still looked at her. Unable to resist, she finally turned her head back to meet his gaze. "I—"

"Is the red in your hair natural?"

Cord's question caught her completely off guard. "You can see it?"

"Yes, but only in the bright sunlight. I noticed when you showed me to the suite yesterday."

She swallowed hard at the appreciation in his eyes. "It's natural. I understand my great-grandmother was a redhead. Mom said I was a carrot top when I was born, but obviously that didn't last." Now she was rambling. What did he care about what she looked like when she was born? She needed to focus.

"Hey, Leah! About time you come for some good malasadas!"

Relieved for the distraction, she waved to Melia, a good bartender and a great friend.

Cord lowered his head very close to hers. "Someone you know?"

She swerved away then mentally kicked herself for her

action. She tried to hide it by stopping. "That's Melia, a friend of mine. She works for Keoki—George—but you should know she's unattached."

Cord's brows lowered in confusion. "Why is that important?"

She clasped her hands together, not sure exactly how to phrase the reality of life in Olino. "I just thought you should know because there's a dearth of single men on this side of the island, and, well, you're new." Being diplomatic when many of the Hawaiian women were not made it hard to explain. Her explanation was at best weak, based on his perplexed look.

Suddenly, understanding dawned, and he flashed her a wide smile. "Miss Leah, I do believe you mean I'm fresh meat."

She cringed at his wording, but it was true, or almost true. It was more like he was chum to a hoard of ravenous sharks, but she didn't want to say it quite like that. It would be a betrayal of her friends and neighbors.

"Leah, bring the *kane* here and come eat!"

"We better keep walking. She's not above stalking up the beach and hauling us over there." She started toward the bar again.

"What's a kane?"

He *would* have to catch that. "It means 'man'."

He gave a half chuckle. "Are you sure a newly wedded man would be safe from being hauled over?"

She nodded. "Most definitely. Love is respected. The word *Aloha* is used as a greeting, but it actually means love, peace and a kind of oneness with the world. It's hard to explain, but a newlywed would definitely be safe."

Melia came out from behind the beach bar and sauntered

toward them. Her long black hair swayed with her stride, her short floral dress revealing her toned legs and bare feet.

Leah lowered her voice, but didn't look at Cord. "You, on the other hand, are not safe."

"Leah, what's taking you so long?" Melia stopped in front of them, her gaze sweeping over Cord. "I must greet our newest *haole* to the island."

She had the strange urge to step in front of her friend and block her view, but that was silly. "Melia, this is Cord. He's checking out the Puanani for his sister. She might want to get married here."

Melia looped her arm around Cord's and pulled him toward Keoki's. "Your sister is a smart woman. The Puanani is the most romantic spot on the whole island, and once you eat Keoki's malasadas, you'll know this be the perfect place for a lovely wedding."

Leah trailed behind them. She wasn't sure what the delicious fried donut-like pastry had to do with getting married. Melia loved to connect things that had no connection. It made following the woman's logic difficult at times. Now, however, it wasn't difficult at all. Melia was all about Cord.

Chapter Three

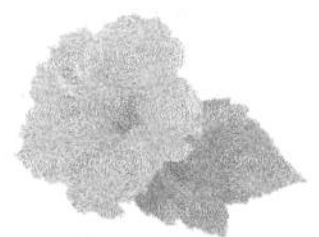

As Cord straddled a stool, Melia walked around behind the U-shaped wood beach bar and settled her hip against the sink behind it, clearly in full flirt mode.

Reluctantly, Leah approached. What was her problem? Melia was her friend and Cord was a hotel guest. He'd be gone in two weeks. Who knew how many women he'd have fun with in that time. In that light, her sudden inclination to keep Melia away from him was completely unreasonable.

She sat on the stool next to Cord's and gave them both her work smile. "As you can see, this is a short walk from the honeymoon suite and would give the newlyweds some privacy."

"If they don't stay in bed all day." Melia winked at Cord.

"I'd rather not think about that." He frowned. "We're talking about my little sister."

Melia gave Cord a look of approval. "Protective. A good trait in a husband."

Leah cringed. "There are also a few other places farther down the beach that a couple could walk to. Plus, in town there are at least a dozen more. I know that doesn't sound like a lot compared to Phoenix, but it is for this area."

Cord's face relaxed at her comment, and he turned from

Melia to her. "The nearest town to our ranch only boasts six restaurants, if you count the fast food place, which I don't."

"We don't have any fast-food places in Olino. We're not big enough, but that's part of what makes this the ideal place for a wedding. Newlyweds are treated almost like celebrities, only without the paparazzi."

Melia sighed. "*Ae*, we love to see happy-afters. It's the ultimate happiness. We all dream of it."

Cord gave the woman a warm smile. "I will admit it isn't something I've thought that much about until Hellion decided to get hitched."

"Hellion?" Leah leaned against the bar made of koa wood to catch Cord's attention.

He turned toward her again. "That's what we call Hailey. You would think with three brothers, she'd have been the mild-mannered one, but she ran us ragged from the day she was born."

That was interesting. What kind of guest would Cord's sister be? Leah really hoped they wouldn't have another out-of-control bride on their hands. The last one had almost caused half the staff to quit, including herself. She was about to ask what he meant by "hellion," but Melia was too quick.

"You mean there are two more like you at home?" Now Melia leaned on the bar opposite of Cord.

Leah took pleasure in the fact that Cord pulled his forearm from the bar top where it had rested. "Not at home. I'm the only one at home. My older brother lives in Phoenix and my younger one is in Tucson. I guess you could say I'm the only homebody."

"If you were mine, I wouldn't want your body anywhere else."

"Melia!" Leah couldn't help it. Even for her friend that was a bit much.

Melia laughed, waving her hand as if to dismiss her comment. "I only having fun. He open the door. I just walk in." She winked, obviously enjoying herself since she'd relaxed into her pidgin English.

Leah shook her head. "I brought him over here to taste Keoki's malasadas. I don't want him to think I lied about how good they are."

"Oh, they more than good. They heaven." Melia reached across the bar and patted Cord's cheek. "You love them, *'ae.*"

As she spun away to saunter out back, Leah sighed. Not all the local women would be as forward as Melia, but others were even more so.

"Don't worry about her. I can handle it. It's actually nice to be pursued for a change." Cord pointed to himself. "I'm the brother who has to do the pursuing, not that I have much time for that."

She relaxed. She didn't want him to be scared off. Not because she liked being around him. No, she was just relieved because the Puanani could really use a bit more wedding business. Besides, he reminded her of home and that made his company very enjoyable. *That and his good looks and tight butt. Ugh. Stop thinking about him in the shower!* She pushed her thoughts aside. "That's hard to believe. Are your brothers that swoon-worthy?"

He laughed. "Heck yeah. Greyson, my older brother is as suave and sophisticated as they come. He fits into the city life of Phoenix perfectly. Wesley, my younger brother has that cocky swagger and boyish charm that the ladies adore."

She smirked. "And how would they describe you?"

"Me? Just like you see me. Ranching cowboy who is as happy having a beer and a rack of ribs at a local bar as a pig in mud."

"That sounds like an honest man to me." It was an impression, more than a judgment, but Cord's smile faltered.

Not pleased to have embarrassed him, if that's what she'd done, she continued. "You said your sister Hailey was nicknamed Hellion. Does that mean she's a bit of a tyrant?" Well, shoot, that didn't come out very well.

"Hailey? A tyrant? Not even close. She's as genuine and giving as you'll ever meet. No, the Hellion part comes from her preference for an adrenaline rush."

Leah frowned. "You mean like a daredevil?"

"Exactly." Cord shook his head. "I remember her as a five-year-old, determined to walk the top railing of the corral fence all the way around."

"Oh, no."

"Oh, yes." Cord grinned. "She fell so many times I lost count, but she conquered that walk before she turned six."

There was pride in Cord's voice. How wonderful it must have been growing up with him as a brother. Her own brother was a couple years younger than her. They were close, but she always felt the weight of being older.

"Her stunts only progressed from there." Cord looked past her, obviously remembering. "Everything from stunt-riding to motocross, that girl tried it and conquered it. Unfortunately, she made a friend in grammar school who loved to risk it all as well, so that just encouraged her."

"Has she calmed down now that she's grown older? I mean, she's about to get married."

Cord's eyes widened. "Calmed down? Just the opposite. The older she got, the riskier her hobbies. She went from jumping out of planes to piloting them." Again his smile faltered, but he shook off whatever bothered him. "I think she might calm down a little now that she's getting married. She really loves Dillon, and he's a good man. We're all hoping he'll be a good influence on her."

Leah's thoughts were spinning as she pictured the bride-to-be. It totally changed her tactics for highlighting the Puanani and Momi. "Is he as much a cowboy as you?"

"Yes." Cord touched the brim of his baseball cap like it was a cowboy hat. "We both work for our families, but his family breeds horses while we raise cattle."

Ah, that was why Hailey could afford to have her wedding on an island. "Your family must be successful if they're planning to ship everyone over to our island for the wedding."

Cord's face froze. "My family?" He looked away. "Yes, I guess so, but I believe Hailey is using her inheritance from our grandmother to help."

Now she'd overstepped. She kicked herself for forgetting how proud cowboys could be. To infer that she'd been questioning his family's ability to pay was incredibly rude. "I didn't mean to pry. I just want to show you what we can offer your sister within her budget. I know some brides save for years for their wedding, so I just want to make sure I can provide her with all she's dreamed of and stay within her means."

Cord grimaced. "I know my sister, and she will spend whatever she needs to in order to have the wedding that she wants. It also means I may find myself in a white tux, floral silk shirt and a fruit basket on my head."

Leah laughed as she pictured the very virile Cord balancing a fruit basket. "I hope it doesn't come to that. On Momi, I think the best we could do is have pineapples shipped over from Oahu."

"Great." Cord's voice held only defeat, but his green gaze sparkled with mischief that reminded her of the natural pool called Queen's Bath on Kauai.

She held up her hand in pledge and forced herself to appear serious. "If your sister decides to have her wedding here, I promise I will do my best to talk her out of any fruit-bearing headwear."

At Cord's equally serious expression as he nodded, she broke out in laugher. His lips quirked up before he, too, lost it and laughed.

Shoot, she could stare into the man's smiling eyes all day and not care if she ever went back to work.

"Here you are." Melia sauntered toward them, a plate of malasadas balanced on her hand. "Heaven on Earth. I guarantee it."

Leah forced herself to smile at Melia. "And here I was told *Momi* was heaven on Earth." She winked at her friend.

"It is, but these are, too." Melia's smile was all for Cord as she placed the dish in front of him.

"Hmm, they look like there could be a cricket hidden inside."

At Melia's horrified expression, Leah chuckled. "It's an inside joke."

Melia finally glanced her way, only this time she raised her eyebrows. "Inside joke, eh?" Her tone of voice as she backed away from the bar and leaned against the beer cooler made her thoughts clear on that subject. "Only sweet in Keoki malasadas."

When Cord looked at the plate again, Melia crossed her arms and gave Leah a knowing look.

Just great, now her friend was backing off because she thought there was something between Cord and her. That's the last rumor she needed spread about town. She shook her head at Melia. "This cowboy seems to think islanders must eat crickets. My guess is, he watches too much television."

"Hmmm." Cord's hum at his pure enjoyment of the malasada sent a shiver along her skin. What did her mom always say? Oh right, the way to man's heart was through his stomach.

His eyes were closed as he chewed. When he opened them, he held up the large, custard filled donut hole coated in cinnamon sugar. "These should be illegal."

She smiled, thrilled he appreciated her island favorite. "But they're not."

He gave her a skeptical look before taking another bite. When he finished swallowing, he looked accusingly at Melia. "You put some kind of addictive drug in here, didn't you?"

Melia raised her hands. "I don't make them. I just deliver."

Cord turned toward Leah. "You want me to get hooked on these, so I'll convince my sister to have her wedding here."

I'd rather you were hooked on me. Where the heck had that come from? She shrugged. "Whatever it takes."

He took another off the plate and held it out. "Would you like one?"

"I should say no and let you enjoy, but I really can't resist these." She held her hand out.

He pulled the malasada back. "Open up."

"What? No, I couldn't."

"Do you want one or not. If not, I'm happy to wolf all these down myself."

He would have to choose the one food on the entire island she was seriously helpless to resist. She gave him a frown, but he just shook his head.

"Fine." She opened her mouth, and he held the pastry to it so she could take a bite. Carefully, she avoided his fingers. Though the heat in her belly wanted her to lick them, her habitual need to avoid touching anyone was stronger.

His smile faltered as she pulled back quickly, her mouth full of heaven. He popped the rest of the malasada into his own mouth, and she felt her cheeks flush. She glanced at Melia to find the woman smiling at her like she'd just discovered how to make gold from sand and planned to tell everyone who would listen.

As if it was completely normal for Cord to feed her malasadas, he chose another one from the dish and held it out to her.

"No, you go ahead. I can have these any day, but you're only here for two weeks. Enjoy them while you can."

"Good point." He looked at Melia. "Would it be possible to meet the man who made these?"

"For you, anything." Melia winked before heading for the doorway leading to the kitchen in the back. "Hey Keoki! A hot man who wants to see you."

Cord bit into the tasty treat, then licked his lips. "Holy shit, these are good."

Distracted by his tongue, it took Leah a few seconds to respond. "I told you."

"Yes, you did. You have completely gained my trust."

Thrilled at his words, she contemplated what to show him next. As much as she liked being with him, she had a job to do, and he had a mission to fulfill before he could enjoy his vacation. If she was successful, not only would he have a good time and recommend the Puanani to his sister, but he would be back for the wedding.

That idea excited her far more than it should.

Cord wiped his mouth after finishing the last malasada. Already his vacation was turning out to be more enjoyable than he'd expected. First, by meeting Leah and second, with this amazing food. He found himself anxious to see what they could explore next.

Movement in the doorway that led to the open-air bar caught his attention. It wasn't the overzealous Melia who came outside this time. A man as tall and wide as the doorway with dark skin, wide set eyes, a large nose and biceps to rival a bodybuilder stepped out, an apron around his hips. His bulk filled the area behind the bar, which just moments ago seemed spacious.

"You wanted to see me?" His voice was a deep bass and from his serious expression, he didn't seem too happy to be there.

Cord rose from the stool and held out his hand. "I just wanted to shake the hand of the man who made the most delicious food I've had all year, and that's saying something because my Mama is a fantastic cook."

The man's mouth lifted in a smile showing his bright white teeth. "You have excellent taste." As the man's large hand took his own, Cord prepared for a tight squeeze, but the giant simply shook like a normal sized man and let go. "I like a man who can appreciate my food."

"Have you always cooked?"

Keoki, as Melia had called him, shook his head. "Not until I opened this place. It was supposed to just be a beach bar, but I had so many people from the Puanani and the resort farther down the beach asking for food so they wouldn't have to walk back to where they were staying, that I started with a few dishes. I only make what I like to eat because all the leftovers go home with me."

He chuckled. "That's smart thinking."

"I may be big, but I'm not stupid."

Leah interjected. "Keoki opened this bar confident he could handle any drunk."

Cord silently agreed. Even his hot-headed younger brother would tone it down with this guy around.

She continued. "When he started experimenting in the kitchen, he liked it."

"Yeah, I watched a baker make the malasadas at the bakery and decided to try it, but I wanted more flavor."

Melia bumped her hip against Keoki. "He always wants more of everything."

Cord couldn't be sure, but he'd swear Keoki blushed.

"I just wanted to make the best."

"And you do." Leah smiled warmly. "I've had lots of others and no one beats yours."

"Thank you, Ms. Leah." Keoki turned his attention back to him and pointed at his empty plate. "You want more?"

"If we have time?" He looked at Leah.

"There's always time for more malasadas." She grinned, obviously having as much fun as he was.

"I'll go make you some more." Before Cord could say thanks, Keoki had disappeared through the doorway.

He resumed his seat. "I was expecting a fat, older man with a bald head to shuffle out here."

Leah laughed. "You got the bald part right. Keoki is kind of shy."

Melia nodded, her flirtatious manner gone. "Which is why he has me to tend the bar. If someone gets rowdy, I just call him." She wiggled a brow. "And if there's a woman here I think he should meet, I give her a tour of the kitchen."

"Sounds like the man is in good hands."

Melia waved his comment off. "We grew up together. He has always looked out for me, and I look out for him."

"My sister has a friend like that. Her best friend is a man named Austin. They were inseparable in school. This sounds a lot like rural Arizona." He glanced over at Leah. "Right?"

She nodded. "Which is why it wasn't hard to settle in when I moved here four years ago."

He could picture her on a horse following a trail through the cacti. "You said there's a ranch nearby. Do you ride?"

Her dark eyes lit with pleasure. "When I first arrived here I did, but once I'd made friends, my life got a little too busy. I miss it."

Just because a person grew up in Arizona, didn't mean they knew anything about horses. That she rode must explain his immediate comfort level with her. "Then you can ride with me when I go to the ranch. Can we arrange that for tomorrow? I'm thinking after the wedding tour, I'll need a good ride."

Her natural smile morphed into a more business-like one. "You're our guest. I'll be happy to help you with that."

That wasn't exactly the answer he was looking for. What *had* he wanted? Maybe a little more enthusiasm? When he mentioned riding, her reaction had been natural, but then she changed. Maybe he was reading her all wrong. This wasn't exactly his environment.

He looked down at his feet in his brand-new flip-flops. They were as white as his ass. Glancing across to Leah's feet, he could tell she spent some time in the sun. Did she wear a bikini?

"Here you are." Melia placed another plate of malasadas on the bar.

"Can I get these to go?" He ignored Leah's startled expression. "I'd like to enjoy these while I learn about my sister's possible wedding venue. It will make the tour more palatable."

As Melia walked into the back to pack up his treats, Leah shook her head. "Either you're one devoted brother or Hailey is black-mailing you, because it's clear this is the last thing you want to do on your vacation."

"I can't deny it's not something I'd do for anyone except my sister, but even being on vacation wasn't my idea. My father insisted. Hailey just provided me with at least one task. I'm hoping the ranch will provide me with new insights on the cattle industry here. After that, I have no clue what I'm going to do."

Leah's eyes were round with surprise. "Do? Last I heard, a vacation isn't about a to-do list and more about fun. Don't you like to have fun?"

Her question made him pause. "I do. Having a few beers with the guys, driving up to the city for a big game, or a barbeque with friends and family are fun. Day after day focusing on relaxing is just not in my DNA. Honestly, I get bored."

She opened her mouth but no sound came out.

He laughed. "Now I've struck you speechless. That's not good."

"No, no, it's just that I've never heard that before. I'm trying to decide if it's that you really love your job or that you really don't need much to make you happy." Her eyes widened in horror. "Oh, no, that's not what I meant. I didn't mean to imply—"

"I know what you meant." He waved off her embarrassment though he did like how pink her cheeks turned. It brought attention to her lips. "You're right on both counts. I love my work and it doesn't take much to make me happy."

Melia came back with his bag of malasadas. "Here you go."

He took the bag and held it up. "Like these. These will definitely make me happy when I get hungry from learning about what might interest a bride-to-be." He gave her an exaggerated shiver.

Leah smiled tentatively, obviously still uncomfortable about her faux pas.

Nothing he could do would change her mind, so he didn't comment further. The fact was, he was a simple man and it didn't take a hell of a lot for him to be content. He stood and pushed the stool back toward the counter. "Thank you, Melia. It was nice meeting you."

"Oh, it was very nice meeting you, too. Don't eat all those at once." She pointed to the bag in his hand.

"I won't." He turned to find Leah already stepping off the concrete floor that indicated the end of the bar.

He strode up to her and matched his gait to hers. "So where to next? I have no idea what Hailey will want to know, so I'm at your mercy."

She shook her head. "It's not like you have to choose the flowers or taste wedding cakes."

"Wedding cakes? I'd have no problem with that."

She finally looked at him. "Are you still hungry?"

He shrugged. "The malasadas were great, but they have no protein. I usually have bacon, sausage, eggs, toast, oatmeal, and if I'm lucky, coffee cake or Rosalie's famous chorizo muffins."

Leah stopped in her tracks, causing him to have to turn around to face her.

"You eat all that for breakfast?"

"I work hard all day."

"I can tell." Her gaze flicked over his arms. It made him want to flex his muscles like a high school kid. He hadn't shown off for a girl since college. He never had to. Once girls learned he was one of *the* Penningtons, they didn't care much about him in particular.

"Who's Rosalie?" Leah's question caught him off guard.

"Our cook."

"You have a cook?" Her surprise had him kicking himself.

"She cooks for the ranch. A lot of the workers come in at dawn. Everyone deserves a hearty breakfast before heading out."

"Hmm, you must have a pretty big ranch. What do you raise?" She'd begun walking toward the resort again, so he fell into step.

"Beef cattle." He had to watch what he said. Being outside Arizona was the only time he could be himself besides when he was on the ranch. Everywhere else, he was the middle Pennington brother. His older brother took the attention as his due and his younger brother took advantage of it, but that wasn't his way.

"Oh, that makes sense. Cattle take up much more land than horses."

He liked that she knew enough about home without knowing his family that he could have a real conversation with her. "Did you grow up on a ranch?"

She shook her head. "No, but my best friend did. We were inseparable back then. That's how I learned to ride, at her house. While in college, I had hoped to land a job at a dude ranch. I loved the idea of having guests stay on a ranch and help with the day-to-day chores, plus I'd have the additional perk of an occasional trail ride."

"So why didn't you work at one. You'd be perfect." He could easily picture her in a cowboy hat ringing the dinner bell for guests to come chow down.

"I did look into those positions after I graduated, but there weren't many of them and the few I found paid too little."

She started to walk past his cottage, but he needed to drop off his malasadas.

He reached out to halt her, but the second he touched her arm, she jerked away and he dropped his hand. Shit, what did he do? He held up the bag. "I'm going to leave these here."

This time her cheeks flushed bright red. "Oh, I thought you were going to eat those on the tour."

"No. I've decided I want to keep them in my room for a

snack later." She looked away. "Leah, is something wrong?" He could have sworn she didn't find him repulsive, unless he misread her.

She snapped her gaze back to his and her business smile was back in place. "Of course not. You just startled me. I was deep in thought. Go ahead. I'll wait here."

He studied her. Despite the smile, something was definitely not right. "Okay." He turned away. He hadn't imagined her reaction. The second he touched her, she'd flinched. Why?

It reminded him of girl in high school. She'd done the same thing. It bothered him, so he made sure to be friendly toward her and watched out for her. He'd thought it was some kind of disorder until the day he witnessed her boyfriend slap her behind the gym. He's been so angry, he didn't think. He attacked the guy, who unfortunately was much shorter than him and claimed he was the victim. It was his word against the girl's boyfriend and she didn't dare say anything against him.

He was still burning up when he came home from school and told his mom he was expelled for three days. His biggest fear was that the girl would be hurt. His parents immediately drove to the school. He never knew what happened, but he was in school the next day as was the girl, but her boyfriend never returned.

Using his keycard, he stepped into the cool room and froze. Had Leah been in an abusive relationship? Was she now? His stomach tightened with anger. He had no use for men who forced themselves on women in a physical or emotional way.

He set the bag on the one shelf in the room's fridge. For all he knew, it could be she'd acquired a stalker while in Phoenix, but he was guessing. Taking a deep breath, he calmed himself. He was jumping to crazy conclusions, but his protective instincts shifted into automatic. He would add one more task to his agenda while on the island—discover why Leah Pennington was averse to being touched. Hopefully, it wasn't just with him.

Comfortable with his decision, he strode to the sliding glass door. He felt the need to find out about Leah's past and didn't question it. Like he'd told her, he was a simple cowboy. He worked hard, played hard, and followed his gut.

Chapter Four

Stepping outside, Cord closed the door, the click of the locking mechanism telling him he need not worry about his future snack. Leah was where he'd left her, only now she studied her cell phone.

Again, he couldn't help noticing the red highlights in her dark brown hair when the sun hit it so strongly. In her form-fitting, yet fifties-style sleeveless dress, he could easily tell she had nice curves and well-toned, tanned arms. She looked all business in the light purple clothing, but she didn't exactly blend in here, despite the flower in her hair.

He'd like to see her with a cowboy hat and the reins in her hands. Now *that* he could see. He wasn't oblivious to the way she'd avoided committing to going riding with him. He wouldn't let that happen. He wanted to see her in a more natural element for her, as well as for him. Maybe then he could discover who she really was and if something happened that made her so skittish.

Her position as manager of the Puanani made it easy for her to keep people at bay. It was a professional job, but what about her friends? What about when she went to the Cracked Coconut and relaxed. Did that change her reactions? The need to know grew. "I'm ready for the wedding tour."

She snapped her head up and dropped her phone into a side pocket on her dress. "Good. I promise to make it as painless as possible."

He grimaced. "I appreciate that. I'll try not to groan too much."

She opened her hand toward the walkway. "Then let's get this over as quickly as possible so you can enjoy your vacation."

He motioned for her to lead the way, not unhappy that the narrow stone walkway forced him to walk behind her which meant he could enjoy the sway of her hips.

Leah glanced over her shoulder at him. "Are you sure your sister isn't blackmailing you into doing this? You really sound as if it's the last thing in the world you want to do."

Bringing his gaze up from her ass, he chuckled. "It's not exactly blackmail. More like I owe her for something I did that she wasn't very happy with."

"Sounds intriguing. I can't imagine you making someone so angry they'd make you do something you really don't want to do." She walked by the path that turned toward the resort.

He stopped. "Believe me, this isn't as bad as what she could have asked for." He pointed toward the resort. "Isn't this the way back to the Puanani?"

She halted and turned. "That's one way. This is another way. You may want to use this path on occasion."

Shrugging, he strode toward her. "You're the tour guide."

"I promise I won't lead you astray."

Her smile this time was all her, and there was a slight flush in her cheeks, but he had no time to comment since she turned around and continued along the walkway. When they came to the end, it went both right and left.

Leah pointed to a large rambling island house. "That's Auntie and Unko's house. If you come down the path this far, you'll be able to tell easily that that's not the way to the main resort." She moved in the opposite direction. "This is a secret path that most guests don't know about."

Secret path? "Why are we using it now?"

Leah's step slowed as if she were trying to decide how to reply. "I thought you might like some privacy."

"Privacy? From who?"

She slowed to a stop and faced him. "It's hard to explain. You're kind of like a celebrity."

"What?" He shook his head. Either she was complimenting him or she was certifiably crazy. He preferred the former. "I'm just a cowboy from Arizona. I'm not a movie star or famous singer." *But I am one of the Penningtons.* His stomach clenched with doubt. No one could have figured that out yet. And what would it matter in Hawaii anyway?

She looked downright uncomfortable. Clasping her hands in front of her, she grimaced. "No, you're even more exciting. You're a handsome, single man."

It took him a moment to understand what she said, his mind still stuck on the fact that she thought he was handsome. His older brother beat him hands down in that department, but he was no ugly duckling either. That she found him attractive stroked his ego, but he was supposed to be having a conversation here.

She'd mentioned that there weren't a lot of single men in the area when they'd headed to Keoki's bar and Melia had greeted him so enthusiastically. "Are you saying that because I'm a single man, I've gained celebrity status since I arrived?" He found that hard to believe.

She threw him a worried look. "Oh, it's more than that. You're attractive, well-built, and on vacation in an area of Momi where the ratio of single men to single women is about one to twenty-three."

Well-built? He forced his mind to stay focused. "One to twenty-three? Are those census numbers?"

She nodded.

Shit, he thought she was making it up. Still, he'd just arrived and Olino was a large area, at least it looked that way according to the map he'd seen in his room. "But I just flew in yesterday."

She cocked her head. "You know how on a big cattle ranch a bulk of the animals will all hang out in the same area?"

He nodded.

"That's kind of what we have here. Olino may be a good size, but word travels fast and all the cattle will gather."

"I think you may be exaggerating."

She raised her right eyebrow. "Really? Then I'll have to prove it to you."

Spinning back around, she continued down the path, passing the laundry where heat poured from the slatted windows until they walked by a utility closet of some kind. Just before turning the corner into what had to be the lobby, she stopped.

"Wait here." She whispered over her shoulder as if they were on some kind of clandestine mission and would be shot on sight if seen in enemy territory.

She was a hell of a lot more fun than he'd expected to

have in Hawaii, and he hadn't even been on vacation twenty-four hours yet.

Leah disappeared around the corner, but he remained where he was, too engrossed in what she'd do next to think about following her. He didn't want to spoil the surprise.

A minute later she'd returned. "Okay, you can come through the lobby. They've gone to the pool. We can see them from the banquet hall."

"Who's gone?"

She rolled her eyes. "All the women. Our lobby was filled with local women who heard you and Mr. du Bourbon were at the Puanani. Every one of them paid the day fees, too, which is great for Auntie, but maybe not for you and your friend. Unless…"

He forced himself to keep a straight face. "Unless what?"

She cocked her head and ran her gaze from the top of his feet to the top of his head. "Unless you're the type of man who likes to have a harem of women fawning over him." Her voice made it perfectly clear what she thought of men like that.

An inkling of unrest settled between his shoulder blades as he thought of the trouble Phil could get into if that were the case. As for himself, it was one of the reasons he couldn't vacation in his own state. Too many women heard the Pennington name and immediately saw dollar signs. More than once he'd tried to reject a woman's advances politely to no avail.

He frowned at her, his voice colder than he intended. "No. I do not."

Instead of being offended, she smiled. "I didn't think so. In that case, don't question me and follow me closely until we make it to the banquet hall." She reached toward him as if to take his hand then suddenly pulled hers behind her back and spun around. She whispered over her shoulder again. "This way." She put a finger against her pretty lips to indicate he keep quiet.

He would have enjoyed the moment more if she'd taken his hand, but her odd reaction, especially when she'd been about to initiate touching him, confused him.

After skirting the bathrooms on their right, they were in the large open lobby. The local woman at the reception desk looked over, but again Leah put her finger to her lips. The employee nodded sagely and looked toward the other end of the lobby. Then without looking at them, she waved them forward.

That was even more odd. Still, he followed Leah as she half ran across the lobby and into a hallway where she slowed down to a brisk walk. It was easy to keep up with her, and as instructed, he remained quiet until they stepped into a banquet hall, and she closed the door behind him.

He couldn't keep quiet any longer. "What was that all about?"

She strode toward the bank of darkened windows, but still remained to the side of them. "I'll show you."

As he drew closer, his step slowed. *Shit.*

"Don't stand there. If you're too close to the window, they'll see you."

The urgency in her tone had him moving to the side a couple more feet. "Are you saying all those women came here just to meet me and Phil?" He stared at what had to be at least two dozen, beautiful local women. Some wore sundresses, some wore wraps, but most were in bikinis, and all were stunning.

"Look."

He moved his gaze lower to where Leah pointed. Phil, his sunglasses firmly in place, sat on the edge of the pool, his legs in the water. On every side of him was a smiling woman—next to him, behind him, in the water before him. It looked like a harem and Phil was the sheik. There was no way even Phil could reject all but one without causing some kind of problem.

He moved his gaze back to Leah. "So if I went out there, what would happen?"

She rolled her eyes. "Over half of those women would converge on you."

"Over half? Why more than half."

She put one hand on her hip, her eyes dead serious. "Because you're better looking than Mr. du Bourbon."

He grinned at her statement and even with no lights in the room, he could see her flush before she walked toward the door they'd come in. He liked that she blushed so easily, not to mention that she thought him more attractive than Phil. That had to be a first, and something he wouldn't tell his friend.

He may have grown up in wealth, but Phil had been raised in royalty, and there was another whole layer to the man that added to his confidence and occasional arrogance.

"Your sister and her groom could enter from the door we came in, or they can enter over here." Leah was now at the back of the room, obviously ready to get the tour started. "We can add an archway of flowers on the inside of these double doors and then open them when the couple has finished taking photos and is ready to join their guests."

He strode toward her, determined to perform his task

for Hailey to the best of his ability. "Does the hotel have a photographer?"

She shook her head. "No, but there are a couple in the area that we can refer. We only use the best."

He could hear the pride in her voice. "Of course."

She turned away from the door she was about to open and frowned at him. "I'm not giving you a line. I've vetted all the outside vendors myself."

"I didn't mean it as an insult. You appear very efficient, so the fact you have vetted the photographers is not a surprise to me." He watched as the tell-tale blush rose in her cheeks again.

"Oh, I apologize. I'm used to dealing with *haole* who think because the hotel is on an island, it's like a third-world country."

Where he'd gone to college was exactly that way, so he kept quiet and nodded to show he accepted her apology.

She yanked open what looked like a closet door, which stuck at first, probably due to the humidity, and flicked on a light inside. "As you can see, we have a full complement of tables and chairs. The maximum we can do at a sit-down meal is three hundred, but between you and me, I wouldn't go over two hundred and fifty as it feels like people are on top of each other."

Again he nodded, taking in the information and storing it to relay to Hailey later. Closing the door behind him, he followed Leah as she moved farther into the large storage room.

Stopping, she pointed to metal shelving which hosted a rainbow of colored packages. "We have over eleven colors in table clothes and napkins, and we can mix and match as your sister wishes. If she has another color in mind, we have a good relationship with another boutique hotel about twenty miles away and we often switch out colors for particular brides, so there shouldn't be an issue coordinating with Hailey's bridal color scheme."

He scanned the colorful material wrapped in plastic, it all having been cleaned and waiting for the next event it would be called into service for. To be honest, he didn't realize the color of table clothes and napkins was an issue, but then again, he was neither a woman nor getting married. He nodded sagely at Leah, and she turned to another area.

If Hailey could see him now, she'd be laughing so hard she'd fall over. He was just lucky she wasn't here to witness his cluelessness.

Leah moved to another section of the storage room. Though he listened to what she said, he found himself far more interested in her. From her voice, he keyed into her confidence and knowledge, not that he'd doubted that after hearing where she'd gone to school. From the way she looked at him, he could sense her eagerness for his agreement. From the way she walked, he honed in on her femininity as each step was controlled and fluid.

What disrupted her entire image was the movements of her hands. Unlike the rest of her, they were jerky and sudden as if she'd forgotten she could use them and then did, only to decide they were too assertive and pull them back. He'd seen her clasp them together a number of times already and that seemed the only time they appeared to relax.

It reminded him of his horse when he was still a colt. Expresso had been a big foal and when it came to walking or running, he'd had a hard time of it. They'd even called a vet to make sure he didn't suffer from wobbler syndrome or some other disorder. However, just as the vet predicted, once Expresso's legs caught up to his body in girth and strength, he was fine and was now a beautiful animal to watch run.

Leah, though, was an adult. Maybe she'd always had this odd quirk.

"… that is, of course, if Hailey would like an inside reception." She cocked her head in silent question. "We also offer outside banquet space, especially if she's looking for a traditional luau."

He shrugged. "I have no idea, but I'll make sure she's aware of that option."

Leah studied him for a moment. "If I get too detailed for you, just let me know. I'm used to talking to the bride-to-be. I've never had one send her brother to scout out our facility."

He grew uncomfortable under her look. "I'll be sure to let you know. Why don't you show me the outside space?" He glanced toward the windows which showed everyone in the pool now, even women who were probably hotel guests. "That is if we can avoid the pool area."

She gave him one of her personal smiles. "We can definitely do that. We'll just go out the back entrance, the one the bride and groom usually come in." With a conspiratorial wink, she walked toward the double doors.

He moved in front of her and opened one for her. As she passed by, he caught a light whiff of myrtle. Compared to the fragrant flowers that abounded at the hotel, Leah's scent was refreshing. It reminded him of the bushes near a creek back at Ironwood.

"There's a fence here, but it's not as tall as you, so you may need to scrunch down. I'm afraid it wasn't really built to hide people, just keep the island chickens out."

"Not a problem. Compared to a round-up, this is nothing."

She continued to walk ahead of him as he bent over far enough not to let his head appear over the fence.

"Yes, but you're not working today. You're on vacation."

He chuckled. "Don't rush it. I'm still 'working' for my sister."

She stepped into the shadow of another building and faced him. "I can't say I've ever had a guest come to the Puanani and not be anxious to start their vacation. I've had workaholics before, but even they were anxious to relax and recharge."

He shrugged. "I'm definitely not a workaholic. I just don't like being bored."

"Hmm." A gleam came into her eyes. "I think we can make sure you're not bored here. If you like, I can create a plan for your vacation so you have fun but don't get bored." She suddenly looked unsure. "I mean, if you would like that?"

Excitement spun in his gut. "It would be a first, but if you could make that happen, I'd be forever in your debt."

She laughed, the sound playing along his skin and seeping in. "Forever's a long time. How about if you're satisfied with your vacation, you agree to do all you can to convince your sister to have her wedding here."

He stuck out his hand. "You have a bargain."

She jerked as if he offered her a rattlesnake then she let out a breath and placed her hand in his. Her grip was firm and confident as she nodded. "Good. Now let me show you this outside space."

As she pulled her hand from his grasp, he forced himself

to let go. For some reason, he expected her hands to be cold, maybe because she clasped them together so often, as if they couldn't stay warm apart. Instead, her hand was soft and not cold at all.

The urge to place her hand on his bare chest took him by surprise. That was odd since he'd discovered women found what was in his wallet and below his waist the most appealing parts of him, not his chest…nor the heart that beat beneath it.

She stopped on the path not twelve feet away. "Are you coming? We have a lot of ground to cover."

Yes, they did, in more ways than one, and he was very good at covering ground. Grinning, he strode toward her. "Lead on."

Leah turned off her computer. It wasn't as if she'd done a lick of work since she'd finished with Cord. Her mind kept drifting back to his smile, his confident stride, and the sound of his deep laughter. He reminded her so much of home. For four years, she tried to fit in on the island, but she was well aware she was only partly successful.

It had to be her nostalgia for Arizona that had her mind wandering back to him. Though to be fair, if she'd met him at the Cracked Coconut, she'd be more than happy to have a drink with him. They could even walk the beach, maybe listen to the waves as they watched the sunset. He might reach for her hand and—

She pushed away from her desk. She was doing too much daydreaming and not enough work. Standing, she brought her half empty water bottle to the prickly pear cactus she had growing on her bookcase. It had been a thrill to discover the same cacti that grew back at home could also be found on Momi. She gave the little cactus some water before finishing off the bottle and dropping it into her recycle bucket.

Returning to her desk, she made sure she had everything put away and her to-do list ready for tomorrow. Cord would be going to Pono Ranch, which meant she could actually concentrate and find him plenty to do while he "vacationed." She shook her head. Maybe she could show him that vacations weren't just about lying on a beach, soaking in the sun.

She pushed in her chair and reached for her purse.

"Can I talk with you a moment before you leave?" Auntie Loke shuffled in, her pink flowered mu'umu'u making her look like a walking frangipani.

"Of course." Leah gestured to the first wicker chair in front of her desk, but Auntie moved around to the other side of the desk and rolled out the office chair. Not sure what to make of that, Leah stood back and watched as Auntie settled herself behind the desk.

"You're very neat and organized."

Hmm, yes, she was, but Auntie knew that already. The owner of the Puanani never beat around the bush unless it was something she didn't want to talk about. Leah walked to the side of her desk, forcing Auntie to turn if she wanted to face her. "What is it, Auntie? What's wrong?"

Auntie sighed. "I can't have you here tomorrow, which means I'll have to work on my day off."

Her blood froze at Auntie's words. Had someone complained about her? Had she been accused again? Her heart started to race, and she swallowed hard to keep her panic at bay. "Why? I'm scheduled to work tomorrow."

Auntie nodded and gave another dramatic sigh. "Yes, yes, but I must send you to the Pono Ranch with Mr. Pennington. It's his request, and we must make sure he leaves the Puanani happy. His sister's wedding would be so good for us."

Her panic subsided in an instant, and she crossed her arms over her chest. "Auntie, you know it's against hotel policy for workers to date customers."

Auntie's feigned surprise was almost laughable. "No, no. This is not a date. You must show him what a wonderful staff we have and how accommodating we can be. Just be nice to him like you are to other guests."

She raised her eyebrow. "Are you pimping me out?" She was half joking but half serious.

Auntie shook her head vigorously. "No, no, no." The older woman suddenly smiled wisely.

Leah steeled herself. That particular smile never boded well.

"It's just like when you show the brides-to-be around town and help them choose places for shopping and the bachelor or bachelorette party, only this time it's the bride's brother you must show around. I'm sure if he's interested in the ranch then so would be his sister, no?"

She didn't doubt Auntie had another agenda, but she also couldn't fault her logic. "Very well, if you want me to." She tried one last time. "But you could always go, and I could work my regular shift."

Auntie pulled her bulk up out of the chair, leaning her hand on the desk to do so. "No, I can't ride anymore. That's for you younger people." She moved forward and Leah quickly stepped away to allow her boss to pass. "You go and I will handle the staff." Auntie paused at the door, her face absolutely serious. "It would be very good if his sister had her wedding here. We're not so big that we can afford to lose a potential customer."

"I know. I will sell the island and the Puanani to the very best of my ability."

Her boss nodded. "Good. Good." Auntie shuffled out the door without another word.

She stared after the woman. Was the resort having problems, or was there something else going on? She'd been at the resort long enough to know when Auntie was hiding something. Sometimes it was a pleasant surprise, but other times, like when they had to layoff staff during the last low season, it wasn't good.

Finally moving to her desk, she picked up her purse. Hopefully, whatever Auntie was hiding would be good for everyone.

Chapter Five

At the sound of a knock, Cord wrapped a towel around his waist and strode toward the front door. It was too early for his ride to the ranch, and he hadn't ordered room service. He hoped none of the women last night followed him.

Opening the door, he relaxed. "Phil." He stepped back to let his friend inside.

"You disappeared last night without a word. Thought I'd stop by and find out why." Phil walked into the middle of the room. "Homey suite."

It was such a typical response from Phil that he ignored it. He moved to the counter where the coffee had just finished dripping. "Want some?" He held up a cup.

"Sure." Phil pulled out a chair and sat. He wore a sleeveless tee-shirt, board shorts and flip-flops, his hair pulled back in the usual ponytail. He could easily pass for a surfer here on Momi.

Cord handed Phil a cup of coffee and poured one for himself. "I didn't expect to see you this early in the morning. I left around midnight and you were still going strong.

Phil shrugged. "I left soon after I noticed you were gone. It didn't take long to figure out if I wanted any exercise time or time with an old friend, I'd have to get up early. So who did you leave with? I saw you talking to another American, an almond-eyed woman with long chestnut hair."

He'd talked to over a dozen women last night. It would have been impossible not to. After having dinner alone in his room, he'd finally braved the resort and found Phil in the lounge surrounded once again, only instead of bikinis, the women wore bright colored, short dresses. "I think the one you're referring to was Annalise. She's from Florida. She found the attention you were getting 'over-the-top', as she put it. I slipped out, alone, shortly after that. I would rather none of the women here or locally know which room I'm in, so I'm not going to switch rooms. I figure being in the honeymoon suite is the last place they'll look."

Phil saluted with his coffee. "Good idea."

"I saw you with another guest, the rich woman. I think her name was Deidre. You seemed to hit it off. Did you take her back to your room?"

"No, she made too many assumptions because of her wealth."

"How do you know that? Did she tell you?"

Phil grimaced. "Unfortunately, yes. She insisted on the most expensive champagne then proceeded to get drunk. I learned far more than I wanted to know." Phil took another sip of coffee. "She was not the kind of woman who would be willing to share. In fact, she was the opposite, and I imagine there will be a few less women here today, which is unfortunate."

"Share? You still do that?" He couldn't imagine juggling more than one woman in the bedroom, never mind in a relationship. Phil had done it twice while they were in college.

His friend shrugged. "On occasion. It helps keep some of

the marriage seekers at bay." He smirked. "They don't call my island Pleasure Island for its beautiful beaches."

He chuckled. "And as the Prince, you must keep up the reputation?"

Phil's smile turned sly. "I do what I can."

Cord nodded. For all Phil's royal charm, there was a lonely side to him that very few people knew about. Cord considered it a privilege to be one of those people. He didn't begrudge the man his charm. Despite the many women Phil had been with, he always respected them, being honest about where he stood in the relationship. Probably because the man didn't have to worry about going without a girlfriend or two for long.

Somehow, he didn't think any of Phil's female relationships ever lived up to his idealistic expectations, but who was he to judge? *His* mom was still alive and well and a wonderful part of his and his siblings' lives. He couldn't imagine losing his mom as a teenager.

Even at the thought, he caved to an urge to include Phil. "I'm headed out to Pono Ranch this morning. I'm hoping to get a feel for their operation and take a trail ride. Would you like to join us?"

"Us?" Phil put down his coffee cup. "You found someone of interest last night after all? I'm surprised."

Cord walked to his dresser and brought the box of malasadas over. It felt rude to not offer one to Phil. "Don't be surprised, because I didn't. The resort manager here is bringing me over there as part of her duties to the hotel. I'm getting the feeling this place could really benefit from Hailey having her wedding here."

"You mean because so many women in this area are looking for husbands?"

Cord laughed. "No, because they could use the business." He opened the box and forced himself to share the remaining two malasadas. "Would you like a sweet start to your breakfast?"

Phil shook his head. "Already ate in my room. Wanted to fill up on carbs and protein before taking a swim and a run."

Not being able to resist, he picked one up. "You don't know what you're missing. There's a bar a little farther down the beach called Keoki's and that man makes the best malasadas on the island."

Phil gave him a skeptical gaze. "And you know this because you've tasted every one of them?"

He took a big bite of the malasada then raised both hands and shrugged.

His friend shook his head. "Let me know how the ranch is. If it offers an all-out gallop then we could go there another day while you're here."

He swallowed and nodded. Then picked up his own coffee cup.

"I want to stay here and converse with more of the ladies. It feels good to be among other islanders who understand the pros and cons to island life."

Surprised, Cord pulled his mouth away from the edge of his cup. "That sounds like you're looking for a wife."

"Maybe." His friend shrugged.

Shit, this was serious. Phil hadn't said anything about needing to find a wife on the long plane ride over. "Is this something you just thought about or is your father pressuring you."

"Neither. Actually, it was Kai who brought it up."

Cord met Kai, Phil's good friend growing up, at their college graduation. The man had as much presence as Phil, only from what Phil said on the plane ride over, Kai was maneuvering himself politically to become Prime Minister, which Phil completely supported.

"And you're entertaining it?" It was a subject broached at dinner back home on the ranch every once in a while, but with two other brothers, Hailey getting married, and his parents being big supporters of getting marriage right the first time, there was no pressure on him to think about it, even if he was already thirty-one.

Phil finished his coffee and set the cup down. "Let's just say I've opened my mind to it more than I had before, so I'm willing to explore the possibilities. It didn't occur to me until yesterday how well an island woman could adjust to living on L'Asile."

"That makes sense. I guess there are nuances and expectations for living on a ranch as well."

"You're going to a ranch today, are you not?" Phil stood, giving him that sly smile of his.

"I'm going there to accomplish a task and hopefully enjoy a ride, not to look for a wife."

Phil chuckled. "No pressure, *mon ami*. I was just making an observation." He moved toward the sliding glass doors. "I have also observed what a secluded spot you have over here in the honeymoon suite." He wiggled his brows. "Don't worry. I won't reveal your hide-out, my humble friend."

Cord walked over and opened the slider. "Thanks, I appreciate that."

Phil stepped outside, but turned back. "However, I will want a detailed account of the ranch. It may be something I should think about for my island."

"Will do."

Phil turned and jogged down the path before heading along the beach for his run.

Cord closed the slider. He wished his friend all the luck in the world finding the woman who would someday rule his island with him. It was Phil that made him realize how lucky he was. Growing up, he'd been overly aware of his family's money thanks to his first girlfriend. He'd always found it a cross to bear, but after meeting Phil, he'd learned to be thankful that was the only issue he had.

He turned away and moved to the sink to shave. At least he didn't have to think about someday running an island country, keeping it economically stable and living up to traditions while trying to stay abreast with the rest of the world. His own biggest concern was having enough calves come spring to keep the herd growing.

He splashed water on his face just as his phone alarm went off. Well shit, he'd wasted too much time. He dried off and inspected his chin and cheeks in the mirror. Not too much scruff. Hell, he was supposed to be on vacation after all. He could skip a day of shaving. It wouldn't be the first time.

Whipping off his towel, he pulled out his jeans, a long sleeved, buttoned-down shirt, and grabbed up his boots. Just the thought of riding after two days out of the saddle had him whistling.

That he was about to go riding with a beautiful woman just may have added to his pleasant mood.

Leah couldn't stop smiling. It felt so good to be on a ranch again, the wide-open land, the paniolos as the cowboys were called in Hawaii riding in, and the smell of horses. She sent many guests here for a ride, but had never received such an in depth look at the sheep and cattle operation. Cord obviously knew cattle and from the conversations he was having with Manu, the haku or head paniolo, it was clear he was both impressed and interested. Manu opened up immediately. He was always so reserved with her, but Cord had the older man laughing in no time.

She rode behind the two cowboys as Manu answered Cord's questions. Watching Cord's body move with his horse could keep her occupied all day. As much as she didn't think it a good idea that she'd come with him to Pono Ranch, she was totally enjoying herself just watching him in his natural element…or rather, almost natural. Pono Ranch looked nothing like the ranches where she'd ridden horses in Arizona.

Pono was more than a working ranch. It was a tourist attraction, complete with a little petting zoo of farm animals for the children, a café, a gift shop, a wool spinning experience, and trail riding. It even boasted a small pond where visitors could feed the ducks. It's variety of activities was why she sent guests to it.

She didn't pretend to know how to run a ranch, but she loved the scents and the amazing views on this one. Most Hawaii ranches on Momi, like Pono, were set up on the old Hawaiian ahupua'a, which was a pie slice of land that started at the peak of the nearest mountain and ran down to the sea. Pono, which meant *everything was as it should be,* still retained the entire land division, covering what had to be thousands of acres.

The Puanani Resort was in the Olino ahupua'a. Olino, which meant *bright,* was named as such because of the brilliant sunrises. It included the town of Kanoa, or the *tree one,* a number of resorts, and a large residential area. Not many ranches had retained the entire piece of land originally divided back in 1848, but Pono Ranch did.

She, Manu and Cord had ridden out from the barns after an extensive tour of the operations and were almost to the highest elevation. The sea wasn't in view at the moment, but the acres and acres of open grassland with gorgeous blue skies was breathtaking.

Cord looked back to make sure she followed, then asked Manu another question. His regular thoughtfulness had her heart melting. It was so different from most of their guests at the Puanani. People came to the island to cram a lifetime of experience, or rest, into a week or two and they wanted it to be perfect, which meant they expected the staff to do whatever was necessary to make that happen. Luckily, few were as selfish and demanding as Deidre.

"Excuse me." Manu pulled his phone from his belt and guided his horse away a few yards.

She let her mount walk up to Cord's. Seeing him in his typical cowboy gear made him appear even more handsome. She swallowed hard before speaking. "What do you think? It's a bit different from Arizona ranching, isn't it?"

He looked out at the rolling land covered in green grasses.

"It's different, yet the same." He turned his head to look at her. "Some of the challenges are different, but the work is pretty much the same." He pointed toward the horizon. "This is beautiful, but it doesn't call to me like the desert does. It's not home."

She agreed completely, but her job was to sell her adopted home. "No, it's not, but it's perfect for a vacation. Most people like to go somewhere different when getting away from work."

He gave her a self-deprecating smirk. "You're right. Hailey would love it." His face turned serious. "What about you? This isn't home to you, yet you live here."

She wanted to deny that it *was* home, but she couldn't lie. "No, it's not home. I think of it as home-for-now. Who knows where my career will take me next? I have to learn to adapt wherever I end up."

"Is that what you want?" He frowned. "To live in exotic locales and adjust to those places?"

No, I want to go home! "Not necessarily, but I need to be open to the possibility of moving if I want to move up in this industry."

"There are a lot of resorts in the Phoenix and Tucson area. You could move up there, right?"

She looked away. *Not likely.* "That's always a possibility. At the moment I'm happy with the Puanani." She returned her gaze to his. "I'll probably start looking at other possibilities next year or if Auntie decides that she'd like to promote someone. I'm in the highest position at the resort beneath Auntie, so I'd have to start looking if that was the case."

Manu walked his horse back to them. "I'm sorry. I need to head back. There's an issue that needs my attention."

"Anything I can help with?" Cord's offer surprised her.

"This is about a few of our sheep. You don't happen to have expertise in that area, do you?"

Cord chuckled. "Afraid not."

Manu sighed. "Then I guess it's all on me." Though he pretended to be bothered by the task, his eyes glinted with amusement. "Do you think you can find your way back?"

Leah looked back the way they'd come, but the ranch house and barns were nowhere in sight.

"Not a problem." Cord's confidence was appealing. "If we get lost, we'll just let the horses lead us."

Manu pointed to her. "That one will come home no matter what. In fact, when you dismount, you'd better tie her up."

"Got it." Cord nodded.

Dismount? Why would they dismount?

"I'll hand this over to you now." Manu pulled a full backpack from his saddle bag. "Just be back before dark or we'll come looking for you."

"Thanks." Cord hooked the sack around his saddle horn.

"Ms. Leah." Manu tipped the brim of his cowboy hat, revealing his salt and pepper hair, then turned his horse around and kicked it into a gallop.

"I like him." Cord's voice brought her attention back to him.

"What did he mean 'when we dismount,' and what's in the backpack?" Had she missed something? Was Cord delivering tools to another paniolo?

His smile was satisfaction itself as he patted the pack. "We're going to eat lunch out here. I didn't want to rush back to the resort, so I talked to Manu about it while you were in the gift shop. Now we don't have to be back until dark."

She couldn't help but smile at his excitement at spending the day on the ranch, but it concerned her. Riding with a client was pushing the boundaries, but a picnic smacked of a date. She frowned. The last thing she wanted was to lose her job… again.

"You don't look excited."

She plastered her smile back on her face. "No, it's great. I was just thinking about what I had on my to-do list this afternoon. Couldn't remember there for a minute."

He moved his horse closer. "I'm sorry. I didn't consider you might have other appointments."

She waved off his comment. "Oh, no. No appointments. Just computer and phone work. Don't worry, there's nothing that can't wait until tomorrow or if necessary, I can take care of it this evening."

His smile faltered slightly, but he recovered quickly. "Good. Then let's head toward that mountain. I bet the views are impressive."

She nodded as she directed her mare to walk beside Cord's horse, though she was still uncomfortable with how this would look to the other staff and especially Auntie. It was doubtful that Auntie expected her to be gone all day. After all, it was the woman's day off.

Scanning the panoramic view of the rolling land, she spotted a large metal tower and relaxed. Letting Auntie know she'd be back later than expected shouldn't be a problem. She pointed toward it. "I'm surprised the Kamakas allowed a tower in the middle of their land."

"Why not? We have one at the ranch, too. We lease the land to the company. They maintain the tower and it diversifies our income. Unlike Pono, we don't raise sheep and I don't think we have the vegetation they would need, but Manu definitely has me thinking about some other ideas I had for diversification."

She stared at him, not because of what he said, but how he said it. It was another side of Cord she hadn't seen yet. When he spoke like a rancher, his authority came through in his voice and sent tiny shivers of excitement galloping across her skin. She'd always been attracted to confident men, but this was beyond confident. This was downright successful.

He looked away from the tower and turned toward her. "Plus, it's not an eyesore out in the middle of nowhere and the height here probably means it provides a lot of service, which suggests the lease is lucrative."

"Do you have yours on a hill?"

He nodded. "We do. We have a nice butte that was perfect for the tower."

She pictured the buttes she'd seen. They were like Devil's Tower in Wyoming. "How did they get a tower on a butte?"

Cord laughed. "Ours isn't perfect, which made it ideal. It appears that over the centuries, dirt and rock either fell from the top down one side or was pushed up against it. We do get some strong winds where we are. Because of this, one side of it was sloped." He shook his head. "Don't get me wrong, it was still a struggle for them to get that thing up there, but they were determined because it would service so many customers."

"Wow, that's great. I know there aren't many places in the Arizona desert where you can ride and have cell reception. I never thought about it as being a desirable place for a tower since it's so sparsely populated, but if it's high like yours, I can see the advantages to the company."

"And to us." He winked. "My dad used a trained negotiator. He's always taught me that if you're not an expert at something, call on an expert for help."

"That's good advice." And Cord was a good man. Not just good—perfect. How the heck was she supposed to keep him at arms-length when the more she learned about him, the more she wanted to know?

"It looks like level land to that copse over there. What do you say to a short race?" Cord looked expectantly at her. "I can give you a head start if you like."

Oh, now he was being overconfident. Should she take the proffered head start? It's not like she knew the horse she rode. What was she thinking? It didn't matter. She squinted her eyes at him. "What makes you think I need a head start?"

His eyes widened in surprise before he let out a loud laugh, his eyes alight with his humor. "Said like a true Arizonan. Then let's go. Ready—"

She didn't wait. She gave her horse a quick kick to take the lead. Within seconds she heard the sound of hooves pounding the ground behind her. She laughed as she urged her mount faster. "Come on, girl. Show him what you're made of."

She focused on her goal even as her skin electrified at the sound of Cord's voice encouraging his horse just behind her. Flicking the reins, she bent low, keeping the wind resistance down to aid her mare.

Cord's horse drew closer, its snort, as it raced next to her, letting her know exactly where he was. She refused to look, knowing if she did, she'd lose speed. "Come on, girl. Just a little farther."

With only yards to go, Cord's mount pulled ahead and won their impromptu race.

She let her horse slow past the copse of trees as Cord turned his horse back to meet with her. Her heart raced with her exertion as happiness pulsed through her blood. She knew the euphoria was temporary, but it still felt good. She'd forgotten how much she enjoyed riding.

Cord's body was one with his horse, his hands relaxed on the reins, his hips moving in tandem with his mount. His smile was wide and his gaze admiring as he approached. "For a few seconds there, I thought I might lose. Nice run."

She cocked her head. "You sound surprised."

"I am. To be honest, I thought after not riding for so long, you would be rusty, but I should have known better."

She preened at that, though why she should feel so proud that he admired her riding skill was beyond her. Besides, tomorrow she was bound to be a little sore. It had been far too many years since she last rode.

"We're not that far from the top. Are you ready to continue?"

His constant concern for her well being could get addictive. "I'm ready when you are."

Cord turned his horse and set out at a walk. She rode beside him, the large expanse of grassy field a pleasure to travel across. In Arizona, she and her best friend always rode trails that had been worn down between the prickly pear cacti and the mesquite trees.

Thinking about those rides made her homesick. She was

lucky they had so few guests from Arizona stay at the resort or she'd be so homesick, she'd be tempted to leave.

Not that she could go back.

Cord picked up the pace as they neared the bottom of the final incline. When they reached it, he slowed them down again, allowing the horses to take the steep grassy hill as they chose. They must have been as anxious to reach the summit as she was because in no time they arrived.

Cord turned his horse around and she followed suit.

The view took her breath away. Beyond the grassy fields were acres of jungle plant-life followed by the golden beaches spotted with volcanic rock formations. Beyond that was the ocean and the many reefs off the eastern side of the island. The color schemes from bright green grasses to deep green jungle to the gold and black beach bordered by blue waters was a feast for the eyes.

Yet beyond that was the Big Island of Hawaii, Kīlauea smoking in many places with patches of orange lava making a stark contrast against the bright blue sky. "Wow." Her exclamation seemed so inadequate as she stared at the scene. She'd lived on Momi for four years and had never seen this.

"There are no words." Cord's voice was low and soft.

She forced her gaze from the view to him. Even in profile, he was a pleasure to look at, his jaw strong, his nose straight, his cowboy hat shading his high brow. He reminded her of a photo she'd seen in the Western History Museum of a time when cowboys were the backbone of her home state.

He turned his head and met her gaze. "It's like that feeling you get when you're watching the end of an Arizona sunset as the sun lowers onto the desert floor and sprays the sky with orange, pink and purple. Only to be followed by a shooting star as the darkness takes over."

"You're right. It's exactly like that." She'd never heard a man talk about the Arizona sunsets like that. She'd never heard a man talk about nature in that way period.

"This view requires more time. Would you mind having our lunch here?"

At Cord's suggestion, she looked around. There was a grove of *kamani* trees nearby and despite the elevation, it was a warm day, so the shade would be good. "Let's have it under the trees here, so we can enjoy the view and not melt."

Cord nodded and led his horse over to the grove.

She brought her horse to a halt next to his, intending to dismount, but watching Cord was far too distracting as he threw his leg over and jumped down.

He straightened his hat then looped the reins over a tree branch and stepped up to her horse and held its bridle. "Let me help you down."

Sudden panic swept through her. "I'm good." Anxious to get down before he could reach for her, she threw her leg up as she turned to dismount, but in her rush, she didn't clear the horse's rump and her foot made contact, causing the horse to start forward. Her other foot, still in the stirrup, went with the horse and she fell backward.

Chapter Six

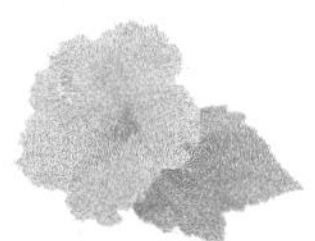

Cord lunged forward, catching Leah before her head hit the ground, his knees taking the brunt of the impact. "Whoa, that's a long way down." His heart thumped hard, making further conversation impossible.

Leah, whose eyelids were squeezed shut as she lay sprawled across his lap, opened her eyes and blinked. "You saved me." The confusion in her voice tugged at his heart.

He nodded, letting his breathing calm some more before attempting speech again.

Her gaze didn't leave his as her eyes filled with water. "Thank you."

At her tears, he found his voice. "Hey, no need to cry. You didn't get hurt, did you?"

She shook her head, giving him a tremulous smile.

He returned it, his heart finally back to a normal beat, which allowed him to appreciate the feel of the woman in his arms. Her face, so close to his, tempted him. He wanted to kiss her, assure her she was safe. But he didn't fool himself. He wanted to taste her lips, feel if they were as soft as they looked. All he had to do is lift his arm beneath her head.

Instead of acting on his urge, he pushed it aside. He

would not take advantage of her scare, nor would he change their relationship in that way until he learned why she was so reluctant to be touched. He hadn't even seen her touch anyone else, not even her friend Melia.

On the other hand, she was definitely touching him now through sheer circumstance. He felt it the second her entire body tensed. As if on cue, she started to roll off him, her feet trying to gain purchase on the slick grass only to slide out from under her, landing her face down on his crotch.

He wasn't immune to the significance of her position and felt himself harden. "Hey, relax. Bring your knees under you."

She did as he instructed, but still used one of his thighs to press on to push herself up, causing his body to become even more excited. To say he was uncomfortable in his kneeling position would be an understatement.

"I'm sorry. I didn't hurt you, did I?" She knelt on the grass, her hair falling out of the ponytail she'd put it in for riding, her shirt half-pulled from her jeans, and her hands clasped in front of her.

It was that last detail that cooled his ardor. "No, I'm fine. I was more worried about you."

She clasped her hands even tighter. "I guess I'm more out of practice than I thought. I used to be able to jump off a horse in a minute." Her hands loosened. "I once jumped from my horse while he was still moving. I was that excited to see my grandfather." Her genuine smile confirmed how relaxed she'd become at her memory.

He lifted a knee to stand. "I bet you were looking for a present." He quirked his lips as he rose and held out a hand toward her, curious about what she'd do.

Her smile faltered and her gaze swept to his knees. "Oh no, you'll have permanent grass stains on those new jeans."

He shrugged, keeping his hand where it was. "I had to break them in one way or another. They'll just get worse working on the ranch anyway."

She lifted her head. "I'm sorry you had to save me, but I'm grateful."

Though she locked gazes with him, she still didn't take his hand.

"Let me help you up." There, now she couldn't ignore it any longer.

She finally looked at his hand and with a deep breath, put hers in his. Once she grasped his hand, she seemed to relax.

As she rose, he wanted to pull her against him, but again he forced himself to remain passive. Two things stood in his way, her aversion to touch and the fact he would only be on the island for under two weeks.

But he still wanted her.

Once standing, Leah released her grasp and scanned the area. "Oh no. Look." She pointed down the mountain where her horse was blissfully trotting back to her comfortable barn.

He laughed. "Don't worry, she'll find her way."

Leah shook her head. "But will we?"

He pressed his hand to his chest. "I'm insulted. Do you have so little faith in my directional abilities?"

She cocked her head and raised an eyebrow. "I don't know anything about your directional abilities. For all I know, you've already become lost at the resort."

"Touché." He nodded. "Then you'll just have to have a little faith."

She pointed. "I'd have a little more faith if your horse wasn't about to leave us behind."

He spun and grabbed the reins just as his horse started to trot by. Idiot. He knew that was a possibility. Calming down the horse, he waited until the other was out of sight before coaxing his animal back into the shade. Tying the reins a bit more securely, he finally faced Leah again. "Now, we can eat. My stomach is growling at me."

"Mine, too."

He pulled the backpack from the saddle. With only one horse, they would either have to walk back or ride double. He actually liked either option.

"How about over here?" Leah stood beneath a tree he recognized as pretty abundant on the island. It was filled with large yellow flowers, and combined with others of its kind, provided ample shade.

"Perfect." He strode to her. "What kind of tree is this? It doesn't leak acidic sap or anything, does it?"

"Ah, you've heard of the manchineel tree. We don't have any of those here on the island. From what I've been told, they're common in the Caribbean. Did you do research on tropical plant life before coming to Momi?" She gazed at him in admiration.

He so enjoyed that gaze he wanted to lie, but he didn't. "No, I can't take credit for doing any research. It wasn't like I was excited to come on this trip. That's why I dragged Phil with me. He's always up for an island." He pulled out the small blanket folded neatly inside the backpack and unfolded it.

She took one end from him and they laid it on the ground. "Then how do you know about the manchineel tree?"

He put the backpack on the edge of the blanket and unzipped it. "I went to the University of the Virgin Islands to get my degree. That's where I met Phil."

Leah had reached her hand into the backpack, but stilled at his statement. "You went to the Caribbean for college? Why?"

Because I was too immature to handle being a Pennington at an Arizona college. "I figured it was my one chance to do something completely different. Besides, I was young and stupid and figured on an island I wouldn't have to study too much." He shook his head. "I was wrong about the studying part, but I was right about it being completely different."

She'd already taken out the sandwiches and napkins.

He pulled out the drinks and sat down beside her, careful not to touch her. He didn't want to make her uncomfortable. "You must have had a similar experience moving here. For me, it made me appreciate home that much more, but I enjoyed the different culture on the island."

Leah held her sandwich in her hands as if she'd forgotten what she was about to do. "When I first arrived and was hit with that hot, humid air coming off the plane, I thought I'd made a huge mistake, but then when I took the cab to the Puanani and saw all the greenery, I felt a lot better. Like you said, it's different."

He unwrapped his sandwich, the tangy scent of barbeque filling his nostrils, making his stomach rumble again. Still, he refrained from taking a bite. "How long did it take to grow accustomed to everything?"

She chuckled as she focused on unwrapping her lunch. "I'm still adjusting, but the more I learn and see and taste," she held up her sandwich, "the more comfortable I feel. Though it isn't home, I know I'll miss it when I move on. Like your island college, this has been my adventure."

He chewed the bite he'd taken. He'd been comfortable on St. Croix, but after four years, he was anxious to return home. Was she? She didn't appear so, though he kept hoping she was.

He took a large swallow of the iced tea the Pono staff had packed for them. Why did he keep hoping Leah wanted to return to Arizona? Was it simply because he felt more comfortable around her since they were from the same state, or was it more?

She interrupted his thoughts. "I never answered your question about these trees. We call them kamani trees. I'm sure there's some more scientific name for them. They don't bear any kind of fruit you can eat, but they're all over, and I love how bright they are— very Hawaiian."

He nodded as he chewed to acknowledge her answer, but he was far more interested in her than in the plant life.

She took a small sip of the tea before continuing. "Did you know Puanani means beautiful flower? Even people's names mean something. Like Melia means frangipani and Ulu means breadfruit."

He smiled at that. "Is he always so forward?"

She sighed. "Only when he's unattached. He needs to find a partner that will marry him. I thought Mr. du Bourbon was going to swing a fist at Ulu's jaw. I can assure you, Ulu is no fighter."

He wiped his mouth with one of the clean bandanas that came with their lunch. "Call him Phil, though I can't tell you what that means. I can tell you Cordell means rope-maker. Nice and simple, like me."

"I'd hardly consider you simple." She gestured toward the fields below them. "You understand how this whole operation works. That's hardly simple."

It seemed so to him, but he wouldn't argue the point. "What about your name? Do you know what Leah means?"

She shook her head as she folded the paper her sandwich came in and tucked it in the knapsack with her dirty bandana. "Every time I think to look it up, I get distracted by something else. I'm not home all that much, so when I am, I'm either cleaning or sleeping." She stuck her tongue out.

The jolt of desire that hit his groin took him by surprise, and he grimaced.

"Exactly." She gave him a warm smile, obviously thinking he agreed with her.

His physical reaction to her just reminded him that he wanted to know more. "Did you buy a home here or do you rent?"

"I rent. Since I didn't know how long I'd be here, I didn't think buying would be wise, and frankly, on my salary, it would be a stretch." She nodded at him as if he'd understand and picked up the wrapping he'd laid on the blanket and put it in the backpack.

Uncomfortable with her assumption, he quickly redirected her. "Since you're not home much, does that mean you go out to eat a lot?"

She cocked her head. "I do usually eat out, mainly at Keoki's, the Cracked Coconut, or a little mom and pop place not far from the Puanani. I've also been known to order dinner from the resort to eat at home." She smiled sheepishly. "I love to cook but cooking for one is no fun."

He tipped his iced tea bottle and swallowed to avoid agreeing or disagreeing. He usually ate at the big house or grabbed a bite with friends. His new kitchen still gleamed, not because he cleaned it, but from lack of use. Rosalie came in and dusted it, complaining it was just for show.

Finishing off his tea, he put the empty bottle into the little vinyl cooler. "Are you finished with that?"

"Almost."

As she tipped her bottle back to finish her tea, his gaze found her slender neck. The urge to kiss her there distracted him.

"There." She held the bottle out, and he took it, but as he did so his fingers brushed hers, and she let it go too quickly, forcing him to grab at it. "Oh, sorry." She looked away as she rose.

Insulted by her aversion once again, he placed the empty in the cooler and then stuffed it in the backpack. What if it wasn't a fear of touching but that she didn't want to touch him?

Placing the backpack on the ground, he rose. Was he reading more into her jerky movements and assuming it was universal?

Leah bent over and picked up two ends of the blanket. "Grab your ends."

The change in subject caught him off guard for a moment. Maybe she didn't hug Melia because she'd been on-the-job and when she ducked under Auntie's hand, she was just checking to see who it was.

"Cord?" She nodded at him and looked toward his feet.

"Right." Bending, he grasped the two ends of the blanket

in his hands. But she had shaken his hand and taken it when he offered to help her up, so it couldn't be an aversion to him.

Folding the blanket in the same direction as she did, he relaxed. It was definitely not him. Maybe it was as simple as a work versus personal space. He folded his end again before she brought hers to him. He took her end, noticing that she avoided touching his fingers. When she bent and folded the blanket up again, she did the same thing.

"I'll take it from here." As soon as he said the words, she stepped away. Folding the blanket one more time, he added it to the backpack before zipping it and hanging it back on his saddle horn. When he turned back toward her, she was taking pictures of the view.

He walked to where she stood. "I don't think a picture will do this justice."

"I know, but it will remind me of today." She didn't look at him. Instead, she gazed at the view, a half smile on her face.

Did she want to remember the view, or like him, remember their day together, a day he was in no hurry to end. He could easily see himself wrapping his arms around her from behind, inhaling her myrtle scent as he rested his cheek against her hair. That's how he'd prefer to remember the view.

She finally looked at him. "Was there anything else you wanted to investigate here?"

"Yes. Manu told me he'd show me the shearing process, which is back at the barns. Without your horse, we'll have to ride double or walk." He'd leave it up to her and see which way she went.

She frowned. "Or you could ride back and send someone for me."

Now *that* he hadn't expected. "I will not leave you out here by yourself." He kept his voice stern, not happy with her suggestion. If it was his sister, Hailey, who could shoot with the best of them, and it was on their ranch, he might consider it—might. But there was no way he'd leave Leah on top of a mountain on a strange ranch with who knew what possible dangers.

She glanced at his horse and quickly replied. "Then we better start walking."

Though he'd expected that to be her decision, he was still disappointed. He nodded and lifted the reins from the *kamani* branch, sending a handful of yellow pedals cascading to the ground as his arm brushed them.

He brought the horse around and joined her. If they had to walk, he would use every minute to learn more about her.

Leah took a bite of the fried dough and sighed. Eating a Keoki malasada for breakfast was the best way to start her two days off. Savoring the sweet for a moment, she closed her eyes. When she opened them, Melia was staring at her expectantly.

"Well, now that you have coffee and breakfast, you tell me what happened at Pono."

She purposefully exaggerated her chewing and swallowed. Then she lifted the coffee cup and took a sip. She'd had an amazing day with Cord. Though she'd done her job by taking him as Auntie requested, the entire day had felt like a date. Their long walk back from the romantic picnic with the breathtaking views had been heavenly. He never stopped asking her questions, and when they finally arrived at the barns, she felt as if she'd been waking from a walk down memory lane.

"Now you stalling." Melia leaned on the bar in front of her.

Yes, she was. She stuffed the rest of the malasada in her mouth. Olino was a tight community. At least most of the Pono workers lived on the ranch, but she didn't know them all and there was a good chance someone may have misinterpreted her trip there—she certainly had.

Last night when she arrived home to her lonely cottage with only some Puanani leftovers in the fridge, she'd kicked herself for not taking Cord up on his offer to go to dinner. Luckily, she'd persevered or today would have been unbearable. It was bad enough that she couldn't stop thinking about him. Her gut said her feelings for him went way beyond missing Arizona.

She reached for her coffee cup, but Melia whisked it away.

"Uh-uh, not until you tell me what you do at the ranch."

"Give me back the coffee and I will."

Melia relented and let her take a sip.

"Cord enjoyed talking ranch stuff with Manu. Manu walked us over every inch of his operation until I thought my feet would fall off. Luckily, he had some horses saddled and we toured the rest of the ranch by horseback. Then I dropped Cord off at the resort and went home. I was exhausted."

Melia gave her a doubtful look. "Fine, so you tell me what you *did*, but what he say? What you say? Did he ask you out? Did you kissy?"

Her friend's questions hit too close to home, and she widened her eyes. "Of course not. You know I can't date him. It's against the Puanani rules. I don't want to lose my job."

"It's a stupid rule." Melia sighed. "Maybe you see him and not let anyone know."

She rolled her eyes. "In this community? Sure, like that would work." Not that she hadn't wished she could do that very thing. There was so much about Cord she liked. Not only did he appear incredibly honest and upright, but he was patient with her and protective. What girl didn't want to have a handsome, sweet cowboy as her protector?

She held up her coffee in salute. "Forget about it. He goes home in twelve days anyway. He's not the type to ask some strange woman he met to come home with him, and when I say 'strange woman,' I'm not referring to the local cadre of single women here in Olino."

Melia pushed back from the bar counter and began to set up for the afternoon. She pulled a bag of limes from the refrigerator. "How you know what type he is? Maybe he all ready to settle down with right woman and the minute he see her it's all love at first sight. He a paniolo after all."

She laughed, shaking her head at her friend's illogical conclusion. "Have you been streaming those black and white movie musicals again?"

"What?" Melia shrugged. "It could happen."

"Yeah, and you could be whisked off your feet by some Polynesian Prince who just won back his island country." She took another swallow of her coffee.

"From your lips to Laka's ears." The woman raised her gaze to the thatched ceiling.

"I don't think a Hawaiian goddess of love is going to be rushing to help you find prince charming." She smiled at Melia to soften her words.

Melia started slicing the limes. "In my situation, I take all the help I can get."

Really? Melia was gorgeous, sassy, loyal and independent. The woman was a catch. "I can't believe you're not taken already."

Her friend stopped slicing for a moment and blew her a kiss. "And that why I love you. Which mean I want to see you with paniolo from Arizona."

Startled, Leah widened her eyes. "Why?" Was it more faulty connections on Melia's part that she'd want that?

"Because…" Melia opened up the fruit tray, gathered up the sliced limes and dropped them in, snapping the lid closed.

"Because why?" That her friend would hesitate to explain was unusual in itself.

Melia pulled the bag of limes from the bar and stuffed them into the fridge then took out a bag of lemons. She plunked them down on the bar, grabbed a lemon and started slicing.

"Melia, why do you want to see me with Cord?"

Her friend finally stopped slicing and looked at her. "Truth?"

"Truth." She tensed. Her friend only used that when she knew what she was about to say would sting.

"You not affectionate enough for our men. You don't touch. You need *haole* like the mainland paniolo. If you stay here, you grow into bitter, lonely old *wahine*."

Her stomach knotted. Wonderful, even her friends thought she had no future on Momi thanks to her stupid issue. She couldn't argue the fact. Every local she'd dated had dropped her after the second date. Her longest relationship had been with an investment broker that had just moved to the island, but even he got tired of her behavior after a month.

Was it time for a change? Did she need to see a psychologist or someone?

"You angry with me now." Melia's frown showed she regretted she'd said anything.

Leah was glad she had. Maybe it was the wakeup call she needed. She forced herself to reach across the bar and pat Melia on the hand. "Not at all. You're my friend and friends tell each other the truth."

Melia's eyes widened then she nodded.

As her friend went back to prepping for the lunch crowd, she pulled out her to-do list for the day. Unclipping the pen from her notebook she hesitated. She should add *find a psychologist* to her list, but something about writing it down made her feel broken. Reattaching the pen to the pad, she dropped it back into her purse. She could fix this on her own.

She was well aware her aversion to touching and being touched had grown worse instead of better. She'd done this to herself. If she could do it to herself, she could undo it. The memory of Cord staring at her as if his touch was repulsive had her stomach sinking all over again.

The look was too close to what she'd experienced in the parking lot her last day working in Arizona. A chill filled her, freezing her to the spot and her eyes misted. She didn't want a man she cared about to ever look at her that way.

And whether she admitted it to anyone, she did care about Cord.

Chapter Seven

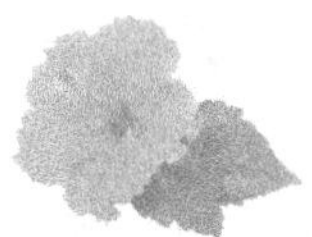

Cord lay on the double-sized lounge chair on his patio. Though he'd hoped to move to a regular room when he'd first arrived, with the women camped out by the pool, he was happy with his current spot. So far none of them had discovered where he stayed, and he wanted to keep it that way.

There was only one woman he wanted to spend time with on his forced vacation and that was Leah Pennington. Unfortunately, she wouldn't be coming to work for the next two days, which shouldn't surprise him. After all, she needed a couple days off during the week like everyone else. At home he usually just took Sundays off, but occasionally he took the whole weekend.

Though she wasn't on the resort, she hadn't forgotten their deal. The typed note slipped under his door that morning informed him he would be picked up at 1:00PM to hike a sleeping volcano and the same note informed him he would be going deep sea fishing at 7:00AM the following day. He looked forward to both activities, but would have preferred it if Leah was with him.

A knock on his door had him rising. He hadn't ordered room service yet. Not ready to admit his suite had been discovered, he quietly walked down the stone path along the side of the house to spy on who might be there.

As he looked over the frangipani bush on the corner, he recognized Phil's short black ponytail as he turned his back. He scanned the area behind Phil to make sure no one had followed his friend then stepped around the bush. "I thought you'd be too busy with the ladies to come hunt me down."

Phil spun, his movement quick from years of required training with what Cord felt were antiques—swords. "Ah, you're still in hiding then."

He nodded. "I'm out back." He turned, assured Phil would follow. As they entered his patio, he grabbed his soda from the lounge and set it on the outdoor table. He held his hand out. "Have a seat. If it's tranquility you're looking for, I can provide it as long as you don't mind the cacophony of birds." He pulled out a chair and sat as his friend joined him.

"I'll take the birds over all the female chatter for a change." Phil set down a half-empty bottle of orange juice. "Not that I mind the ladies' talk. It's just nice to have other sounds to listen to and other scenery to enjoy."

"How'd you get away with no one seeing you?"

Phil's smile was sly. "I excused myself to use the toilet then walked by it and around the corner to the path past the laundry. Through the window I did see one older woman loading sheets into a washer, but I held my finger to my lips. Hopefully, she won't tell the others where I went, if they get that far."

Cord chuckled and raised his glass. "I'm sure your secret is safe unless one of the women is her daughter and she's looking for a son-in-law."

Phil visibly shivered. "I prefer to pick my own wife, not

have one foisted upon me. My father is in good health, and I am yet young."

He raised his eyebrows. "Not as young as you think. I'm surprised your father has not pressured you to settle down yet. I would think at thirty-three he'd be wanting grandchildren to insure the continuation of the du Bourbon lineage."

Phil's face sobered. "Perhaps if my mother were alive I would be married by now, but my father is far too preoccupied with affairs of state."

For a small island country, there was quite a bit of dissention on how to best run it, at least from what Phil had said last time he'd visited Ironwood. "I thought your childhood friend was planning to run for Prime Minister?" He didn't begin to understand how the royal family and a parliament governed a nation. Phil's country operated quite differently than Great Britain's. The du Bourbon king had the final say on everything.

Phil visibly relaxed. "He is, but not yet. Kai needs to be in the parliament longer and maneuver his support."

"I much prefer maneuvering cattle."

As he'd hoped, Phil laughed, the weight of royalty fading away. Phil was far more experienced at persuading people to do what he wished.

"So why the visit? Were you looking for a respite from the ladies or did you have an ulterior purpose?"

Phil opened his bottle of juice and took a swig before replying. "I thought you might give me some advice."

"If it's about cattle, horses, beer or American country music, I'm your man."

Phil frowned. "It's about American women."

Cord lifted his eyebrows in surprise. "Um, I hate to tell

you, but you have much more experience in that department than I do. Much more." He was glad he hadn't laid a bet on what Phil needed advice on because he would have lost the ranch.

For the second time since he'd first met Phil, he looked uncomfortable, his usual suave demeanor suddenly gone, and in its place, the real, uncertain man beneath was revealed.

Cord immediately sobered. "You know I'll help in whatever way I can."

Phil nodded but didn't say anything. Instead, he stared at the bottle he kept turning in his hand.

He knew Phil well. They'd been housemates for four years. Living together and experiencing all the school and island had to offer had made them close. Phil would choose his words carefully.

Finally, his friend looked at him. "I'm perplexed by the American woman, Annalise. She's from Florida, which I know little about and I'm not sure it's important. She's single, yet she shows no interest in getting to know me."

If it was anyone else, Cord would have laughed, but Phil's need to be liked by women went far deeper than ego. "Have you been introduced?"

"*Oui.*" That Phil slipped into French revealed his total focus on the subject. "Yet beyond the cursory pleasantries, she's ignored me."

"Is she here with anyone? Maybe she has obligations. She could even have a boyfriend back home. She could also be getting over a bad break up and is in that phase when she hates all men." He'd run into a few of those before.

Phil's face lightened. "I had not thought of any of those

possibilities. She's here with Deidre. Perhaps through a sense of loyalty, she doesn't wish to be tempted by me after I showed no interest in her friend."

Cord couldn't imagine any woman being that close to the selfish Deidre, but it was a possibility. "That could be it. I think what's important is that you don't take it personally. After all, you have all the rest of the ladies anxious to get to know all about you."

"This is true." Phil finally smiled. "Now if you were to come to the pool, you could take at least half of them off my hands." He held his hands out before him as if he could hand women over just like that.

Cord laughed, far more realistic than his friend about his own magnetism, which was minimal without the Pennington money behind it. Then again, Leah did say she thought him more handsome than Phil, and he'd take that over a lame horse any day. "Sorry, my friend, they're all yours."

"Why? Could it be an attractive, confident resort manager from your home state has caught your eye?"

Leah had definitely caught his eye and more. "I admit to enjoying spending time with Leah, but I'm only here a couple weeks. I don't see how anything can come of it." He held up his hand as Phil opened his mouth to speak. "And no, you know I'm not like you. A vacation fling is not my style. If she were working in Arizona and we met, I would definitely pursue this, but in this situation where we can't really see where a relationship could go, it's doomed to end before it begins."

"By your standards this is true. However, you've only spent two days with her. If you like her, I think you should stay open to the possibilities."

Even as Phil said the words, he wanted to agree. He and Leah had a connection that was far more advanced than anyone else he'd ever dated. He felt comfortable with her like they had been together for months. He'd never had that before.

"I admit, spending time with her is making this vacation-slash-reconnaissance mission much more palatable. She's off for the next two days, so I won't see her. That's probably good, so I can focus on my mission here. I was thinking of asking her to show me something else Hailey might like."

He leaned forward. "We've gone to the ranch, which was very enlightening. I'm hoping to convince my father of a new idea I had after visiting it. Leah's lined up a volcano hike and deep-sea fishing for me, both activities something Hellion would enjoy. Any other ideas?"

Phil stared at him so hard, he looked over his shoulder to make sure it wasn't because a woman had found them.

"*Imbécile*, all women love shopping. You must have her take you shopping."

He let his head fall into his hands. Of course. He should have thought of that immediately. Hailey loved to shop. Lifting his head, he grimaced. "Thank you, my friend. You're right. Guess I didn't think of it because it's one of my least favorite activities."

"But you will do it so you can spend time with this manager, *non*?"

He shook his head. "I'll do it for Hailey."

"And for your heart."

He kept shaking his head as if he could convince himself that Phil was wrong, but he wasn't. He wanted to spend more time with Leah.

Phil stood. "*Mon ami*, if you feel something, you have an obligation to yourself to follow it through."

He leaned back in his chair and raised an eyebrow. "And you say this from experience?"

Phil didn't laugh. "I do. Unfortunately for me, no woman has held my heart since my *maman*, but it doesn't keep me from exploring the possibilities. I never want to regret missing *the one*."

At Phil's words, his gut tensed. What if Phil was right? "Then to put your mind at ease, I'll see where this leads, even if it's a dead end to the sea."

"*Bon*. Now I will leave you so that I may continue to enjoy all that the Puanani has to offer." As Phil wiggled his brow, Cord laughed and waved him off.

Phil strolled through the beach gate and started to jog back toward the resort.

Cord sobered. He'd never thought about 'the one.' He only thought about ulterior motives and when he'd discover them. He hadn't thought of himself as cynical, but now that he looked back on the few relationships he had since college, he'd always been expecting the other shoe to drop, which meant, he'd always held a piece of himself back.

He finished the last of his soda and set the can back on the table. He could thank Brittney Nicholson for that, his high school sweetheart who'd crushed his heart. But that was in the past, over a decade in the past, and it was time he put that part of his life to rest.

It would be a lot easier if people in Arizona didn't immediately recognize his name. A quick internet search was all it took to confirm he was one of *the* Penningtons. Had Leah not bothered to check? That she hadn't made him both excited and anxious.

He'd have to tell her if he thought they had something by the end of his vacation. Until then, he could enjoy her for who she was, and she could learn about him without the bank account added to the mix.

Happy with that thought, he picked up his empty can and walked into the honeymoon suite to prepare for his hike.

Leah closed the door to her office. No need for anyone besides Ulu to know she'd come to work early. That she'd woken up earlier than usual with Cord on her mind wasn't a surprise. On her days off, she avoided the resort like a saguaro cacti forest, but she couldn't wait to see him again, even if it was just to tell him what his next adventure would be.

She hoped he liked the hike and the fishing. Momi didn't have an active volcano, and right now she couldn't arrange for him to travel to the Big Island to see Kilauea because its last eruption was too recent. From his description of his sister, there was no doubt she would do that and maybe it would be possible when she came for her wedding. If she came.

Sitting down at her computer, Leah pulled out her folder on approved vendors. There was so much more she could have Cord experience. She'd like to give him a mix of exciting and calm experiences, from waterfalls to museums. Since his last was—

Her phone rang and she glanced at the caller. "Ulu, what's up?"

"I hope you don't mind, but I sent him down to your office. Hmm-hmm, he does have a nice ass."

"What? Who are —"

"Gotta go."

She stared at her phone and shook her head. Who could be looking for her at this hour? It was barely seven. Setting her phone down, she rose from her desk, prepared to meet either an angry customer or a new vendor wanting their business.

A knock sounded on her door, and she straightened her dress. "Come in."

At the sight of Cord's freshly shaved face underneath his cowboy hat, her tummy did a happy dance. "Hello. I didn't expect you to be up this early."

He took his hat off and held it in his hand as he closed the door.

She'd never thought of her office as small, but with him filling it, it suddenly felt very intimate.

"I took a chance you might be in. I didn't want to waste any more time."

Her heart lurched. Did he miss her while she was off? He was all she'd thought about.

"I know Momi has a lot to offer and I only have nine days left. I want to make the most of them, for my sister's sake, of course."

She hid her disappointment behind a smile. "Of course." She moved behind her desk. "I was just looking through the day's possibilities based on what's open and what might have availability."

He didn't sit on either of the chairs. Instead, he moved to her side and rested his hip on the corner of her desk. "I thought you could show me the town."

"Kanoa?"

"Yes. I understand there are a lot of shops and bars there. We both know my sister would love to go shopping with her new groom in tow, or possibly let the groom have a bachelor party there?"

"Certainly." She should have thought of that. "I'd be happy to call a taxi to bring you to town. I have a map that will help you find your way around." She opened the second drawer of her desk, but he stopped her with his hand on her arm.

She jerked away, unable to help herself. Quickly, she covered her reaction by rubbing the back of her neck. "You don't want a map?"

"No. I'd like you to be my tour guide."

Her tummy went from dancing to full-out somersaults. "I'd love to, but I'm the only one on duty right now. Auntie took today off since she worked for me earlier this week when we went to Pono Ranch."

Cord stood. "Actually, Auntie sent someone to cover for you."

Huh? Since when did guests make arrangements for employees? She worked hard on the staff schedule to make sure everyone had the days off they wanted while the resort was still fully staffed. "It's not that easy. If—"

"Why not?" Cord stood at her door, his hand on the knob.

"It's complicated. There are personal schedules, staffing needs, and with the added day visitors, I need to be here."

Cord shook his head and opened the door.

Unko, Auntie's husband, stood there with his niece, Wena.

"Oh, wow. Wena!" She came around the desk, but halted before giving the young woman a hug. "It's so good to see you. I heard you graduated."

Wena, her long black hair neatly pulled back from her face, but still left cascading down her back, smiled. "I did." She glanced at her uncle behind her. "Unko and Auntie said I could spend this summer learning about the Puanani and how it operates."

Leah smiled past the lump in her throat and kept it by sheer force of will. "How wonderful."

Unko, whose graying hair did nothing to take away from his stature, nodded toward Cord. "I ran into our guest here yesterday, and he mentioned wanting to go into town. He said you'd been a great tour guide so far, and I figured you could show him around today while I give Wena the tour and explain some of the fundamentals."

He waved his hand. "I know I don't know half of what you know, but maybe Wena could spend some time shadowing you after she gets a taste of the basic mechanics?"

Again, she kept her smile, her stomach twisting tighter than a rattlesnake ready to attack. "I'd love that." She could see her days at the Puanani were numbered already.

"Very good. Then I'll tell Ulu to call me if there's anything that needs tending to, and you show this young man all that our wonderful town offers. Hosting his sister's wedding would be a real honor for the Puanani."

She nodded, clasping her hands in front of her as she fought back tears.

"Thank you so much." Wena waved before turning to follow her uncle down the hall.

Cord, thankfully, cued into the fact that she wasn't herself and closed the door behind them. "What's wrong? As soon as they turned around I thought you were going to break into tears."

She turned away, not sure how much longer she could keep that from happening.

"Did I do something wrong?"

At his question, she had to face him. The last thing she wanted was for him to feel guilty about something he had nothing to do with. "Of course not."

The relief in his face soothed her tattered heart. That he cared so much about hurting her weighed in his favor right now. Defeated, she couldn't keep up her work persona any longer and sagged into her chair. "It has nothing to do with you and everything to do with me, or rather with family."

Cord pulled the chair from in front of her desk over toward her. Spinning it around, he straddled it and gave her his full attention. "Tell me."

She gazed into his concerned eyes and caved. "I have to look for a new job. My days here are coming to an end."

His brow furrowed in confusion. "Did you figure that out just now, or did you learn this before I came in?"

"Just now, but I knew the day would come. I just didn't expect it this way."

"I don't understand, but I want to."

"I shouldn't bother you with my troubles."

He gave her a crooked smile. "But you will…I hope."

How could she resist? Maybe if she hadn't just had the

wind knocked out of her, she could have, but his concern and total focus on her was too much to resist. "Wena just graduated from the university. Last I knew she was wavering between a degree in hospitality or a degree in interior design. That she's here and plans to spend the summer learning about the Puanani means they're grooming her for my position."

"What? They can't do that? You have a lot more experience than she does."

Cord's scowl made her feel better in a way, as if she had a champion for a change. "Unfortunately, they can. Blood is thicker than experience in tight-knit communities such as this. For better or worse, Auntie and Unko will replace me with Wena when they feel she's ready."

"I don't like it." Cord's hand gripped the back of the chair like he planned to pick it up and smash it over someone's head.

"You don't like it?" She chuckled half-heartedly. "Believe me, I'm not in love with the idea either."

"I wish I could make this right for you." Cord's sincere gaze had her queasy stomach settling.

"I appreciate that. It just surprised me. If I landed this job, I can land another and I know Auntie will give me a wonderful recommendation. I've learned a lot working here. I'll just have to update my resume and start looking."

"Is there anything I can do to help?"

Where was he when she was being fired from her last job? She so could have used a knight-in-shining-armor like him then. Or rather a cowboy in chaps with a lasso to rope up the bad guys. She smiled at the thought. "Yes, there is something you can do."

"Name it."

He made it so easy to smile. "Let me take you on a tour of Kanoa. That will take my mind off my new life direction."

Cord stood, flipped the chair back around and set it against the wall then held out his hand. "It would be my honor."

Her heart did a little dance at his gallantry, and she made herself take his hand. At his warm grasp, she felt cared for and protected all at once. She must have really been plowed over by Wena's appearance to feel so much simply from his grasp, but even as they left her office, she didn't try to release his hand as he walked her past a grinning Ulu and out to the parking lot.

Chapter Eight

Cord opened the car door for Leah and shut it after she sat behind the wheel. He was excited, angry, and hopeful all at once at Leah's news. He was excited to be spending the day with her, but angry that she could be pushed aside so easily.

What had him hopeful was the chance that she might move back to the mainland, maybe even Arizona. That alone had him much more open to the possibilities of a relationship of some kind. He simply refused to acknowledge that she could as easily move to China for her next position. His mother had always said worrying was useless.

Sliding into the passenger seat, he gave her a thumbs up, and she drove them to town.

Once she'd parked, he jumped out to get her door, but she was too fast. "This is the very western end of town. I'm going to show you every nook and cranny."

That she didn't mention his sister was a relief. He'd seen her with her professional façade in tatters, and it appeared she was in no hurry to rebuild it, which fit him perfectly. He wanted to know Leah—the woman from Arizona, not Leah—the manager of a Hawaiian resort.

"Is there a place nearby that we can have breakfast? I'm in the mood for something a bit heartier than a malasada."

She gave him a shocked look before laughing. "You better not let Melia hear you say that."

He grinned as he shook his head. "No, ma'am."

"I know just the place to go." She led them down a side street.

It contained small shops selling everything from floral wraps to plumbing parts. When they reached the end of the street, it opened onto a large square. In the center was a farmer's market.

"This way." She pointed to the right.

He followed her as she threaded her way through mostly locals past a bank, a place with a sign that said Shave Ice, and a clothing store that had all Hawaiian prints in the window before stopping at a place called Onolicious. He opened the door for her and took off his hat as they entered the sparsely populated place.

Leah strode directly for the back and another door. He reached around her and opened it. Outside, he put his hat back on as he scanned the jungle oasis. Verdant plants covered the concrete walls that closed in the large courtyard. Bright pink and orange blooms filled the air with a sweet scent and the water fountain against one wall provided a tranquil sound.

A dozen tables filled the space and only two were empty. Leah stepped up to one of them, and he quickly pulled out her chair for her.

She stepped away as their arms almost brushed. "Thank you."

He clenched his teeth together to keep from remarking

on it. Now wasn't the time. She was upset, and he wanted her to trust him. Purposefully ignoring the seat opposite her, he took the one next to her. There was so much he could read in her body language. He felt as if he were taming a wild mustang with Leah, always afraid she'd pull back and run off.

"If you'll allow me? I'll order for you."

He grinned. "I trust you. Just remember, I'm a simple cowboy from Arizona and I'm starving."

Giving him a ghost of a smile, she nodded authoritatively. "I know exactly what you need."

He leaned back, crossing his ankle onto his knee and watched her as the waitress came over.

"We'll have one Loco Moco and a SPAM® and eggs." She glanced over at him. "Coffee?"

He nodded. As soon as the waitress left, he spoke. "I probably should have told you I may be simple, but I'm not big on SPAM®."

She chuckled. "Don't worry. That's for me. I actually never had it until I moved here. I don't order it that often, but once in awhile I'm in the mood for it, like now."

He raised a brow. "Then I have to ask. What is Loco Moco?"

"It's a breakfast fit for a paniolo."

Paniolo is what they called the cowboys on the island. "In other words, I'll see when it arrives."

"Yes, and I expect you to eat every bite."

"Yes, ma'am."

She smiled. "Now what kind of shops did you want to review? Did you have anything you need to get while we're here?"

He shrugged. "Probably the kinds of shops you would like."

"Me?" She frowned in confusion.

"Sure. You're a woman and you're from Arizona. That makes you more qualified than me."

She cocked her head. "When you put it that way, I can see your point." She tapped a finger on the table. "If I were visiting here on my honeymoon, I'd want mementos from my trip, something authentic, maybe some jewelry, and probably a book on Momi. There are a bunch of books on the other Hawaiian Islands, but you can only find books about our island here."

That told him a lot about her that she wasn't interested in the touristy items and was interested in actually reading about the place. "I should probably get one of those books to entice Hailey to come here."

"Do you think she might pick the Puanani based on what you've seen so far?"

He stared into her excited brown eyes. Had she already forgotten that her days of employment there were numbered? "Would it still be important for you even if you weren't here anymore to oversee the arrangements?"

She opened her mouth then shut it quickly. From where he sat, he could see her clasp her hands beneath the table. Her whole demeanor seemed to shrink. "I guess not. It's such a habit to want what is best for the resort that I forgot."

He kicked himself for bringing her down again. "I don't know what Hailey's going to do, but I'm glad she sent me here to scout out this island for her." He smiled, refusing to let her brush away his obvious interest in her.

She blushed. "It's not like I grew up here, but I'm happy to show you—oh, thank you."

The waitress set down a plate of SPAM® with a sunny-side egg on top. It actually smelled pretty good. Then she set a large plate in front of him and at the first whiff, his stomach growled. He grinned. "Perfect."

Leah smiled smugly. "Told you."

He examined his food. Brown gravy covered a fried egg which sat on top of a hamburger patty perched on a pile of white rice. Cutting a piece of egg and hamburger, he dipped his fork underneath to include the rice and popped a chunk into his mouth.

The savory flavor satisfied his taste buds as he chewed, the unique textures a new experience. He caught Leah watching him and swallowed. "This is good."

"Do you think it will be enough?" She made it clear she doubted he could eat it all.

He looked at the plate as if seriously considering her question. "If it isn't, I can always order another."

She laughed, the sound reassuring. If he could keep her laughing, maybe she'd forget about the fact that technically she was working.

As they ate, a comfortable silence ensued. The food was too good to interrupt, and the fact Leah didn't feel the need to fill in the silence made him more confidant that she was comfortable with him.

After they finished breakfast, they walked around the square. Leah was a wealth of information told from the perspective of a mainlander who had moved to the island. It enabled her to both find the local culture interesting and see it from a bird's eye view.

"Every one of these shops will deliver to the Puanani. We are one of only three resorts they will do that for." Leah's pride showed in the lift of her chin.

"I'm guessing that's thanks to you."

Her cheeks flushed a bit. "Yes, but it wasn't my idea. I found out when shopping here the first time that they were already delivering to one resort, so I made it my mission to get the Puanani on the list."

He wanted to tell her how lucky the resort was to have her, but since they would be letting her go to hire a relative, that caused his blood pressure to rise, so he didn't mention it. "I'm not surprised. You strike me as someone who can be very determined."

She stopped. "Only when I'm absolutely sure that I'm on the right track." She rolled her eyes. "Unfortunately, that's not very often." She turned toward the shop where they stood. "This is one of two jewelry stores in the square. It's reasonably priced and the owners are good people. I had a couple who hadn't bought their wedding rings before flying over for the wedding, and they had a good experience. I've had other guests shop here and were very happy with their purchases."

"Is jewelry shopping a normal activity for your guests?"

She looked at him in surprise. "No offense, but you don't get out much do you?"

He chuckled. "I told you. I'm a simple cowboy. I've never bought jewelry for a woman."

Her eyes widened. "Not even for your mom?"

He grimaced. "Technically yes, in that I gave Grey the money, but Wes and I always let my older brother handle the choice of item. He's good at that."

"Then we need to go in. Someday you may want to buy a woman a piece of jewelry, and I promise you if you don't pick it out yourself, not only will she know, but she'll be upset with you."

"Really? Then lead the way." The fact was, for the first time, he was sincerely interested in what a woman would like, and not just any woman.

The shop had a handful of customers, all obvious tourists. He'd bet over half the store's income was generated from tourism. An attractive female worker approached them. "Can I help you find something?"

Leah shook her head. "No, we're just looking." After the woman nodded with a smile, she moved away and Leah leaned a little closer to whisper. "She thinks we're together. I'll go look at watches, so you can view the jewelry. Don't be afraid to ask to look at it or what the price is."

He nodded to show he understood then enjoyed watching her as she meandered over to an area that displayed the very finest watches. He only knew that because his brother had given him one last year on his thirtieth birthday. He saved it for special occasions.

Seeing that Leah was engaged in conversation with a worker, he walked toward the closest counter. It had a variety of necklaces. Despite how professional Leah dressed, he'd noticed she only wore small earrings. Her neck begged to have a necklace draped around it. Something that would fall toward the center of her chest, which he tried not to focus on too much when with her, but it wasn't easy. She had the perfect curves.

"Were you looking for something in particular?" Another

worker had moved to where he stood looking down at the display of colorful gems set in gold or silver. Some even had colored gold.

He shook his head. "I'm just getting ideas."

The woman looked past him. "I'm sure she'll love whatever you pick out."

He didn't disagree verbally, but he still didn't feel as if he new Leah that well. If she left this island for another one, would she want a reminder of where she used to live? Would she prefer something that reminded her of home? He didn't even know if she preferred gold or silver.

He smiled. Yes, he did. She wore silver. The few times he'd seen her with bracelets, they were silver and her watch was silver. It could be white gold or platinum, but she didn't seem like the kind of woman to spend months of paychecks on jewelry.

He looked over at her. Now why did he think that?

She turned at that moment and caught his gaze. She smiled then turned back to talk to the man showing her watches.

"I wouldn't bother."

Cord turned to the man who had spoken to him. "Excuse me."

"Leah. I wouldn't bother buying her anything. You won't keep her around that long."

He studied the mainlander. The man had thick blond hair, a trimmed beard, mustache and a narrow face. He wore a collared shirt and tie, but no jacket.

Forcing himself to keep the growing anger from his voice, Cord looked the man directly in his blue eyes. "Why wouldn't I keep her around?"

The man turned his head to glance at Leah then lowered his voice. "I think she's a virgin. She can't stand anyone to touch her. Trust me. You won't even get a kiss from her."

Cord fisted his hands to keep them at his sides instead of moving toward the man's face. He may be able to afford any damage to the premises he might cause, but he doubted very much that one punch would be enough. Instead, he lowered his brows in confusion. "I have no idea what you're talking about. Maybe it was just you she didn't want to touch."

At the man's smug look, Cord looked past him and held out his hand. "Leah, could you come over here a minute." He nodded toward his hand.

Leah's face went from surprise to her professional smile in a second. Immediately, she strode across the store and grasped his outstretched hand, much to the astonishment of what was obviously a former boyfriend.

"Richard, I see you've met Cord."

Richard swallowed his surprise before turning toward him. "Nice to meet you." The words were said out of habit, his focus still on Leah.

"What are you doing here?" Leah kept her hand in his though she didn't move closer.

A smug smile formed on the man's face. "I've come to buy an engagement ring."

Leah's smile changed to something more genuine. That in itself, helped undercut some of his anger toward the man.

"That's wonderful. I'm so happy for you." She turned toward the woman Cord had been talking to. "Please show my friend your engagement rings."

The woman nodded and walked around the counter.

Leah faced her ex-boyfriend. "I hope you find the perfect ring for her."

The man nodded, clearly confused by Leah's reaction to his news, but he obediently followed the store worker.

Cord squeezed Leah's hand in his. "Let's get out of here."

She nodded and allowed him to lead her outside. The next store front was a pest control company and the one after that was a hardware store, but next to that was exactly what he was looking for.

Entering Pele's Volcano Bar, he kept Leah's hand in his and led her upstairs to the covered deck. He walked to a table near the front and pulled out a chair for her. Silently, she sat, and he waved a waiter over. After ordering a couple of drinks, he sat. "So Richard is an ex-boyfriend."

Startled, her eyes rounded. "Why do you say that?"

"He basically let me know that before you came over."

She looked down at her hands in her lap. "Oh. We only dated for about a month." Her gaze found his. "I'm really glad he found someone. We didn't work out."

"Why?" He had a hunch, based on Richard's comments, but he needed to hear it from her. He wanted her to trust him enough to explain.

She shrugged. "It was my fault. I just didn't feel comfortable enough with him."

He studied her, wanting to push her, but not wanting her to revert into Miss Resort Manager on him. "Tell me."

Leah's gaze was interrupted by their drinks arriving.

He waited until she'd taken a few sips of her drink then laid his hand on the table between them, palm up. "Take my hand."

She looked around the bar.

He had no idea what she expected to see, but the few other couples that occupied tables were too engaged in each other. He wanted them to be just as focused.

She finally returned her gaze to the table and stared at his hand. "Why?"

"Humor me. Just take my hand. You did in front of Richard."

"That's because I got the feeling you wanted us to look like a couple. You did, didn't you?"

He nodded.

"Why?"

"I'll tell you if you take my hand."

She frowned, but she placed her hand on top of his.

He clasped it gently, the feel of her skin against his felt right. It wasn't the only thing he noticed. Once she laid her hand in his, she relaxed, almost as if the idea of touching made her more nervous than actually touching.

Her gaze moved from his hand to his face. "Okay, so why did you want Richard to think we were a couple?"

"Because he saw me looking at you and told me not to bother buying you anything."

Her eyes widened. "Why would he think you would buy me something?"

Probably because of the way he was gazing at her. "More to the point. Why would he tell me not to bother?"

Her brows lowered. "That's probably because we didn't work out."

He shook his head. "No, he told me why."

Leah looked away, but not at anything in particular, and started to slip her hand from his, but he held tight.

"He said you can't stand anyone to touch you."

Her gaze snapped to his. "He said that?"

He nodded, watching her closely. At first she appeared hurt, but anger quickly surfaced.

"How dare he? Maybe it was just him I didn't want to touch." She lifted her chin slightly as if happy with her point.

He hesitated to respond. He had two ways he could go here. One was to agree with her. After all, she didn't owe him anything. But his heart refused to listen to his brain and he shook his head.

She immediately deflated, her eyes lowering, her shoulders slumping.

He kicked himself but couldn't let it go. "I've noticed it as well. And before you say it, it's not just me. You ducked beneath Auntie's touch, didn't hug your friend Melia, and refrained from touching Wena when you were clearly happy to see her."

She didn't look at him, and he could almost feel her need to clasp her hands together, but he still held on.

"Every time someone hands something to you or you hand it to them, you're careful to keep from touching them." He squeezed her hand until she looked at him, her brown eyes showing a sadness that worried him. "Why, Leah? Has someone in your past hurt you?"

He forced his hand not to tighten at the thought of her in an abusive relationship. Her caring heart deserved better.

At the slow shake of her head, his muscles relaxed, but his mind remained alert.

"Then why?"

She sighed heavily. "I've never told anyone here what happened. I didn't want to see people every day who knew."

His heart stilled, and he had to take a deep breath to force it to beat again. There was a very good chance that if he made her reveal her secret, she wouldn't want to see him the rest of the time he was here. He didn't want to risk that.

But his gut was telling him that not only did he need to know, but she needed to confide in someone. What if he could help her? "You won't see me everyday once I leave for home, and I promise I won't say anything to anyone."

She remained silent as he gently brushed his thumb over the back of her hand, hoping she would see that he took this seriously.

Finally, she spoke. "Why do you want to know so much? I know Melia and Ulu and even Auntie have noticed, but they didn't ask."

He gave her half a smile. "I feel at home around you, like we've been friends for a long time. Friends help each other."

She shook her head. "I'm afraid no one can do anything about what happened."

"Leah." He stared into her eyes. "Tell me."

"Fine, but just remember, I told you there's no way to fix it."

"Understood." He admired her as she sat straighter as if facing her nemesis head on. It reminded him of a wild bull spinning to attack the man that thought to ride him.

"I lost my job at the Scottsdale Gardens Resort because I was accused of sexual harassment."

"What?" He'd planned to keep silent, but the idea was so ludicrous, even after knowing her only a few days that his mouth got ahead of his brain.

She nodded, her brow puckered. "I didn't remember doing

anything wrong. I was never a touchy-feely kind of manager, but my supervisor said there was too much proof, and human resources had told her they were going to recommend I be fired. She suggested I resign before they could do that."

The pain of her dismissal flashed across her face, her eyes turning almost copper.

Then she snorted. "What really sucked was I was about to be promoted to her position, and not only was that off the table, but thanks to the gossip mill in the hospitality industry, I knew I couldn't get another position in Arizona…" She took a deep breath, her hand tensing against his. "I had to apply out of state. When Auntie hired me, I swore I would watch every movement I made so I wouldn't cause the same issue again by accident. I guess I over-compensated."

She shrugged as if it was nothing, but her grip on his hand said otherwise. "Now it's a habit I can't seem to break. Maybe because I don't want to. Deep down, I'm still afraid of doing something wrong."

Cord stared at her. The shock of what she'd been accused of far smaller than the ache he felt at her life now. To see her, a competent, smart, beautiful woman, destroyed by a false accusation had his jaw so tight, he couldn't speak.

"I may have been able to keep this strange problem I have relegated to work, if…"

As her voice trailed off, a deeper anguish seemed to take over. "If I hadn't run into the man who'd accused me on what ended up being my last day of work." She shivered as if the memory swamped her like a tidal wave and left her raw and cold.

"What did he do?" His voice was just above a whisper, his anger growing exponentially.

She moved her gaze to their clasped hands. "It wasn't him. It was me. I was walking through the parking lot on the way into work. As soon as HR started the investigation, I had to move to the evening shift since he worked during the day. The hotel manager had called me to tell me to come see her before I started the shift because the investigation was complete. I was beyond nervous, and thinking the worst, I was a bit misty-eyed. I guess I wasn't paying attention to where I was walking and I bumped into him."

She licked her lips, but kept her gaze lowered. "When I said excuse me, I realized who I'd bumped into." She paused then looked up at him, the hurt in her eyes so clear he had to force himself not to look away. "It wasn't what he said, so much as the look of disgust in his eyes as he recoiled from me that sucked the air right out of my lungs. He yelled that I was stalking him outside of work now and he'd go to the police, but it didn't really register. All I kept seeing was that look in his eyes. I felt like a worm. I never wanted to see that look in someone's eyes again. When I went into my supervisor's office, she gave me the option of resigning, which I did." She gave him a sad smile. "Despite all that, one of my new hires, Sheena, gave me a hug goodbye and told me I was the best boss she ever had. That was so sweet, but I felt so uncomfortable."

She sighed. "I thought I could keep from touching those in my workplace and still have a personal life, but I was wrong. I know. I'm an oddity." Her shoulders fell and her hand relaxed within his, as if she'd given up and accepted her fate.

"No." The word was ground out between gritted teeth. That she blamed herself was not something he could allow.

Forcing air into his lungs, he made his jaw work. "Whatever you may think, this is not your fault."

She shook her head and gave a sad chuckle. "I'm afraid it is."

He squeezed her hand. "Who accused you?"

"It was my front desk assistant manager. He said I routinely touched him, and he didn't like it. He said it made him uncomfortable and he didn't want to come to work. Another of my front desk employees said he'd witnessed it. He said I touched my assistant manager's back and leaned over him when viewing the terminal and that I often brushed by him, making contact. I had no idea I had done any of that. My supervisor, to her credit, interviewed every front desk employee, but the evidence was clear."

His mind sped. "Did they have cameras?"

She nodded. "Of course, but the angles were wrong to prove or disprove anything. They weren't really set up for that. At first, I thought it was laughable, but as they continued to investigate and it took longer and longer, I knew it was serious."

"Did this man ever tell you he didn't like you touching him?" Though Cord couldn't imagine that.

"No. He told my supervisor he was afraid to tell me because I favored the women over the two men under me."

Cord forced himself not to roll his eyes. "What happened after you left?"

"What do you mean?"

"I mean, who took over as front desk manager? Who ended up with the promotion?"

"Oh. The banquet manager got the promotion and my assistant manager became front desk manager, but that would have happened anyway if I was promoted. I really don't think it was to get ahead at the resort."

He wouldn't argue the point, but something about the whole affair wasn't sitting right. What he hated most was that Leah was left with an unreasonable fear of touching anyone… and he definitely wanted her to touch him.

Lifting her hand in his, he leaned over and kissed the back of it, a move Phil practiced on a regular basis, but one he'd never had the urge to do before. "Thank you for sharing that with me. I promise I won't tell a single person here on Momi."

She gave him a real smile then. "Thank you."

"Can I ask another favor of you?"

She raised her brows and cocked her head. "Hmm, I'm not sure. You may have used them all up."

He placed his free hand against his chest. "Please, tell me that isn't true."

She pretended to seriously think about it. "First, tell me the favor."

He gave her his most charming grin. "I enjoy holding your hand so much, I'd rather not let go. Would you mind continuing our explorations holding hands?"

Her gaze froze, and he quickly added. "Especially since Richard may be around the square. I want him to realize he missed out on a great woman."

The blush that stained her cheeks worried him that she'd move back into manager mode again like she usually did when he embarrassed her with a compliment.

Chapter Nine

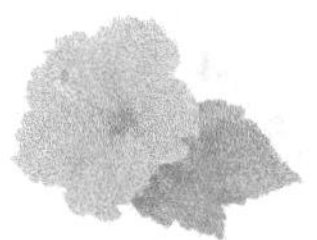

Leah cringed inside, not because she didn't want to hold Cord's hand, but because she wanted to and couldn't. She pulled her hand from his grasp and placed it in her lap, wishing he didn't look so crestfallen. "I would like that, but I can't."

"Why?" His direct green gaze was hard to turn away from.

"It's Momi."

His brows drew together. "Momi?"

"Yes." She nodded trying to figure out how to explain it. "Momi and Olino in particular. It's hard to understand. Remember how on your first day here we had the lobby full of women?"

He nodded.

"That's because news travels really fast in Olino. It's kind of like its own community. Back in 1848, all the Hawaiian Islands were divided into pie slices, or ahupua'a, which gave each Hawaiian king a piece of land for his people that had a bit of every ecosystem. Each one was given a name, like Pono. Over the years, many of these ahupua'a have been divided further like here in Olino, but the community of the original division is still very tight knit."

"That sounds like the 'estates' on St. Croix. The old sugar

plantation borders are still used to divide the island and many people have communities within them that are like extended family."

She smiled in relief. "Exactly."

He shook his head. "But what does that have to do with holding my hand?"

Her stomach knotted. She'd hoped he'd understand, but her women's intuition was telling her that even if he did, he wouldn't like it. "Olino is a tight knit community. If I'm seen holding your hand around town, it would be everywhere by dinner time. Auntie would hear of it, and I could be out of a job far sooner than I want to be."

"I didn't get the impression that Auntie minded you showing me around." He raised his brow, the challenge clear.

"Showing you around and holding hands are two completely different things, especially when the Puanani has a strict policy on employees dating guests."

His brows lowered and he opened his mouth to speak, but she held up her hand.

"Please, I don't want to leave another job in disgrace."

He stared at her a minute as if trying to decide what to do. Finally, he gave her a quick nod. "I understand."

Though relief loosened the knot in her stomach, her heart wished it could be otherwise. In just a few days, Cord had wormed his way under her defenses and made her wish for a more normal life.

He looked out onto the square where the bustle of everyday life continued. A passing interest to him.

She, however, would always be on the outside looking in.

When he turned back, his smile had returned. "I believe

you were going to show me where I can purchase a book on the history of Momi."

She nodded, happy to have them back on normal ground… if anything in her life could be considered normal.

Leah walked into the banquet hall to check on the set up for the Akoni family reunion luncheon. The tables were set with alternating green and yellow table cloths and similar cloth napkins. At the center of each was a single glass vase with woven *lauhala* around it, adding more green color to the room, and which would soon sport bright yellow orchids.

Immediately, the memory of her and Cord having a picnic lunch under the *kamani* trees on Pono Ranch surfaced. Her whole body warmed as she remembered his smile. Even yesterday afternoon she'd basked in that smile once they'd made it through her confession. She trusted him with her secret here on Momi, and it didn't really matter if he told anyone in Arizona because her life there was over.

On that thought, she glanced at the clock on the wall and quickly moved to the back doors. The flowers should be arriving any moment. Her staff was busy putting the final touches on the room, so she opened the double doors at the back only to discover Cord and Phil standing outside.

"Leah." He grinned. "I was just telling Phil about how you had an event today, and I wouldn't get to see you."

"It was more a complaint than a telling." Phil rolled his eyes, finally seeming somewhat human to her.

She could feel her cheeks warm at his statement. "Well,

here I am getting ready for a big family reunion." She refocused her gaze on Cord. "What are you doing back here? You have a dive soon." She looked past him. "They should be here any minute."

He chuckled. "Yes, *we* know, but Phil didn't want his lady friends to know, so he snuck away early and called me from his hiding place here to keep him company until the van arrived."

She turned to look through the banquet hall windows at the other end of the room to see the pool crowd meandering a bit. All except Diedre, who had the attention of her two favorite island men. "I think they're getting restless." She turned back to the men to find Cord whipping his gaze up to meet hers. Was he checking out her butt?

Ignoring the thrill that gave her, she glanced down the drive again, now looking both for his van and her flowers. "I'm sure your ride will be here soon."

"I don't mind waiting." Cord raised his brows, hopefully. "Are you sure you can't join us?"

She looked at Phil who just shook his head.

"Cord, as you can see I'm working. Besides I never learned to scuba dive in the desert of Arizona."

Phil chuckled. "*Oui, mon ami.* Not everyone spends their college years on a beautiful Caribbean island."

"And not everyone gets to grow up on one in the luxury of royalty."

She snapped her gaze to Phil, who frowned at Cord. Oh boy. She wasn't supposed to know that.

Cord appeared contrite. "I'm sorry, Phil. I'm so comfortable around Leah, I didn't think."

She hastened to assure Phil. "I promise not to say a word to anyone, especially Diedre."

After shooting an exasperated look at Cord, Phil nodded to her. "I would appreciate that. I wish to enjoy my vacation."

"Of course. We can be discreet here." The sound of a vehicle pulling into the driveway had her looking away. "Oh, my flowers are here. If you will excuse me?"

The men strode out of the way of the truck, and she quickly signed for the delivery. When she next looked up, it was to see Cord waiting for Phil to climb into the van. Just before he stepped in, he looked back at her and waved.

Her heart warmed and she waved back.

"Someone you know?"

Wena's voice behind her had her spinning around. "Just a couple guests going scuba diving. Is everything under control?"

"I'm not sure. I was checking the table settings like you asked and there's no spoon for dessert. Didn't you say they had ordered *haupia*?"

Quickly, she followed Wena to review the tables and then followed up with the kitchen. The coconut pudding-like dessert definitely needed a spoon.

Her day continued to be busy, which she appreciated because it kept her from thinking about Cord...too much. All the activities she'd planned for him were chosen with his sister in mind, which meant they were a bit on the dangerous side.

At the time, she hadn't thought she'd worry about him, but she did now, which was silly because not only was he a grown man, but she'd vetted every operation herself, and they all had excellent safety records.

Still, as she handed Nani the paperwork on a tour for the

Randolphs, she breathed a sigh of relief when the scuba van finally arrived in front of the lobby and Cord stepped out. He was followed by Phil, who then leaned in the open driver's window and handed the female driver a business card and pen. She'd bet that woman would be calling him very soon.

She should go back to her office and turn off her computer before Cord saw her, but she just couldn't seem to make her feet move.

"Earth to Leah." Nani's soft voice broke into her trance.

"What?"

"If you stare any harder, he'll be able to read your thoughts."

She forced herself to look away. "I was just pleased they made it back in one piece. We both know tourists are not immune to shark bites."

Nani gave her a soft smile. "I hear cowboys aren't their cup of tea."

"Now why would—"

"Oh please. It's so obvious."

She stiffened. "I swear I'm not seeing him. That's against policy."

Nani's face softened. "I was just teasing."

She glanced toward the entryway at the sound of Cord's voice. "I better get back to my office."

"Leah, wait."

She ignored Nani and strode toward her office, panic riding up her spine. She couldn't be seen with Cord again or she'd be out of another job…even if she was soon to be out of job anyway. She also did a miserable job at hiding the fact she was attracted to him. She didn't need another disgrace.

Closing the door behind her, she quickly turned off her computer and set her agenda for the following day's tasks next to it. Tomorrow she'd scheduled cliff diving for him and Phil. What had she been thinking? If she recalled correctly, after that was ziplining and then parasailing. Jotting a note to find a safer activity for the day after that, she dropped her pen and grabbed her purse.

Once outside her office door, she listened, but didn't hear Cord. Quietly, she tip-toed to the front lobby. After a quick scan proved no one was there, she headed across it, waving good bye to a confused Nani as she almost ran to her car. The sooner she left for home, the easier it would be to resist temptation.

Why did temptation have to come in a six-foot, brown-haired cowboy with the nicest smile and the biggest heart?

Cord swung off the platform of the zipline, the tree tops whizzing by as he sped down the final run. Instead of enjoying the scenery, he just wanted it over with so he could get back to the Puanani. It was the opposite of how he'd thought his "vacation" was going to go.

He lifted his feet up and came to a halt as he stood on the platform, the spotter ready to help him. He thought he'd want to go home as soon as he'd learned what he needed to know for Hailey, but as the last two days sped by with no more than a glimpse of Leah, he'd seriously thought about extending his stay. He needed to see her. Talk to her.

He'd swear she was avoiding him, but every time he saw her she was knee-deep in work. He had to respect that, especially after what she revealed to him. Still, he'd hoped they could spend some time together. He'd even stealthy come to her office near the end of the day yesterday, only to find it locked, and when he'd checked the parking lot, her car was gone.

Unbuckling his harness, he gave the spotter a quick smile of appreciation. The note under his door had said tomorrow was parasailing. He would refuse to go if she didn't go with him. Phil had already said he wasn't interested. Maybe he could help Leah with her work. He just wanted to spend time with her, so he could figure out how he felt about her.

Grabbing the rope, he lowered himself to the ground to find Phil waiting for him.

"You look like you're about to knock down these trees with your bare hands. What's wrong?"

It took him a moment to get out of his head and focus on what Phil said. He shrugged. "Just frustrated."

Phil looked at the zipline. "I thought everything went smoothly."

He waved away the experience. "That was fine."

"Ah, it's the *belle femme.*"

He'd never taken French in school, but after living with Phil for four years, he'd picked up a few of his phrases and *pretty lady* was one of them. "Yeah."

Phil nodded. "I can commiserate. Come, let us have a libation."

It was still afternoon, so Leah would be busy. Maybe talking to Phil would help him figure out exactly why he was so irritable. "Fine."

Phil patted him on the back and led the way down the

path to the small building where they'd been given instructions. Their car was waiting for them, though their driver was not a woman today. After negotiating a side trip to a bar, they were on their way.

He was glad that Phil remained silent because his own thoughts felt as if they were bouncing off the inside of his skull. He was *never* irritated. Not even when a ranch hand didn't listen to instructions. It just wasn't who he was. He was the easy-going brother. Wes was the hot head and Grey hid it well.

What the hell was wrong with him? Was it simply Leah, like Phil suspected? If so, why would she be irritating him when all he wanted to do was spend time with her? It made no sense, especially because he'd just met her nine days ago. He couldn't shake the feeling that time was running out.

The car pulled off the paved road onto a sandy one then stopped in front of a small beach bar. It was everything Phil asked for, quiet and local. After telling the man to come back in a couple hours, they doffed their shoes and walked through the sand.

On the beach, a couple families enjoyed the water while the scent of fried SPAM® wafted toward them. It made him smile as it conjured up his memory of having breakfast with Leah, who enjoyed the Hawaiian staple.

After grabbing a couple beers, they snagged a small picnic table in the sand.

Phil lifted his bottle. "To beautiful women."

"To amazing women." He clinked his bottle against Phil's, ignoring the man's raised brow as he swallowed the cold brew.

"So, *mon ami*, what is it about the pretty manager that has you frustrated?"

He took a swallow then set the bottle down, rubbing the condensation with his thumb as he stared at it, as if expecting it to tell him what his problem was. "I don't know. As you suggested I gave her a chance and I like what I'm discovering."

"Does she appear to like you as well?"

"Yes. I'm pretty sure about that because she confided in me."

Phil took another swallow. "Then what's the problem?"

He looked out at the ocean, the waves crashing far from the secluded beach. "My problem is I want to spend every day I'm here with her. It's as if I'm addicted to her."

Phil nodded. "*Oui*, the blossoming of love is always so."

He laughed, the action loosening some of his tension. "And how the hell would you know?"

"Oh, I have it on good authority."

He shook his head. "Whether good authority or not, the fact is the woman has a job to do and doing well in her chosen field is very important to her. I respect that in her, but in a weird way I also resent it because she can't spend more time with me. Yet I don't want to jeopardize her job either." If he caused her to be let go, he'd never forgive himself.

"What's wrong with the nights? Surely she doesn't work then as well." Phil wiggled his brow.

Cord grabbed up his beer and took a swallow before answering. "That's the bigger problem. It's against the Puanani policy for employees to date guests."

"Who said anything about dating? I'm saying—"

"Careful what you *are* saying." Anger at his longtime friend took him unawares.

Phil held out his hand. "I meant no disrespect." He lowered

his voice. "Your actions speak louder than your words, *mon ami.* You think she may be *the one* and you'll move mountains for her."

He widened his eyes at his friend, who simply nodded sagely. Was that it? Was he headed toward the L-word with Leah? He *did* want to move mountains for her. He wanted to have the man that accused her, fired. He wanted to restore her reputation in Arizona. He wanted to help her succeed in any way he could. Was that the reason for his frustration? "And if this is how I feel? What can I do?"

"Move mountains."

He shook his head. That wasn't helpful. "I'm not sure I follow."

"You say even if you have time, you still have the problem of the hotel rules, *oui*?"

"Yes."

Phil grinned as he lifted his bottle in salute. "Tell them that if they don't bend the rules for your *amour* then you and I will leave and stay at another hotel so you can see her."

Cord stared at Phil. He'd known the man was smart, but that was brilliant in an underhanded way. He had no doubt Auntie would not want to lose their business. After all, he was staying in their most expensive room and Phil planned to be there for at least a month. "You're a genius."

"So I've been told." Phil winked and took another swig of beer.

He laughed, his tension gone as he envisioned the next four days spent with Leah. "Don't let it go to your head."

Phil raised one eyebrow as a slow smirk raised his lips. "Too late."

"Hmm, yet you don't seem to be making headway with one of the ladies here. Was it Anna?"

Phil lost his smile as he shook his head. "No, Annalise. Anna is far too plain for a prince."

He had to be kidding. Cord widened his eyes and stared at Phil as if he'd grown horns. "Would you really let a woman's name keep you from getting to know her?"

"It's a moot point. Annalise is the one I wish to know better now." Phil's gaze strayed to the ocean water. "She has hair the color of chestnuts, amber eyes that glow with unknown depth and a voice as sweet as the mourning doves on my island."

Well, hell, he hadn't seen Phil get this poetic the entire time he'd know him. Sure, there'd been a couple analogies regarding the women he'd met, but he always stayed to the trite comparisons. This was completely new. He needed to tread carefully with his advice. "Is it that she's not interested in you that has you so intrigued or is there something about her that makes your gut tighten and your tongue stick in your mouth whenever you see her?"

Phil frowned. "My tongue does not get stuck and…" He trailed off as if realizing something. "She's different. She does not need to say a word, yet she's noticed. When she does speak, it is with measured intent as if she wishes to be careful of everyone's feelings. And when she smiles, *mon dieu*, it fills the soul with peace."

"And this is an American?"

"*Oui*, I too am surprised." Phil took another swallow before setting his empty on the picnic table. "I need help my friend. This is one woman I must know."

"You have far more experience than I have, but I'll do

my best." He finished off his own beer, stood and pulled out his wallet. "Next round is on me. This is going to take some serious thought and that's thirsty work."

At Phil's slumping shoulders, a posture he'd rarely seen on the man, he smacked him on the shoulder. "Don't lose hope. Between the two of us, I'm sure we'll figure out a plan to win the beautiful Annalise's heart. If that's truly what you want."

Phil's blue gaze turned bright, and he sat straighter. "I have conquered far greater tasks." He waved his hand. "Fetch the beer. We have work to do."

He smiled as he strode toward the bar. What if they both found their *one* on the same island thousands of miles from their homes? He slowed at the thought. Maybe that was exactly what they both had needed, to step away from their regular life and assumptions in order to be open to new possibilities.

He continued toward the bar. He liked the idea of new possibilities.

The ride back to the Puanani hadn't gone quite as planned thanks to a flat tire. As their new driver headed toward the hotel, the sun had already set and Cord's frustration grew, knowing he'd missed another evening with Leah.

As they pulled into the resort, his hope rose. Leah's car was still in the parking lot. Excited that he hadn't missed her, he jumped from the car, letting Phil take care of their payment. Striding up the steps to the lobby, he didn't notice the "Queen Bee" as Ulu dubbed her, standing on the top step until it was too late. "Good evening, Deidre."

She looked past him. "Is Phil with you?"

He nodded before continuing to walk by.

She grabbed his arm. "Hey, what's your hurry?"

He stopped and forced a smile. "I'm hungry."

Her gaze swept over him from his t-shirt to his sneakers. "I bet you eat a lot."

"Yes, ma'am. If you would excuse me?" He looked meaningfully toward Phil, who approached them.

"Of course. Don't be such a stranger at the pool." With that parting remark, she turned her attention on his friend. Poor woman didn't have a clue that Phil was not the least bit interested in her. His sights were on her friend. If she were to realize that, it would royally piss her off.

Once inside the lobby, he nodded at the night clerk and headed down the hall to Leah's office. Her door was closed, but there was a light shining underneath. He knocked, hoping she wasn't somewhere else on the resort.

"Come in." Her voice sounded distracted.

Opening the door, he found her frowning at the computer, her fingers tapping at the keyboard.

"I didn't expect you to still be working."

At the sound of his voice, she looked up and smiled. With a sigh, she sat back. "Technically, I'm not. Just trying to force my resume to look somewhat intelligent."

He meandered toward her desk then leaned against the corner of it, inhaling her myrtle-like scent. She always smelled so fresh, even when she looked tired. "It's true then? Did Auntie tell you they want Wena to manage the hotel?"

She shook her head. "No, but I can read the writing on the wall. I'd rather get a jump on this than be caught without a job.

Depending on where I'm hired, I'll need every cent to get my belongings off Momi and to my next destination."

He sincerely hoped her next destination was somewhere in the western half of the United States. His brother owned a private jet, which could make seeing her a reality. "If you need a fresh set of eyes to look it over, I'd be happy to review it."

Her eyes widened. "You would? Do you know anything about the hospitality business?"

"No, but I know you and I could probably suggest ways to make you look good on paper. You already look great in person. Once you land an interview, they'll be so impressed with your intelligence, they'll offer you the job."

The blush on her cheeks at his compliment made her even prettier. Still, he steeled himself for her to revert to manager mode. She always did after she blushed.

She surprised him, smiling tiredly instead. "I'd appreciate that. Let me print out what I have." Leaning forward, she tapped a couple keys.

She really had no clue how pretty she was. In her form fitting, sleeveless, pale yellow dress, with a neckline that accentuated her collarbone, she looked classy, curvy, and very smart. Her dark brown hair barely brushed her shoulders and instead of a flower, she'd worn a matching headband that showed off her delicate ears when she turned her head.

Rolling to the credenza behind her, she waited for the pages to print, giving him a perfect view of her long legs and bare feet. She had left her sandals beneath the desk.

A growl from deep in his stomach was almost loud enough to be heard over the printer, which gave him an idea. "I'm going to head back to my room and shower. I'll order us some dinner and I'll read your resume afterward. Just bring it over."

Not wanting her to find a reason not to come, he strode for the door.

"But if you wait—"

He didn't let her finish. "My stomach refuses to wait, and I know you haven't had dinner yet. Let's take some time on this. We want to get it right." He opened the door to the hallway. "Besides, I need to talk to Auntie Loke tomorrow about something and I want your input, so we can help each other out." Ducking out into the hall, he closed the door, leaving her with her mouth open and her eyes wide.

Pleased with his spur of the moment plan, he strode into the quiet lobby, smiling like a fool as he passed the night receptionist and continued out the back entrance toward the honeymoon suite. As he came to the end of the path, he glanced at Auntie Loke's house. Something told him she was going to be fine with him dating her hotel manager, especially as she planned to keep the business in the family.

That Leah would lose her job to an inexperienced family member went against everything he knew to be right, and he contemplated finding a way to help her keep it, but even as he headed for his room, his gut told him meddling in that way would piss her off. He had no doubt she would land on her feet, he just wanted her to land back in Arizona somehow.

Once in his room, he ordered dinner and took a fast shower. He dressed in a pair of shorts and a loose Hawaiian button-down shirt that Leah had picked out for him the day they were in town. Then he grabbed a beer and stood at the sliding glass door to his patio. He could just make out the white tops of the waves breaking over the reef as the resort's lights reflected off the crests.

A knock pulled him away, and he opened his front door. As the waiter brought in the meal and placed it on the small table, he wondered if it would all fit. He probably shouldn't have ordered when he was so hungry. When there was no room left and dessert was still on the tray, he took it and put it in the empty refrigerator.

Tipping the man well with the request that he not tell anyone he was staying in the honeymoon suite, he lifted the lid off a small cold plate and inhaled the aroma of salmon and tartness. His stomach growled loudly, even drumming out the sound of the air conditioner.

"Hell, I'll never make it." Pulling the dish from the table, he brought it to the nightstand, sat on the bed and started to eat.

When he finished off the *lomi-lomi* salad and there was no knock on the door, he started to worry. What if she sent an employee to drop off her resume?

No, she wouldn't want them to know that she was looking for a job yet. Though she could simply put it in an envelope.

He glanced at the time on his phone, which sat on the dresser. What time had he arrived? How long had it taken for the food to be prepared? What if she left and went home?

"Shit." Ever since his conversation with Phil, spending time with Leah had taken on a desperate tone. He needed to relax. Just because she could be *the one*, didn't mean she was.

A knock on his door had him tensing. Was it an employee or Leah? Opening the door, he found her standing on the step and all his doubts disintegrated. He grinned, opening the door wider. "I had no idea what you like besides malasadas and SPAM®, so I ordered a few things."

She smiled uncertainly and walked in, careful not to brush against him. It took all his willpower not to pull her into his arms—he was *that* relieved to see her.

"A few?" She stared at the table covered in dishes.

He closed the door. "Actually, this one is empty." He lifted the metal lid to prove he told the truth. "I was really hungry when I ordered, so I may have ordered too much, but there's a fridge in the room, and you're welcome to take home any leftovers."

"I wasn't hungry when you suggested this, but the minute I walked in and smelled the sticky chicken, my mouth started to water." She dropped some papers on the bed and moved to the table.

He stepped up and pulled her chair out for her. "I'm not sure what I ordered except for the Hawaiian burger."

She chuckled. "Let me guess. You think it's a hamburger with pineapple."

He pulled out his chair and sat. "Of course. What else would it be?"

Her brown eyes sparkled with amusement. "You'll see."

And he did. Pineapple was completely absent on his burger, but there was a large slice of SPAM® on it, which she offered to eat for him, but he wanted to show her he was open to new experiences. Luckily, he found he enjoyed it. He kept the conversation light, telling her about Phil's many conquests throughout the last couple days with a bit of exaggeration.

He had to admit he was surprised at how relaxed she was.

He'd thought she was avoiding him, but it must be that she simply was that busy. "Did you have another event today?"

She shook her head. "No, but I had to check the end of the month figures, create the schedule for next month and correct a few mistakes Wena made on the reservation system. I put her at the front desk to get a taste of that. Unfortunately, I forgot to warn her about Deidre and the woman made her cry."

He pushed his last empty plate to the side. "I ran into Queen Bee when Phil and I returned from ziplining. If I'd known she'd made Wena cry, I probably wouldn't have been so polite. There's no excuse for that."

"Is Phil interested in Diedre?"

"Not even a little. He has his eye on someone else."

Leah placed her utensils on her plate and wiped her mouth. "I'm surprised she's still running after him then."

He shrugged. "Phil's that way. He can be nice to every woman he meets, rich or poor, young or old, nice or…"

"A bitch."

He grinned. "I wasn't going to say it, but yes."

She laughed. "I'm counting on you not to tell anyone that I *did* say it." She pushed back her chair. "Would you take a look at my resume now? There's really no one else here I can have look at it, and it would make me feel better to have another opinion. I made a few more changes before printing out a couple copies."

A couple copies? What would they both need a copy for, unless she didn't want to get too close by reviewing the same one? If he ever got a hold of the asshole who accused her of sexual harassment, he wouldn't be accountable for his actions. "Let me clear this away."

She raised her brows. "And put it where?"

He scanned the room. They had a minor problem. Walking to the slider, he flicked the switch light up the patio. "Why don't we go outside? I doubt there's anyone nearby that would hear us. Or I can take the dishes out there."

She rose. "Oh, no. You don't want the dirty dishes outside. You'll be inundated with critters by morning."

"I see your point."

She picked up the papers and a pen from his nightstand, and he opened the door for her. This time when she sat, she couldn't avoid sitting next to him because there were only two chairs, though she did place one copy far away from her.

He picked it up and moved his chair next to hers.

She gave him a hesitant smile as if he was someone she'd just met.

They were beyond that now and hopefully would grow more so over the next few days. He placed his hand palm up on the table between them.

She looked at it and then met his gaze.

He raised one eyebrow in expectation.

A silent battle of wills ensued until she finally sighed and placed her hand in his. "How are you going to write with me holding your hand?"

He picked up the pen with his left hand. "I'm a lefty."

She squinted her eyes at him. "No, you're not. You signed the credit card receipt at the restaurant the other day with your right hand."

His heart jumped that she was that observant of him. "Busted, but no problem." He released her hand, stood, placed the chair on the other side of her and put his left hand on the table.

Laughing, she grasped his easily. "You *are* determined."
He smirked. "More than you know."

147

Chapter Ten

Leah couldn't believe some of the great insights Cord had on her resume. Once she made the revisions, she was confident she could at least snag a few interviews. Next, she'd have to start looking at what openings were available.

Cord pushed back his chair. "Now that we did all that work, would you mind taking a walk on the beach with me?"

She tensed. If someone saw them...

As if he knew her thoughts, he rose with her hand still in his. "It's almost midnight and it's dark. I doubt anyone will be there."

Midnight? Time with Cord seemed to fly by. She wasn't even tired, yet when he'd first come to her office, she'd been ready to crawl into bed and go to sleep. She had to admit, he was pretty determined while still understanding her position. To have such a good man want to be with her was hard to resist.

She stood. "I would like that, but if anyone is there, you have to promise to release me. She held up their clasped hands.

He lowered his head as he brought her hand to his lips and kissed it. "I promise."

A flicker of anticipation leapt from her hand to her heart

even though she felt bad. "I know it seems silly, but on such a small—"

"Shh, it's not silly. I understand. I follow the rules as well and think I've figured out a way to get around them."

"You have?" Hope filled her chest but she squashed it. What did it matter? He only had four days left on Momi, then he'd leave.

He nodded smugly. "Yes. Phil and I will move to another hotel for the rest of our stay. Then I can see you without you breaking any rules."

"What? You can't." She liked having him close by and the thought he'd be gone bothered her. Four days was still four days. "I mean, Auntie would be so upset." And probably blame her in the process. Had she screwed up again?

"Good. That's what I'm hoping."

Her heart pounded. "I don't understand?"

"Leah, I don't want to cause you any trouble, but I do want to spend every last minute of my vacation with you, so I'm going to tell Auntie why I have to leave the Puanani, and of course, Phil will come with me. If she decides that she's okay with you and I spending time together, then we'll be happy to stay."

Her stomach unknotted. She had no doubt that Auntie would be okay with it because the woman was all about money and love. She looked sideways at him. "That's a very underhanded idea."

"I know. Phil came up with it, but I had nothing else."

Despite every reason that came to mind for them not to do this, including the small inconvenience of 3,000 miles of ocean and land, her heart thrilled. "Why are you so determined to spend time with me?" She had to ask because it had never happened before, not even while she'd been in college. She'd always been the one more interested in the man than the other way around.

He lifted his other hand toward her face and she jerked back, unable to help it. At the concern in his eyes, she wanted to cry.

Cord squeezed her hand. That helped her to stay still as his other cupped her chin. "Because I really like you. There's something right about us together, and I want to find out why."

Even as hope grew that he felt it too, he lowered his head. She quelled the urge to pull back again and as his lips touched hers, she practically melted. His kiss was gentle and light and over as soon as it started.

She must have closed her eyes because when she opened them, she found him studying her.

"Are you ready for that walk?"

Walk? She blinked. Oh right, a walk on the beach. "Yes." Her voice came out as half sigh, half whisper, which must have pleased him because he gave her a kind smile before dropping his hand from her cheek.

Cool air brushed against her heated skin where he'd held her face, shedding a sudden light on the contrast of her life before and after her disgrace. Even as he moved toward the gate, her hand still firmly in his, a slow resentment began to build inside her.

She'd always blamed herself for what had happened, sacrificing all human touch and numerous relationships. The blame hadn't changed, but a new anger grew at what her life had become because she'd allowed it.

Luckily, Cord opened the gate and motioned her ahead of him. In a way, maybe he could be the beginning of a new era for her, whether they had a chance or not.

At the thought of nothing further happening between them, her belly tightened. For the first time in four years, she was determined not to let her stupid past get in the way of her future.

Cord fought the need to punch something, anything, at the damage done to Leah's psyche. It reminded him of approaching a badly mistreated horse, something he'd only experienced once and never wanted to again. Then, as now, he wanted to hit something.

It didn't matter that the woman next to him hadn't been abused physically because it was clear that mentally she had been. He had no doubt that she wasn't to blame. Someone had either misinterpreted her actions or had outright lied.

At that thought, his hand must have tightened on hers because she looked up at him.

"Is something wrong?"

He didn't dare try to smile, so he shook his head. "No, it's just a little dark right here. Maybe you should guide us."

Her brows lifted as she nodded. "There will be some light up ahead because of the resort's lights. Just keep straight."

He let her lead, forcing himself to think of other things like the sound of the water lapping against the beach, the fresh scent of the woman beside him and the feel of her warm hand in his. The temperature was perfect as a light breeze brushed across their path.

When they reached the water, he halted them, looking down one end of the beach then the other to make sure they were alone. He didn't want Leah to have to deal with island gossip before he spoke to Auntie Loke. It wasn't hard to see the beach because as Leah had mentioned, the resort lights bathed it in a peachy glow.

He turned them away from the resort and started toward Keoki's bar and the darker areas of the beach for privacy.

"Did you have beaches like this where you went to college?"

Her question, coming from out of the blue, surprised him, but the memories rose to the surface quickly. "Yes and no. They were a different color, much whiter. Instead of lava rocks breaking them up, we had old coral. But they were similar in that there were resorts, local beach bars and private homes along them and the water was just as warm."

She sighed. "That must have been a great place to attend college."

He grinned. "It was. That's where I met Phil. We were roommates in the dorm the first semester then rented a house together."

"A house?" She slowed. "That must have been expensive. Was it on the water?"

He cringed because it was. "Yes, but like here, there were really nice places to rent and real dumps. One we looked at had the bathroom in a separate building."

She chuckled. "Sounds perfect for a couple of college men."

"You're right, but we didn't take it. It made me think of the old west outhouses." He shuddered to make clear what he thought of those. "In a way, you're having a similar experience to mine but without all the studying."

She groaned. "I'm glad I earned my degree, but I definitely don't miss that. It would be hard to study when so much fun is right outside."

"Yet, you said you haven't had time to go riding."

"I know, but that's not a bad thing because I'm busy having fun with friends."

They were drawing closer to Keoki's. The bar was closed up tight and the area dark except for the residual light from the Puanani and a resort farther down the beach. He finally asked the question he was most curious about. "Do you ever go home to see your family?"

She halted. "I've been home once a year. More than that and I'd get too homesick. It's hard enough to come back here. Though it's a beautiful paradise, it's not home."

Now that was what he'd been hoping to hear.

"Was it like that for you when you went away to college?"

He turned toward her. "Yes, but I also knew it was only for four years."

"Looks like that's what it will be for me, too, except I won't be going home." She sighed.

He took her other hand before she could pull away, though she did jerk at his sudden touch. "There must be somewhere in Arizona you can work. Maybe in another area of the state?"

She shrugged. "I won't say that's impossible, but in order for me to move up in my career, I need to work in one of the cities and my reputation in those is mud."

Even in the limited light, he could sense her complete

hopelessness. "And you want to move up so you can earn more money?"

"Not exactly. Yes, I wouldn't mind being able to put more away and take a few vacations myself, but I want to learn more. I want more responsibility. I want to be challenged. I know that sounds weird, but that's just how I'm wired."

"It doesn't sound weird at all. That's exactly why I wanted to go to Pono Ranch, to learn more and see if there was anything new that we could incorporate back at Ir—the ranch. So where do you think you'll work next if not Arizona? California? New Mexico?"

She laughed. "Oh, I don't think I'll have much choice. Based on what I want to do next, the timeline, the number of openings available, and if I'm qualified enough, I could end up as close as the Big Island or as far away as Dubai."

His gut clenched. He didn't want her in Dubai. That was halfway around the world. She had to be closer. Their values were too similar. It was no wonder he felt good around her. He wanted her in his life for more than four days. Pulling her hands around his back, he stepped closer.

Her face tilted up to keep his gaze. "Cord?"

Letting go of her hands, he wrapped his arms around her slowly, aware of the slight jerk she made as he rested them on the small of her back. "I'm going to kiss you now."

He had no idea if telling her he would touch her more would help, but her sudden intake of breath had him believing she just might want him to. Lowering his head, he brushed her lips lightly like he had earlier, only this time he wasn't going to stop until she wanted to stop.

Increasing the pressure on her lips slowly, he licked at

them, enticing her to open to him. As her mouth did, he forced himself to move slowly, pushing his tongue past her lips and tasting her for the first time.

It was all he could do not to moan aloud. Her taste, mixed with the red wine she'd had at dinner, filled his head. Leaving his arms loose about her, he took his time to explore her mouth. He wanted to savor every inch of her sweetness.

When her hands tightened against his back to pull him closer, he swallowed a groan. Her breasts, now crushed against his chest, were soft and warm. Her belly, where his growing erection pressed, made him want to move his kisses there.

She pushed her tongue into his mouth, and he retreated, allowing her the same liberty she allowed him.

Unfortunately, or fortunately, she was no novice, and as she sucked on his tongue, he grew uncomfortably hard. He wanted to be inside her, surrounded by her, loved by her.

Loved? Even as the thought occurred, a peace settled into his bones. This was definitely a woman he could love.

Leah broke their kiss and stared at him.

He couldn't read her in the dark, but the ambient light reflected her gaze.

"You're a very special man, Cord Pennington."

The sound of his last name coming from her lips was like a bucket of cold water in his face. He needed to tell her that he was one of *the* Penningtons. "Leah, I—"

"Don't. I know you enough. You can deny it all you want, but you *are* special. In fact, I think so much of you that I'm asking you to help me."

Shit, he'd do anything for her. "Of course."

"Touch me."

His throat closed at the enormity of her request. It was both an honor and a risk that scared the hell out of him, but it was worth it. He nodded without saying a word, not sure he could.

Leah moved her hands from his back and awkwardly looped them around his neck.

Once she'd touched him, she relaxed into him, revving his body up another notch. He turned his hands so his palms were flat against her back, pleased that she didn't twitch.

Lowering his head slowly, he kissed the corner of her mouth, her cheek and her jaw.

Voluntarily, she leaned her head away, offering her neck. He accepted the invitation, tracing light kisses beneath her ear and along the pulse that beat so fast. When he reached the spot where her neck and shoulder met, he gave it a harder kiss, the spot teasing him with every dress she'd worn.

Slowly, he moved one hand from her back to the side of her waist, marveling at her curves. As his lips found the top of her shoulder, he skimmed his hand along her ribs. He ran kisses up the inside of her biceps while letting his hand brush the side of her breast.

She shivered, but instead of pressing closer to him to avoid him, she turned her body away, giving him more access.

By now his other hand had her ass in a tight grip as he forced himself to stay in control.

When her lips found his chest where his shirt had parted, he sucked in his breath. *Keep it slow. Rein in your own need or you'll ruin it.*

Despite his pep talk to himself, he couldn't stop his hand from moving over her breast and cupping it. As he gently squeezed, his cock jumped against her belly, obvious in his loose shorts.

She pressed against it even as she dropped one arm to pull his shirt to the side to lick his nipple.

Holy shit. His breathing didn't seem to know what to do, racing then stopping as she laved him. Hoping she liked the same, he brushed his finger across her nipple, feeling it harden beneath the fabric of her dress and bra. He wanted her clothes off. To touch all of her and feel her against his own nakedness.

As her little teeth started to nibble, he couldn't take it and pulled her against him, forcing her to look up at him. He kissed her, his tongue breaching her lips and telling her exactly how much he wanted her, as if she couldn't tell with his cock grinding into her.

She moaned in the back of her throat, sending his need higher and beyond what he could control.

Breaking the kiss, he stepped back from her, his heart racing as all his blood pounded with need.

"Cord? Did I do something wrong?"

A chuckle tried to get past his dry throat but it came out garbled. "No." He took a few deep calming breaths. "No, I just needed to breathe." He grinned. "You literally take my breath away."

She seemed unsure, but with the limited light, he couldn't tell. He'd just convinced her to spend time with him. He wasn't going to assume any more than that. He held out his hand, intending to continue their walk. At her hesitation to take it, he knew he'd made the right decision to stop things before they got out of hand.

Though she did finally touch him, he was more determined

than ever to make her comfortable before he gave into his need…no matter how uncomfortable that made him. "Let's head back. You have to work in the morning, and I've kept you out late."

She nodded. "You're right. I still need to go home and make the changes on my resume."

He gave her a warm smile. "I hope my input helped. You deserve a great position."

"Thank you. It's really nice to have someone in my corner."

They walked along in silence, the waves crashing out on the reefs and disintegrating as they rolled toward the beach to move the water's edge a couple feet on the sand. The sound was soothing and having her with him felt right.

As they came to the Puanani, he stopped before making the turn that would bring them back to his room. He stepped in front her. "I'll talk to Auntie in the morning. If she lifts the rule for you, will you go parasailing with me?"

She shook her head.

He frowned, his gut tensing with disappointment. "Why not?" Hadn't he cleared the way for them?

"I can't. I have to work. We have a baby shower tomorrow afternoon. It's going to be very busy and Wena doesn't know enough to oversee everything."

Of course. He should have expected that. "When is your next day off?"

In the peach hue of the resort lights, Leah's teeth gleamed. "I have the following two days off."

"Good. Don't plan anything. I mean, if you haven't already." What an idiot. She had a normal life beyond his vacation plans.

"I have no plans except grocery shopping and errands."

He was so anxious to spend time with her, he'd help her vacuum if he had to. "Then could you switch the parasailing to a day later and come with me? I don't want to go by myself and Phil needs to attend to the ladies because he's already heard grumbling with him gone the last two days."

Leah's hand tightened around his. "I've never gone parasailing."

"Really?" He widened his eyes. "What about all the other adventures you've been sending me on?"

She smirked as she shook her head. "Nope, just the horseback riding. I was scheduling what you said your sister would like and what would prove to you that a vacation didn't have to be boring." She released his hand and spread her arms wide. "It's all about what the customer would like, not about me."

He stepped closer to her. "And if the customer wants *you*?"

She dropped her arms before bringing one hand up to point at him, but stopped just short of touching him. "This customer will have to wait until the day after tomorrow."

Both her words and her distance bothered him. Their time was so short.

"Now I need to get home." She turned toward his suite.

"Of course." He opened his arm toward the path and she started forward. Disappointment rode him hard. He just needed to be patient.

With only four days? And what if after four days neither of them were sure what they had. Could he let it end?

Halfway up the path she stopped and waited for him. As he halted next to her, she took his hand with hardly a twitch and smiled up at him. "I knew something was missing. Just took me a moment to figure it out."

His mood lifted, and he gave her hand a light squeeze. Then again, maybe they *could* figure this out.

When they reached the patio, he opened the gate for her. The copies of her resume were still on the table beneath the lava rock they'd placed on them to keep them from blowing away.

She picked up the one with her corrections on it and turned to face him. "Thank you for this. I'm actually excited now about finding a new opportunity."

Being partly responsible for her happiness made him proud. "I'm glad I could help." He walked her through the room and to his front door. Before opening it for her, he stopped. "I'll see you tomorrow."

"Unfortunately, I have a big event tomorrow."

"Even if I have to track you down to your office, I'll see you."

She smirked. "Be careful none of the ladies see you or you may not make it to my office."

He lifted his hand and cupped her cheek. That she barely flinched had him excited in a whole new way. "Good night, Leah." He lowered his lips and kissed her gently.

She deepened the kiss immediately, so he followed her lead.

When the urge to press her against the wall grew insistent, he broke it off. "See you tomorrow." His words were just above a whisper.

She swallowed and nodded before slipping out into the night.

After she left, he stared at the closed door. He didn't need four days to know he wanted a relationship with her. He was kidding himself to think he still had to decide. The question was how *she* felt and how to make a relationship possible if she did feel the same.

Striding back outside to the patio, he grabbed up the other copy of her resume. There had to be a way to find her a position in Arizona. If anyone could give him ideas, it would be Grey. Then again, even Hellion might have an idea or two. She knew everyone, even the owners of a nudist resort.

Shaking his head at the idea of Leah working at such a place, he opened the slider and set the resume next to his phone on the end table. Tomorrow, he had work to do.

Chapter Eleven

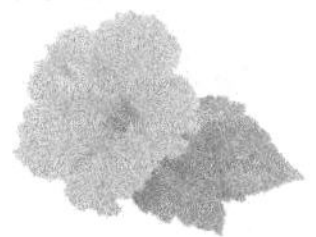

"Hey, Leah. Try not to look so happy to see me."

She glanced up to find Melia sauntering over in a short, flowered dress that hugged her curves beautifully. As her friend made her way to the table, both men and women noticed.

The Cracked Coconut was Momi's biggest combination local and tourist bar. Nestled between two boutique resorts in Hele, it was always busy. Of course, the live bands, beach access, and "no shoes - no shirts required" policy didn't hurt either. It's warm koa wood furniture was accented with pale blue cushions, every table boasted a candle inside a tall glass, and its wide thatched roof gave it the island vibe.

She smiled at her friend. "I *am* happy."

Melia pulled out the chair next to her at the small round table. "I don't think so. I see you sulking here and think, something bad happen."

"I'm not sulking."

"Uh-huh." Melia waved over a waiter. "Two Lava Flows." After he took the drink order, she zeroed back in on her subject. "Tell me why you glum."

She chuckled. "I'm not glum. I'm actually quite happy."

"Except…"

"Fine, except I didn't see Cord all day, and he said he would see me today."

Melia's laughter filled the air, causing more than one male head to turn. "Lady, you funny. I thought you don't want to see him because you lose job."

Even as Melia mentioned it, Auntie's conversation with her that morning had her smiling. "Auntie gave her blessing and lifted the rule, not just for me but everyone at the resort. That was *my* stipulation."

Melia nodded. "No surprise. Auntie's priorities straight. Love first, then work."

She shook her head. Melia was a true romantic.

She must be herself as well because she really did miss seeing Cord. She'd like to think it was because he'd set up the expectation, but even if he hadn't, she would have wanted to see him.

"You hunt him down?" At Melia's question, she rolled her eyes.

"Of course not. I had work to do."

"Then why you think you see him?"

"Because he said he'd see me today."

Melia, who had taken a sip of her drink, shrugged. "Day not over yet."

"It is for me. It's not like he knows where I live or has my phone number or has any idea I'll be here at the Cracked Coconut tonight."

"Maybe. Maybe not." Melia sipped on her drink, her brown eyes dancing with mischief.

"Wait a minute. What do you mean? You're practically laughing. What do you know?"

Melia stirred her drink as if it was the most important task ever and cocked her head. "Maybe I know some handsome paniolo come see me today."

Her heart skipped a beat. "Cord came to Keoki's?"

Melia laughed as she nodded. "He want to know two things. How to make malasadas and where he find you tonight." Her friend wiggled her brows. "He only got one."

She held her breath. "Which one?"

"Oh, Keoki never tell his recipe."

She couldn't believe how quickly her heart started to race. She scanned the crowd but didn't see Cord. She looked back at Melia. "Did he say he was definitely coming?"

Her friend nodded, her smile wide.

She looked down at her short-flared skirt of pink hibiscus flowers on a white background and her white tank. "I should have worn something nicer."

Melia wagged her finger. "Paniolo don't care about clothes. Bet he prefer none better." She winked and laughed again.

Her cheeks warmed as she remembered exactly how much Cord had felt just last night. She'd been totally lost in their passion, but he'd kept it from going too far. It had been too long since she'd been with a man. How did she know if she really wanted him or was just starved for—

"Wow. He one hot 'dude'."

At Melia's exclamation, she looked up to see Cord making his way through the tables at the front. Dressed in his cowboy hat, western shirt, jeans and cowboy boots, he had every woman in the place staring.

He stopped at their table and tipped his hat. "Ladies, may I join you?"

She nodded, her breath caught in her throat, keeping her from jumping up like she wanted to.

"Yes, yes." Melia rose and moved over one chair.

Cord smiled at her friend before his gaze came to rest on her. "I hope you don't mind." He sat. "I didn't have a chance to see you earlier, so I asked Melia where you lived."

"I not tell him." Melia shook her head.

Leah couldn't take her eyes off Cord. "No, I don't mind. I'm glad you're here. It's more enjoyable to be with you when I'm not at work."

He grinned. "I'd hoped you'd see it that way."

Melia leaned forward and lowered her voice. "You better claim you territory or you gonna lose him speedy."

"Huh?"

Melia motioned toward the bar with her head.

She glanced over to see three female tourists eyeing Cord. She looked back at her friend who raised her brows in question.

Of course. She returned her gaze to Cord and forced herself to touch his shoulder. It felt awkward, but once the warmth of his body heated her hand through his shirt, she relaxed. Leaning toward him, she kissed him on the cheek.

His hand immediately caught her chin, which made her start, but he held on and turned his face to brush her lips with his own.

When he let go, she smiled. "I'm really glad you're here." She didn't want to just say the words, especially after almost pulling away from him, so she ran her hand down his arm to clasp his hand.

His wide grin told her he appreciated her attempt. "Now,

what should I have to drink? Preferably not fruity." He lowered his brows in a mock scowl.

Melia waved her hand and in no time, they had a drink for Cord. He'd barely taken a sip when the Hawaiian band started up again and he stood. "Come on, ladies. If there's music, we have to dance."

A cowboy who wanted to dance? Right then and there she thought she'd died and gone to heaven. Could the man get any more perfect?

He led them both out onto the deck area where a large open space in front of the band invited people to dance. The hanging lights in small wood cages that hung from the trees made it appear as if they danced beneath the stars.

After a few fast dances where she tried not to stare at how well Cord could move, the band slowed it down.

Melia started to walk away. "You two dance. I need rest."

She watched her friend head back toward their table. When she turned back to Cord, he opened his arms but didn't move forward to embrace her. His message was clear. It was up to her.

Taking a deep breath, she stepped closer, bringing to mind how good it felt to be in his arms last night. She placed one hand on his shoulder, barely flinching. Determined, she reached her other forward. Though she hesitated, she grasped his hand in hers.

The smile he gave her at her success made her feel warm all over and stupid proud of herself. With his help, she finally had hope that she could undo the damage she'd done over the last four years.

"It appears Melia didn't get to rest after all." Cord's warm breath against her ear as he guided them around the dance floor sent a shiver of desire racing through her.

He turned them so she could see Melia dancing with a dark-haired tourist dressed in typical island-wear.

"I'm glad. She deserves to find someone special, too."

He didn't exactly hesitate in his moves, but she sensed a stiffening in him.

"Too? Who else has found someone special?"

She pulled her head from his shoulder and gazed into his dark green eyes. Swallowing, she finally admitted it out loud. "I have."

Instead of relaxing him, he seemed to grow even more tense. "Do you think Melia would mind if we cut out now?"

She shook her head, hoping he wanted to spend more time alone with her.

"Good." He let go of her except for his hand still on her back as he guided her off the dance floor. He stopped the waiter and paid him for their drinks, then touched her back again, but she stepped away.

She wanted to cry. Why couldn't she stop this habit?

Cord wasn't deterred. He touched her back again, and despite another twitch from her, he continued to guide her out.

Once they were in the parking lot, he stopped. "Your car?"

Of course. "This way." She moved in the direction of her car, Cord following her. *If he reaches for me again, I will not flinch.* She unlocked the passenger door then turned only to find him boxing her in, but not touching her.

Her heart leapt with worry at the tension radiating off him. Was he upset by her confession of how she felt about him? Or was he getting tired of her avoiding his touch. He certainly lasted longer than most.

"Leah, I—"

She was afraid of what he would say. "I'm sorry. I know this problem I have is aggravating. It's aggravating me, too. I just wish it would stop." Her vision blurred as her frustration with herself got the better of her.

She couldn't see his eyes very well, but she could tell his face was coming closer. In the next instant, he was kissing her, their lips the only place they connected. He hadn't given her room to move away, so the contact was smooth and relief washed through her.

As his tongue stroked her own, relief turned to much more and without thinking, she found herself leaning into him. Her heart raced as their bodied touched. She wanted to be with him so badly. She made her hands wrap around his waist, pulling herself closer.

With more control than she had, he broke the kiss and leaned his forehead against her own with no flinching on her part. At the small victory, she opened her eyes to stare at his lips.

"Leah, I would like you to take me back to the resort so I can undress you and touch every part of you until you can enjoy my touch."

A tightening started low in her belly that had nothing to do with frustration and everything to do with excitement. *I already do enjoy your touch, but I know you can't be sure of that.* "I'd like that."

He lifted his head away and looked at her. "Are you sure? I know this could be hard for you."

She wanted to deny it, but he was right. Still, she couldn't imagine making love to anyone else. "I am, if you're sure you can deal with my…"

"Minor idiosyncrasy?"

She nodded, grateful for his positive spin on such a negative problem. "Yes."

He moved his hand from her car and brushed his knuckles lightly across her cheek, even though she moved her cheek away at first. "For you, I could deal with a lot."

Warmth, embarrassment, and hope filled her. Where had this man been all her life? "Thank you."

He shook his head, stepped back and chuckled. "No need to thank me. Just seeing you naked and in my bed will have me wanting to thank *you*."

She widened her eyes as excitement sped straight to her core. She swallowed hard, but no sound would get past her throat. Instead of responding, she sidled along the car and practically ran around to the driver seat.

As she drove, he rested his hand on her thigh, burning her through her light skirt even though he didn't move a finger. By the time they pulled in at the resort, she was almost too excited to stand. Her palms left sweat marks on her steering wheel and her mind kept bringing up the image of Cord's naked butt as he stood in the shower that first day.

Her car door being opened startled her, and she raised her hand to her chest.

Cord stood there with his hand held out.

Right, she needed to get out of the car if this was going to happen. She placed her hand in his very slowly, avoiding a twitch, then looked up at him with a smile, happy in her tiny triumph.

He helped her out but didn't let go of her hand as he closed the door. As he walked her toward the lobby, her mind finally kicked into gear and she stopped them just outside the open entry. "Wait, let me make sure the lobby is empty. I don't feel like sharing you tonight."

He raised his eyebrows. "Just tonight?"

"Very funny." She smirked at him before releasing his hand and walking into the lobby. Wena was at the front desk for night duty.

"Aloha and welcome to the Puanani." Wena smirked as she greeted her with what every employee was supposed to say when guests checked in.

She nodded her approval. "Everything going okay?"

"Yes, but even if it wasn't, I have strict orders to call Auntie because you're off the clock." She looked past her. "Is he with you?"

Of course, Auntie told her. "Yes. Are all the ladies occupied?"

Wena nodded. "Yes. Most of our neighbors went home and our French guest took those staying here out to Huaka's for a luau."

"Good. Have a good night then." Striding back to the entry, she slowed. Cord stood in profile, looking out at the parking lot. The peach glow of the resort lights surrounded him, but his features were in shadow. She could see him sitting on a horse, watching a sunset in Arizona, his eyes shaded by his cowboy hat as he enjoyed the final rays of the day. Her heart took a giant leap. She was falling for him fast.

He turned and looked at her, his teeth showing as he grinned.

She hurried forward and reached out her hand, focusing on how much she wanted to touch him and being rewarded when she didn't shy away.

She could do this!

They hurried across the lobby like two kids planning mischief before slowing as they walked along the path to his suite.

Opening the door for her, he let her precede him before he took the "do not disturb" sign and hung it on the outside and closed the door.

She stood in the middle of the room, having turned on the light, suddenly unsure how to start this. She didn't have to think about it long.

Cord threw his wallet and keycard on the dresser and stepped up to her. He halted before touching her. "I need you to know that I'm not into vacation flings or anything like that. I've asked you here because you mean something to me."

If her heart wasn't already a puddle of melted butter, it would be now. She raised her hand toward his face, forcing it past her hesitation to cup his cheek. "I think I know what kind of man you are. I don't doubt your intentions, and you shouldn't doubt mine. You mean something to me, too." She pushed away her conscience reminding her of the miles of ocean between them and focused on the roughness of his jaw against her hand.

He turned his face to kiss her palm even as his hand grasped her wrist. With nowhere to go, her hand didn't move much, but it would have. Irritation rifled through her. She just wanted it to stop.

"Don't."

She snapped her gaze to his. "What?"

"Every time you flinch, you tense up afterward. I understand that you will and why it happens. I also understand you find it frustrating, but I'm okay with it. I think if you just relax and enjoy, it will eventually fade. But I doubt that will happen tonight, and I'd rather you enjoy our time together than be frustrated by it."

"You're right. It's just that—"

Before she could finish the thought, he wrapped his arm around her and kissed her. She did jerk but it didn't matter because his tongue had her relaxing into him even as a totally different tension built in her belly.

Her hands were trapped between their bodies, but it didn't keep her from moving them over his chest. As her fingers brushed against a button, she found a new purpose for her roving hands. Remembering the feel of his chest beneath her mouth, she pulled the material aside, even as his hand roamed over her back and beneath her tank top.

He broke their kiss and let her go, stepping back.

Before she could ask why, he'd whipped off his hat, setting it on the dresser, and pulled his shirt over his head to throw it on the floor.

She stared, trying not to drool over Cord's naked torso. His chest muscles were well developed and beneath them his washboard abdominals actually had her fingers itching to run over them.

He stepped back to her. "I want to feel you without clothes between us."

She wasn't sure if he was asking permission to undress her or not, so she crossed her arms and lifted her tank over her head, throwing it toward the chair in the corner. Cord's gaze flew to her breasts covered in her strapless bra. She hadn't planned to see him tonight, so it wasn't her fanciest, but it also wasn't padded and her nipples stood out clearly against the white nylon material.

Cord reached his hand forward, and though she jerked at first, he stroked his finger across both her hard nubs. "May I?"

She had no idea what he was asking, but right now she'd say yes to anything, so she nodded.

He ran his hands along the band of the bra, around her back to unclasp it. At the feel of his bare hands on her back and moving toward the front with the bra, her nipples hardened further in anticipation of his touch.

But he didn't touch. When his hands reached her arms, he let them fall to the side as he dropped the bra, though his gaze riveted on her breasts.

"Touch me." His words were low and husky and sent a thrill shooting through her.

Lifting her hands, she pushed through her hesitancy and laid them on his chest. Hard and warm were her two first impressions. She ran her hands over his pectorals, down the rippled abs then up and over his powerful shoulders and biceps. His muscles contracted slightly as she touched them.

The urge to press her breasts into him was too hard to ignore. She slid her arms around his back and pulled herself against him. At the contact, warmth settled between her thighs.

She moved her hands lower to slip beneath the waist line of his jeans, but she couldn't go much farther with his belt around him. Forcing herself to move back a little, she found his belt buckle and started to unclasp it.

His hand on hers stopped her, so she pulled away.

He wasn't smiling, his gaze intense. "I want to touch you."

She shivered but not from the air conditioning. "Yes."

He lifted his hand and brushed his fingers across her nipples. Though she flinched, she had little time to be upset because zings of pleasure traveled from her breasts to her core, completely distracting her.

Once his hands were on her, they didn't seem to want to leave. He cupped both her breasts, rubbing his thumbs across her hard nubs, building the tension inside her. When he moved his forefinger to join his thumb and rolled her nipples, she thought her knees would give out. She grabbed his wrists without a thought—anything to stay standing.

Cord looked at her. His brow lowered in concern.

She smiled contritely. "You make my knees weak." It was a confession she'd never made to a man before, but his solicitous manner had her feeling comfortable with it.

His prideful smile would have caused her to laugh if she wasn't so anxious to make love. He stepped back. "Turn around."

He wanted her back? Confused, she did as he asked. When his hand brushed her lower back as he unzipped her skirt, she stiffened. She was too grateful that her reaction didn't bother him to get upset at herself. When her skirt fell to the floor, she stepped from it. She didn't move, waiting to see if he'd take down her pink flowered panties.

He didn't touch her. Was he staring at her? The idea was heady.

What she didn't expect was his arms wrapping around her waist, which caused her to jump. He pressed his fully naked body against her, his cock hard digging into her lower back. She grinned. At least she knew he found her attractive.

His hands moved upward once again to play with her nipples. She held onto his arms, thankful for his support at her back. When his fingers on one hand pinched her nipple, she moaned as her opening filled with moisture.

As if he knew what he'd done, he moved his other hand over her belly and into her panties.

She held her breath as his fingers moved through her patch of curls and finally between her legs.

Cord's mouth descended on her neck at the same time his fingers found her readiness and explored her folds.

Her heart raced as pleasure swept over her. It had been so long since she'd been touched by someone else that her body felt tighter than a milkweed wisp. As his fingers moved her wetness upward over her hard nub, she shuttered at the stimulation. "Oh…yes."

Cord's fingers didn't stop between her legs or on her nipple as he held almost all her weight, his erection pushing against her.

She tried to stop it, but it had been so long that her orgasm rushed over her like a tidal wave. She let her head drop back against Cord as pleasure swept away her thoughts and her strength.

When she opened her eyes, Cord had her sitting on the bed. She looked down as he knelt before her, pulling her panties from her legs. "I'm sorry. I couldn't wait. It's been so long."

His hand paused before he finished removing her clothing, then he stood. It put his cock even with her face, and she licked her lips.

"No." As he said the word, she looked up at him. His jaw was tight and his gaze intense, but he was focused on her mouth. "I want to be inside you."

Her whole body sighed and revved at the same time. How odd was that? Not interested in delving into the feeling, she scooted back on the bed and opened her arms. "I want you there, too."

He stalked to the side of the bed and pulled a condom from the drawer. Quickly rolling it on, he moved back to the end of the bed and gazed at her body. His jaw twitched before he knelt between her legs. As he lay out over her, she barely jerked at all and instantly touched him, resting her hands on his waist.

He lowered his head, and she welcomed his kiss at the same time he found her entrance. Slowly, he pushed into her, gliding inside until she was complete. It was as if her whole life had happened for that one moment.

Chapter Twelve

Cord forced himself to move slowly, but as Leah's very tight sheath took all of him, one phrase echoed in his mind.

The one.

His gut said he could never let her go. Lifting his hips, he pulled away as her sheath grasped at him, making it clear in his mind that this was meant to be. He started a slow rhythm, pumping in and out. Their tongues tangled until his thrusts grew rapid.

Lifting his head and breaking their kiss, he gave into his need to watch her as he brought her to orgasm. Her eyelids closed, her cheeks flushed and small excited sounds escaped from between her parted lips as he rocked them.

She was beautiful in every way. He wanted to see the pleasure he brought her, but when her vocalizations grew louder until her eyes squeezed tight and her sheath spasmed around him, he lost it all, throwing his head back with a yell as he came.

He pumped into her, the feelings of ecstasy surrounding him but not blotting out the woman with him as her pleasure fueled his own. When he slowed, he became even more attuned to her signals, her sheath relaxing and her breathing slowing. Opening his eyes, he gazed at the woman he *loved.*

He welcomed the feeling as one he'd always wished for but never expected after his first few attempts to find the right one for him. It hadn't taken long to discover that his family's wealth would always stand in the way.

He tensed. He had to tell Leah. He should have told her sooner, but he'd focused so much on her, that he'd failed to explain. He had no doubt that she wouldn't care. He knew money was not a motivating factor for her beyond getting paid appropriately for her work.

"What are you thinking?"

Her voice brought his gaze back to her eyes. Her deep brown eyes reminded him of that moment in the desert just as the sun set and everything turned a dark brown. He almost chuckled as he realized her eyes matched the dark cocoa color of his horse. "I was thinking how much I like your eyes."

She grinned. "I like yours, too. They remind me of Christmas."

He raised his brow. "Christmas?"

"Yes. They're the exact color of holly."

He wasn't sure what to say to that.

"I like Christmas." She winked.

He chuckled, but then stopped as his balls tightened with his movement. "And I like you."

She lifted her hands and placed them on his back. Again, it was the initial contact that was hard for her, but she moved her hands downward and squeezed his ass, causing his cock to react inside her.

"I like your butt." Her mouth quirked up on one side as she wiggled her eyebrows.

"You do, huh?"

She nodded.

"Too bad." Before she could respond, he wrapped his arms around her and rolled them over then plastered his hands on her curvy ass. "Because I like yours."

As she laughed, she contracted around him again. "Then I guess we'll just have to take turns."

Cord woke to find Leah curled on her side away from him. Nowhere were they touching, though they'd fallen asleep with him spooning her after they'd made love again. Even in her sleep, she reacted to touch?

To test his theory, he moved his body against hers. She didn't jerk at all nor did she wake up. Pleased to know that her habitual avoidance of touch was only in her conscious and not her subconscious, he proceeded to kiss her awake.

Since they had all day together, he wanted to make the most of it. When his numerous kisses across her soft skin didn't get any reaction at all, he pulled the sheet off them and ran his hand over her hip and thigh.

Still, her breathing remained even. She was a serious heavy sleeper. That could definitely be to his advantage. He moved his hand up over her stomach to brush it across her only available nipple, her arm completely covering the other one.

Circling the tip, he watched as the areola pebbled and her peak grew hard. He grinned at the change in her breathing. Continuing to play, his own body reacted when her hips pushed hard against him.

Glancing at her face, he saw no change. Maybe she thought he was a dream.

Her hips pushed against him again, and he stopped playing with her breast to stroke his hand down to her thigh. When her leg lifted, inviting him in, he looked to her face again to find her smiling. "Good morning."

"Good morning." She opened her eyes and met his gaze. "That's a very nice way to wake up."

"I agree."

"What time is it?"

He glanced at the clock on the end table next to the bed. "It's almost nine. You slept a long time."

"I slept really—wait, did you say nine?"

"Yes."

She pulled her leg off his hip and sat up. "They're coming to pick you up at 9:30!"

"What do you mean pick me up?"

Leah scrambled out of bed and ran to the shower, turning on the water. "The parasailing company. Remember, you said you wanted me to go with you today. I don't even have a bathing suit with me, and there's no time to run home."

He finally left the bed, stifling his disappointment that they wouldn't be having breakfast in bed like he'd hoped. It was his fault for wanting a busy vacation. After all, she did to make the arrangements he'd asked for. He definitely wasn't going to ask her to cancel it. They could always lay around in bed tomorrow. "I saw a gift shop in the lobby. I'll buy you a bathing suit."

She was about to step into the shower but paused. "No, I couldn't let you do that."

He nodded. "I insist."

Her gaze roved over his body from his messed-up hair to his bare feet and everywhere in between. "Okay." Grinning, she stepped into the spray and began to wash with the hotel soap he'd been using.

He sat on the bed and watched. It was far better than television, not that he'd turned that on since he'd arrived on Momi. By the time she finished and came out to wrap a towel around her, he was so hard he wasn't sure he could stand.

Grabbing another towel and capturing her hair in it, she stepped away from the shower. "Your turn." She looked at the clock. "You only have fifteen minutes. I'll dress and order some breakfast to eat in the van." She gave him a shrewd look. "Think you can be ready by then, cowboy?"

At the challenge in her gaze, he forced himself to rise, pleased to see her gaze lower to his obvious hard-on. "I can, can you?"

She sucked in her breath, nodding absently.

He grinned before striding to the glass shower and walking into the still running water.

He was as good as his word, and they were able to sneak into the gift shop and purchase a blue flowered bikini for Leah without anyone seeing them. Or rather almost no one. Just as they were heading out of the lobby, he spotted Deidre walking toward them. He grabbed Leah's hand and ran around the corner of the building, pulling her into his arms, packages and all.

Before she could say a word and give them away, he kissed her. She relaxed into it quickly, and he didn't stop kissing her until he heard the van pulling into the resort's driveway.

At Leah's look of confusion when he drew back, he

grinned. "Our ride is here." She blinked before understanding dawned and a slight blush crept into her cheeks.

He loved that about her. There was so much to love about her. He planned to convince her that he was equally loveable for the entire next forty-eight hours.

Leah couldn't stop smiling. Her day with Cord was the best day of her life so far. The morning had been spent parasailing before they went back to his room to shower and change for lunch at Makanalani's, a very nice restaurant that had squeezed them in as a courtesy for all the customers she'd sent their way. The food truly was "heaven's gift" as the name implied.

Now, on the spur of the moment, she'd suggested taking the trail to Pu'ipu'i, her favorite waterfall on the whole island. It was on the sunset side, so it took a while to make the trek, but if she didn't miss her guess, they'd be in time for the sunset glow.

Though Cord's cowboy boots weren't the best for the trail through the jungle, he was making it work. Of course, her flat white sandals that she'd worn with the new sundress he'd bought her at the Puanani gift shop, weren't much better, but they were going slow. They had plenty of time.

Besides, she liked the look of him in his long sleeve shirt completely unbuttoned and loose over his jeans. She'd told him he could take it off before they started the climb, but he'd refused, saying he might need it for a pillow if he got tired. He had eaten a very large lunch.

She thought she'd had a lot of new adventures when she

first moved to Momi, but being with Cord added a whole new dimension to her life. If only she could forget he would be leaving soon.

"Do you think you'd go parasailing again?" His question broke into the cacophony of bird song this deep in the jungle.

The parasailing, after the operator had strapped them in, had been a full-on adrenaline rush. "In a heartbeat. Thank you so much for making me go with you. That was spectacular."

Cord held her hand as they walked through the thick foliage. "Believe me, it was my pleasure to have you beside me. Hellion would love that, though I'm not sure about Dillon. I think he likes to keep his feet on the ground."

She snapped her head around. "You never told me that."

His grin turned sheepish. "I just remembered now."

He let go of her hand as they had to walk single file between two large lava boulders, but she could still feel him close to her. "Exactly how long have Hailey and Dillon been engaged?"

He didn't answer until the path widened again and he'd taken her hand. "About two months now."

She halted in her tracks. "How long have they known each other?"

He shrugged. "I'm not sure. A few years I think. His mother kept trying to set Hailey up with Dillon's older brother."

Now it was starting to sound like a soap opera.

"But it was probably about a month after Hellion decided he was her man that she reeled him in." He looked away as if the subject made him uncomfortable.

"That doesn't seem long enough to know you want to spend the rest of your life with someone."

He tugged her forward. "I don't know. My mom and dad had only known each other a week before they fell in love. Hailey fell fast, but it took Dillon a bit longer."

This time she was positive she saw him grimace. "You don't like Dillon?" That surprised her because Cord was so easy going. She couldn't imagine another man getting under his skin. If he could be friends with a man who was French royalty, the problem must stem from Dillon.

Cord still didn't look at her. "No, not at all. He's fine and exactly what Hailey needs. Is that the waterfall I hear?"

She wasn't oblivious to his sudden change in topic. "Yes, that's the sound of Pu'ipu'i. I like this waterfall because it's not super high and narrow. This one is short and wide, but the pink bougainvillea flowers and lime green florescent moss makes it the most beautiful, in my opinion."

"I highly value your opinion, so I have high expectations." He finally met her gaze. "And so far, you've exceeded every one of them."

Her cheeks heated at the warmth in his eyes. She hadn't had any expectations the day he checked into the Puanani, so he'd completely blown her away. She tried to pull her professional persona together for a response, but she couldn't. "I'm so glad because you've been more than I'd ever even hoped for."

He grinned and opened his mouth, but she tripped on a root and started to fall.

Cord kept her from hitting the moist ground by lifting their linked hands high and grabbing her around the waist with his other arm.

Though she stiffened, he still pulled her against him. "If you wanted a kiss, all you needed to do is ask."

She started to shake her head but stopped as a devilish smile formed on his face. "You caught me."

He lowered his head. "Literally." Then his lips were on hers. She held on as his tongue swept through her mouth, igniting fires no amount of water could put out. Every part of her body came alive. It didn't help that all she had on was a thin sundress and with his open shirt she could feel his warm skin through her clothing.

The sudden flutter of wings and a loud high-pitched call sounded right next to them.

Cord broke the kiss. "What the heck?"

She grinned. "Shh, it's an 'apapane. It's a male. He's trying to impress a lady."

"So am I." Cord's frown disappeared.

She pointed as the bird sang again. "He's right there."

Cord turned around, keeping one arm wrapped around her waist. "Wow, with those red feathers, he should have no problem. He's better dressed than I am."

She placed her hand on his bare chest, pleased that she hadn't hesitated. "It's what's inside that counts the most. But I have to admit, I'm very attracted to the outside as well."

He nodded toward the bird. "Hear that buddy. You have competition."

The bird cocked its head then let out another piercing trill.

Cord raised his free hand. "Fine, you win."

She laughed, causing the bird to fly farther down the path. "We're close. He's a flower follower. He sucks nectar from the flowers around the waterfall."

He loosened his hold and took her hand again. "Then we better follow him."

Her whole chest warmed at his silliness. She'd simply never a met a man with so many great attributes and no ego at all.

Their red-feathered friend knew his bounty and with a few more flits ahead of them, he flew up to seek out the bougainvillea above the wide, double waterfall.

Cord stopped. "This is impressive."

She leaned against him. "I know. It's not as high as many of the waterfalls on Momi, but it's so wide and so beautifully framed by the flowers, that it's my favorite."

"Gentle." He studied the water. "The water flows over the rocks as opposed to crashing down from a high elevation." He pointed. "See up there. It's like the double drop is part of the natural journey."

She moved her gaze from the water to Cord. He'd nailed it. That was exactly why she'd always loved Pu'ipu'i, but could never quite explain why. "Yes."

"I think Hailey would like this even without all the drama."

At the mention of his sister, she finally asked what she'd been curious about since he'd arrived. "Why did you come to Momi to check out the Puanani for your sister? You said you don't like vacations, and I know you didn't like learning about the wedding details. There's something you haven't told me about this trip."

Cord grimaced. "You're right. It's hard to admit, but I screwed up and hurt my sister. This is my payback."

She could think of worst punishments for screwing up, like losing one's job. "What did you do?"

Stepping away from her, he didn't look at her. It was such odd behavior for him that it worried her.

"I went back on my word."

She sucked in her breath. For some people, she knew that wasn't even worth mentioning, but for Cord, it was huge. "You broke a promise to Hailey?"

He nodded silently.

Oh, heck. That wasn't good. "And it involved Dillon?"

He finally looked at her. "Yes. I misjudged him."

If his sister could see Cord now, she'd know he was truly remorseful. Leah hated seeing him like this. She knew what it was like to have done something wrong and feel regret. Walking over to him, she laid her hand on his cheek with barely any hesitation. "What's important is that you've learned from your mistake and your sister is happy.'"

He nodded, his face finally relaxing into his usual smile. "And not only have I investigated everything for Hailey, but I met you."

Her heart fluttered at the warm look in his eyes, eyes so green they may very well rival the moss on the waterfall. "I'll always be grateful for that. Is it wrong that I'm pleased you messed up?"

He pulled her into his embrace. "If it is, then we'll be wrong together. I could never regret this. Leah, I—"

Her heart jumped at what he might say, but her mind didn't want to know and she pulled him down for a kiss. He gave in at once, and she lost herself in the taste of him, ignoring the warning signals her brain was trying to send her.

When he finally pulled away, he looked over her head at the beauty that surrounded them. "No wonder our bird friend likes this so much. It's not only beautiful but peaceful. Why is no one else here?"

She shook her head. "Sometimes locals come here on the

weekend, but mostly it's like this. Tourists want to see the high falls that Hawaii is known for. We have two of them here on Momi. But little Pu'ipu'i is too mellow."

"Can we walk down there?" He turned her so he could point where he wanted to go.

"Yes. There's actually a narrow trail because of the pool of water that collects at the bottom and slowly flows downstream. It's like an infinity pool only natural."

"Lead the way." He gave her hand a tug.

If he thought this was beautiful, wait until the sun hit the right point on the horizon and lit up the moss. She forced herself to let go of his hand as the trail was far too narrow. Funny how quickly she'd grown accustomed to having his hand in hers.

Using one hand to keep her balance by sliding it along the black wet rock on the side of the falls, she made it to the bottom without falling.

There was a large shelf just above the natural pool.

As soon as he stepped onto the shelf, he looked up at the waterfall. "It's even more impressive from here. I hope the locals never share this with tourists. This kind of beauty needs to remain unspoiled."

She smirked. "But you're a tourist."

He strode toward the edge, but stopped to look at her. "Yes, but I'm with you, so that doesn't count." He turned back to stare into the clear pool of water and she joined him.

"What do you see?" She scanned the water for fish or a brightly colored rock, but didn't find anything.

"I see skinny dipping."

She looked at him in shock. "You're kidding."

He shook his head, then moved to the back of the shelf and proceeded to take off his shirt.

"Cord, what if someone comes?"

He laughed. "You said no one comes out here during the week and since the daylight is waning, I doubt anyone will start up the path now. Aren't you hot after our long climb?"

She cocked her head. Part of her was surprised but another part of her was excited. It wasn't as if she'd be on the island for much longer anyway, so even if someone did happen upon them, her embarrassment wouldn't last forever. "Oh, what the heck."

He grinned at her as he toed off his boots. "Good, because I hate swimming alone."

With her adrenaline revving anew at their daring, she kicked off her sandals then placed them on a rock far from the spray. Pulling her sundress over her head, she folded it and set it on her sandals. Without giving herself time to think, she reached behind and unclasped her bra, adding it to the pile.

Turning back, she found a completely naked Cord watching her. He took her breath away for a moment as he stood, his back to the falls, his eyes focused on her as if she were the only woman on the planet.

"You're beautiful." His words were husky, sending desire shooting through her veins like a firework.

Without hesitation, she removed her panties, placed them on her pile and walked up to him. The mist from the waterfall moistened his skin and made the hair on the top of his head wave. She felt like they were Adam and Eve in the Garden of Eden, though not quite as innocent.

But as she looked in his eyes, she was positive their hearts were pure. At that moment, the sun hit the waterfall through the small break in the trees and the moss lit up like green glow sticks. "Look."

"I am."

At his words, she almost forgot what she wanted him to see…almost. She raised her hand and pointed beyond him. "No, the waterfall."

He turned toward the pool. "Magic."

She walked up to him and grasped his hand.

He looked down at her. "That's what you bring to my life. Magic."

She gazed into his eyes, silently wishing they could have this forever.

"Ready?"

She nodded. "It's going to be cold."

"Good. I need a cold shower about now."

She laughed as they swung their hands and jumped.

***

Cord sat at the table on his suite's patio. After two days of never leaving Leah's side, it felt odd to be alone. After their waterfall experience, something had changed. He felt it. She was coming to love him.

The following day they'd spent half in his room and half at the resort down the beach, jet skiing. And finally, last night, a dinner cruise on a yacht to watch the sunset. It couldn't have been more perfect. He was more sure than ever that she was ready to talk about continuing their relationship.

He expected a call from Grey, who'd promised to put

out some feelers in the Phoenix area. Hailey had also agreed to check into Tucson and see what she could find out. There had to be someone who would hire Leah. He couldn't imagine the entire state's hospitality industry knew of the complaint against her.

Popping the last of the malasadas in his mouth from the dozen they'd bought yesterday, he contemplated their options. Leah was on the hunt for a new job. He'd ask her to look in the states surrounding Arizona, if the worst-case scenario with her reputation was true.

First, he had to tell her he was one of *the* Penningtons, so she'd understand that he was willing to come to her wherever she landed. He'd tried twice more in the last two days, but they were interrupted both times. She would need to go into this relationship with her eyes wide open. He may be the least known of his siblings, but the word would eventually get out that he was seeing her.

He took a final swallow of his coffee. No, it would get out that she was his *girlfriend*. That's what he would want the public to know. He was ready to take it a step farther, but he wasn't completely sure where she was. He was almost positive it was the distance thing that kept her from saying what he longed to hear. He had just under twenty-four hours to figure it all out.

At the sound of his patio gate opening, he turned, expecting to see Phil, who would be looking for an update. Instead, he watched in stunned silence as Diedre sashayed toward him in her polka-dot bikini and a pink and white sunhat to match. At the last minute, he rose. "Ma'am."

Chapter Thirteen

"**Y**ou're a hard man to track down." Deidre oozed triumph.

He shrugged. "Probably because I didn't want to be found."

She pulled out the chair next to him and sat, crossing her legs, her toe nails painted pink and white as well. "But I found you."

He resumed his seat, curious as to what she wanted. "Yes, you have. What can I do for you?"

The woman lowered her dark sun glasses and stared at him in disbelief. "Surely you know that I would entertain having dinner with you."

He pulled on the manners his mother had taught him and choked down the bark of laughter that tried to escape. "I'm sorry, I was unaware, and I'm flattered. However, I only have one night left here and I'm otherwise engaged."

She waved her hand. "Oh, I know they have had the manager of this place showing you the sights, but I would think you'd want to have at least one evening with someone of your own social class."

He stared in shock at her implication and a slow anger began to build. "I'm sorry, ma'am. I don't understand what you mean."

Deidre smiled like a cat who found the cream. "Oh, you don't have to hide it from me. It can be our little secret. I even fell for your common cowboy guise at first, but you can't hide who you really are Cordell Pennington. Like always attracts like."

He fisted his hands beneath the table, thankful he wasn't standing because the urge to throw the woman off his patio was almost too hard to push away. They were no more alike than a saguaro cactus and a lava tube. "I appreciate you keeping my secret, but like I said. I'm not free for dinner tonight."

She stared at him as if she could figure out whether he was lying or not. "Too bad." She rose. "Then maybe we can get together later. Your friend Phil has a nice way about him, but he's far too generous with his time. You, I think, are much more like me. More of a one-on-one person."

She was right about that and the one he would be with was Leah. He rose. "I'm afraid my time is taken until I leave, but it was nice meeting you."

The woman frowned as she stood. "Are you spending more time with the manager?"

There was no way he'd let this woman make problems for Leah. "I'm not sure if Phil told you, but I'm here for my sister and I have a few items to wrap up."

She squinted her eyes at him. "Really? Don't insult me by making up such a pathetic lie. You don't know what you've turned down."

She turned on her heel and stalked through his gate, letting it bang shut behind her. He shook his head. She was obviously someone who only believed what she wanted to believe.

Turning, he picked up his empty coffee cup and walked into his room. At least Diedre knowing where he was and who he was wouldn't do too much damage on his last day. Just to be safe though, he should probably head down the beach until Leah got off work.

At the thought of seeing her again and talking about future plans, his mood lifted. Maybe between jobs, she could come meet his family.

The buzz of his phone interrupted his planning. "Hey, Grey." He sat on the loveseat and leaned back, throwing one arm up on the back. "I'm guessing you have news."

"I do, but you won't like it."

He tensed. "Why?"

"Your girlfriend was telling the truth. I only talked to two of my contacts, one in northern Peoria and one in South Phoenix and I'm sorry to say but Leah Pennington's name is mud. They all know about the sexual harassment allegations and believe she was fired."

His heart sank. "What about Hailey?"

The pause was long. "She talked to a few people in Tucson and found the same thing."

Grey's hesitation was telling. "But there's more." Cord leaned forward, his gut tightening.

His brother's voice lowered. "Did you ask Hailey to check into a nudist resort?"

He raised his brows. "No, I didn't. Why? I know she's friends with someone who works there."

"She is? Why? Is she vacationing there? I'm not sure mom and dad would be thrilled about that."

Now that he realized what Greyson was thinking, he

relaxed a little. "No, or not that I know of, but I wouldn't put it past her. Dillon's sister-in-law works at Poker Flat Nudist Resort. Why? What did she say?"

At the mention of Dillon, Grey sighed. "Hailey said they aren't big enough yet to need a manager beyond the owners, but she did say that a requirement to work there was that a person has to have screwed up. If you ask me that's a pretty dumb way to choose employees."

He didn't disagree, but he wasn't sure he agreed either, so he kept silent on that. It would have been the perfect place for Leah…except for the nude part. "Has Hailey chosen an island for you to investigate yet?"

"No. But she said last Sunday at dinner that she'd found the perfect place for Wes to check out. He wasn't there, so she didn't expand."

He'd been chosen to go first simply because he was Hellion's only brother who lived on the ranch and she saw him more than the others, but now he was very glad she'd chosen him to come to Momi. "I'm sure we'll hear about it."

"If I know Wes, it's the only thing we'll hear about for months."

He chuckled. Their younger brother didn't do anything halfway, not even when it came to complaining. "Thanks for looking into that. I was hoping she'd blown it out of proportion, but I guess not. Would you mind if I started using your private jet a bit more after I return?"

"It's that serious?" Grey sounded surprised.

"Yeah, it is. I'm not going to let miles stop this from continuing. I think for the first time in my life, I'm happy about our family's wealth."

"About time. Hey, I have another call. I'll catch you at dinner Sunday."

"Right. Thanks, Grey." He ended the call and dropped the phone on the couch. That was that. There were no possible jobs for Leah in Arizona. Not that they couldn't try, but if she worked in another state, he'd just fly there. He refused to let her job and his family ranch keep them from what they could be.

She was *the one* for him. Now he just needed to convince her of that.

Leah finished the last of the food orders the chef had submitted and closed out the screen. Not hearing any footsteps in the corridor, she took out her phone to check her personal email. There were twenty-two more job alerts to go through. She'd already sent out fifteen resumes, but that was just the start.

Scrolling quickly through the jobs, she paused at one listed in Phoenix. Shaking her head, she continued on. An email from a resort in Colorado had come in. Breathless, she opened it.

Her heart leapt at the request for a phone interview. She'd gone through dozens of phone interviews to get her job at the Puanani, but maybe all her added experience would make the process a little faster.

Excitement raced through her veins. She needed to tell someone or burst.

Cord. He was the one she really wanted to share this with. She'd have to caution him to take it as no more than a good sign and not to expect that she would get the position. If she got through the phone interview then she'd have to fly out for an in-person interview.

Closing her email, she rose. She had to tell him right now. He said he'd be hanging out at his suite all day. She should wait until dinner tonight, but she was too excited. Striding out of her office, she nodded at Ulu and headed out to the pool. It was much faster than going around back.

Besides, there were a few less women today now that they realized Phil was not in the market for a wife. She'd bet they'd be inundated if word got out that he was royalty, but she'd never let that slip. The Puanani's reputation was at stake.

"Leah."

She'd almost passed the pool when she heard her name. She sighed. She'd hoped Diedre wouldn't see her, but no such luck. The woman just couldn't let her pass without asking her for something. Turning, she walked to where Diedre lounged. Io was just handing her a drink. "Hello, Diedre. I see Io is taking good care of you."

The woman nodded as if it were her due. "He's a good man."

The man in question smiled but didn't join the conversation.

Diedre took off her glasses and stared at her. "I hope you weren't headed to the honeymoon suite."

Leah's stomach sank. She should have known Deidre would find out where Cord was staying eventually. At least it was his last day. Even at that thought, her stomach lurched.

"He's not there."

She blinked, getting her mind back on the conversation. "He isn't?"

Diedre smirked. "No. Mr. Pennington is now aware that

we know where he's staying, and I got the distinct impression he'd hoped to avoid that."

She nodded. "Yes, he liked the privacy."

Deidre gave one of those high society, condescending laughs. "Of course, he did. With so many women not of his class at this resort, it's no wonder he stayed in hiding."

"What are you talking about?" She was only half paying attention since her excitement would have to wait until Cord returned. Unless of course Deidre was lying. How would she know what Cord was doing today?

"Really, Leah. You don't have to keep his secret with me. He admitted he was one of *the* Penningtons from Arizona. All of us know each other. It just took me a while to see-through his cowboy façade. They do own the largest cattle ranch in the state after all, so it was a perfect disguise. But don't worry. I won't tell these ladies." She swept her hand toward the tourists around the pool, Phil noticeably absent.

Deidre was crazy if she thought Cord was from that Pennington family. "You do realize, Deidre, that not everyone with the Pennington name is related. My last name is Pennington."

Deidre laughed. "Okay honey, if you say so." She turned away, obviously dismissing her.

How odd that Diedre thought Cord was wealthy. Maybe he told her that to get her off his case. Obviously, she'd found him.

Not deterred, she continued to the honeymoon suite only to find Cord gone. Her good news would have to wait until later. It wasn't as if she could go traipsing down the beach while at work.

Returning to her office the back way, she double checked her personal email on her phone again then put it away. If only she and Cord didn't live so far away. The heartache she was sure to suffer when he left was too close now. She knew what she was getting into. Maybe if she landed a job in the west, she could contact him. See if he'd moved on. It was the one reason she'd held back. No matter how much they each might want it, they couldn't ignore the thousands of miles between them and with her looking for a new position it could be even more.

Unless…unless she landed in a state with ranches. There were plenty of those. Then he could hire on at one of them! Her idea gave her heart hope and she entered her office even more anxious to talk to Cord. How he felt about her idea would tell her a lot about how he felt about her.

Sitting at her desk, she opened her work email and found a message from a new vendor who wanted to work with the Puanani. Immediately, she searched the internet to see what customers thought. But as she read the reviews, the seed of doubt Deidre had planted grew. It couldn't hurt to do a quick check and put her mind at ease.

She'd only looked up the Pennington family once, after the first time someone asked her if she was one of them. She had hoped to discover they didn't have any daughters so she could easily respond next time she was questioned, but as it turned out, they had one. She didn't pay attention to any brothers since it was the female she'd focused on.

Typing in the words Pennington and Arizona, she waited for the results. Within seconds a list of articles came up. She clicked on images and scrolled down. Just as she thought, Cord was no—

She froze, staring at a slightly fuzzy picture of a giant check and the Pennington family standing on one side with a group of people on the other. It had been taken years ago, but even with the cowboy hat shading his face, she swore it was Cord. She clicked to find the caption.

Left to right in the back were Greyson, Wesley and Cordell Pennington. In the front was Hailey and her parents.

She shook her head. Why wouldn't he have told her? She clicked back and scrolled farther. Hailey and Greyson dominated the photos, but there were a few very clear pictures of Cordell Pennington.

Her heart contracted as she slumped back, staring at the screen with blurry vision. She'd trusted him with her most private secret. Her biggest embarrassment. Her most vulnerable issue, and he couldn't tell her he was one of *the* Penningtons?

Why? The word kept repeating itself over and over? He didn't think she was trustworthy enough? He didn't want her to know he had money? She didn't mean that much to him? He was leaving so he saw no reason?

She clasped her hands. They'd made love and she didn't even know! Was it just sex for him? No, not the Cord she thought she knew. It was probably because he felt bad she was so messed up. If it meant more than that, he would have told her.

Oh God, he'd purposefully lied to her! His mention of Rosalie at the ranch he "worked on." She was his family's cook. No wonder he got uncomfortable when she asked about Hailey's budget for the wedding. He didn't want to tell her.

Her mind flew, memories of every conversation pulling up other ways he avoided talking about his wealth. Her stomach squeezed so hard she coughed at her own stupidity. It was one thing if he'd done it when they first met, but as late as four days ago, he'd hedged about Hailey's reason for not getting married in Arizona, which she had mentioned would make it easier financially on the family.

He never said his sister wanted it to be a private affair without news crews and the local paparazzi interrupting!

She squeezed her hands, refusing to cry. It was her own fault. She'd let her guard down because he was a cowboy and then he was so nice. She'd ignored the fact he was a guest and she was the resort's manager. Once again, she had no one to blame but—

Her phone rang.

Unclasping her hands, she pulled it from the side pocket of her dress. It was Melia. She cleared her throat. "Hey. What's up?"

"Sorry to bother you at work, but your cowboy needs someone to save him. The local ladies found him and he's buried."

Save him? She scowled. "Let them have him. I gotta go."

She ended the call. It may be her fault she'd trusted him, but she certainly didn't have to make his last day easier on him.

Despite her anger, her heart lurched that she wouldn't see him again. Why couldn't she have just followed Auntie's rule?

Furious with Cord and herself, she rose. She had work to do. Stalking out of her office, she stopped at the reception desk to pick up the mail, then strode down the hall to the banquet room. They had a bride-to-be flying in the next day, and she needed to be sure the three sample cakes would be ready.

She needed to be sure of a lot of things until she could go home and let her heart break as it wanted to.

Cord strode down the beach, his heart in his throat. Leah was pissed at him for some reason and he had an idea of why. He also knew who told her. Running up to the resort, he strode between the buildings to the pool area.

"You." He pointed to Deidre before he'd even reached her.

"Me? Oh, I'm so glad you came to your senses before you left. One night is better than none, right?"

He kept his fisted hand at his side. He would not hit a woman…ever. "What happened to 'our secret'?"

She had the nerve to shrug. "I only keep secrets for people who are a nice to me."

"Believe me, right now I'm being very, very nice to you compared to what you deserve."

The woman whipped off her glasses. "Don't tell me what I deserve. I don't care who you are in Arizona. You're still well beneath me. You're clueless what an honor it was for me to even talk to you."

He stared in disbelief. The woman had no grasp of reality. This was a waste of time. He needed to find Leah. Without another word, he continued toward the main lobby.

"You should have been much nicer to me Mr. Pennington." Deidre called out behind him, but he ignored her. He had only one purpose now. Find Leah.

As he came into the lobby, Ulu glanced up and smiled. "Hello, handsome."

"Where's Leah?"

"Oh. She headed for the banquet hall. Is everything okay?"

Through gritted teeth he answered. "No, thanks to Queen Bee."

He caught Ulu's scowl as he passed the reception counter and strode for the banquet hall. Had it really been less than two weeks when Leah had first taken him down the very same hall? Even then he'd been interested in her.

Before he made it to the door, Leah came out, her head down as she read something in a folder she held. He grasped her shoulders to keep them from colliding.

She jerked away forcefully at first, but on seeing him, her eyes rounded and she took another step back. "What are you doing here?"

"We need to talk."

She shook her head. "No, I don't think we do."

He wasn't letting her pass. "Yes, we do."

She frowned at him. "I think the time for talking was *before* you took me back to your room."

She had a point, but he couldn't give in an inch. From the set of her jaw, she'd already drawn her own conclusions, and he needed her to erase them. "I tried to tell you before then, but we kept getting off the subject."

She clutched the folder to her chest. "And you couldn't simply bring it up?"

"I started to many times."

"Of course, why tell *me*? Why would you want *me* to know? After all, I'm just the manager here."

His gut tightened. What was wrong with him that he

hadn't told her? "That's not fair. You know you're much more than that."

She waved her hand. "Okay, a vacation fling, then."

He moved toward her to grab her shoulders, but she backed up against the closed door, and he dropped his hands. "I don't have vacation flings. You mean a lot more to me than that."

Her face crumpled. "But not enough to tell me who you were."

"I did. I'm Cord Pennington. There's nothing more to tell. My family's money is not me."

She stared him in the eyes. "So, if that's the case, why couldn't you tell me?"

He fisted and unfisted his hands, his personal hang-up now seeming like a giant canyon between him and her. "Because I've never been comfortable with it. Well, not exactly never."

She didn't say anything. He didn't blame her. She was probably afraid if she interrupted, she'd give him another excuse not to tell her.

"I never thought about it growing up until high school. I was dating this girl for over a year. I thought I was in love and that she was the one I would marry. You know, the person you go to prom with?"

Leah didn't nod or make a sound, forcing him to continue.

"It wasn't quite prom yet. In fact, it was homecoming, the homecoming game which I wasn't going to make, except I got home early with my dad after a long day of driving back from Yuma. I quickly showered, changed and drove to the game before it ended, intending to surprise Brittney. I knew where she sat in the bleachers, so I walked underneath them until I saw her boots."

He paused as the memory, replayed so many times, came into focus again. "I reached up to tug on her ankle, but before I touched her, she laughed saying, 'That's not going to happen'."

"I waited, curious about what they were talking about. Hoping it had something to do with me. It did. Her friend asked her why not, and she said she was going to be the richest graduate from Valle Verde High after she married me. At first I was thrilled to know she felt as much for me as I did for her."

Leah's brows lowered, but still she didn't say anything.

"Her next words killed it. She said that she wouldn't have had sex with me if I wasn't rich. She told her girlfriends to get their priorities straight, too. Money then looks then money." His stomach didn't tighten like it used to. The wound was old and the lesson well learned. "I broke it off with her the next day. Ever since then, I've been reluctant to let anyone know I'm one of *the* Penningtons."

Leah's face didn't change. She must see that like her, he had just fallen into a habit that caused him to make stupid decisions.

"So, what you're saying is you thought I would be as shallow and money hungry as that high school bitch."

He sucked in his breath. "No. Not at all. I just wanted you to know why it's so hard for me to tell anyone who my family is. It's a habit to hide it. Like hiding the fact Phil is royalty."

Her lips twitched, but a smile didn't appear so much as a grimace. "I see. I'm good enough to keep Phil's secret but not yours." She shook her head. "Never mind. It was my mistake for falling for you. You'd think I would have learned by now to follow the rules of my employment."

Shit, when she put it like that, he really did come off like an asshole. "Leah, listen, I'm sorry. I didn't do it to hurt you. Actually, I planned to tell you tonight. I want you to know what you'd be getting into if we continued our relationship."

Her eyes widened in disbelief. "Continue? I guess we don't have to worry about that now." She started to move past him, but he couldn't let her.

Grabbing her arm, he held her there. "Please, Leah. I want to continue this. Don't let my wealth sabotage my heart again."

Her hard look softened and her eyes filled with tears. "It's not your wealth that screws you up, Cord. It's your head." She pulled away and strode out into the lobby.

Fuck, she was right. Why couldn't he just get over it? Millions of people would love to have his problem. There had to be a way to save this. Leah was worth whatever it took. He strode back into the lobby, but she was nowhere to be found.

He looked at Ulu who pouted. "She said she'd fire me if I told you where she went."

"I messed up."

"It certainly appears that way."

He just stood there with no solution staring at Ulu. "I don't know how to fix this."

"But you want to fix it, right?" Ulu cocked his head.

He nodded. "More than I want to breathe."

"Good." Ulu smiled. "You find your friend and meet me at Keoki's at six. We fix this."

He stared at the man, not sure if he really meant it.

"Oh, please." Ulu rolled his eyes. "I'm single, not desperate…yet." He winked before raising his hand and waving him away. "Now shoo and go find that other hunk. I know that woman better than you do and between you and me, she *needs* us to fix this."

Leah set out the photos on the table in the banquet hall and pretended she didn't know that Cord would be leaving in a few minutes.

She pretended she'd slept last night, despite vacillating between crying in her pillow and punching it, switching between wondering if she was making a mountain out of a mole hill and hoping she never saw him again.

Rearranging the photos of the banquet room made up for wedding receptions for the fourth time, she finally clasped her hands together. It was for the best.

Cord leaving would have hurt anyway. This way maybe she wouldn't pine for him or try to find a new position closer to Arizona. She'd applied for one in London just this morning, just to prove to herself that she could cut the ties.

She glanced at the clock. Was he outside waiting for his taxi? Despite her resolve, she walked to the back doors and opened one.

Her breath caught at the site of him talking to Phil who would be staying at least another two weeks. Phil had seen the wisdom of staying in the honeymoon suite and had his bags quietly moved there early in the morning even though housekeeping hadn't cleaned the room yet.

Cord nodded at something he said. Dressed in his jeans, boots, and cowboy hat, he was ready to return to his life in Arizona. His wealthy ranch life.

A yearning to go with him hit hard, but she clasped her hands and held tight. That was his life, not hers. He'd never said he wanted her to come to Arizona. He'd only said he wanted to continue their relationship.

She'd discovered that morning that he'd tried to extend his stay but Ulu had told him there were no rooms. She'd never realized how protective Ulu could be and had thanked him. It didn't matter if he stayed. It didn't matter if she could forgive him. He lived in Arizona and there was no work there for her. It was just as well.

Phil noticed her and pointed.

Her heart leapt. Would Cord turn around?

He did.

She forgot to breathe as he stared at her. *I loved you.* The words flew through her mind as she gazed at him, wishing everything could have been different.

Then he touched the brim of his hat and turned back to Phil.

Swallowing new tears, she stepped into the banquet hall again, closing the door behind her. The sound seemed so final.

Straightening her shoulders, she forced herself to return to her office, ignoring the hurt that settled in her chest. On the way through the lobby, she stopped at the reception counter where Nani was just handing room keys to a new check-in. When she finished, Leah stepped behind the counter. "Is Wena still in the laundry?"

"Yes." Nani studied her face.

She quickly looked down to grab the note she'd left at reception. "When she comes back, ask her to come see me."

"Of course." Nani touched her arm.

She flinched but forced herself not to pull away.

"Is something wrong?"

She shook her head. "No. Just have a lot going on right now. I'll be taking an early lunch today." So she could be on her first interview call. She'd had great responses, even hearing from places she hadn't applied to. She loved the electronic job board sites. They were so much better than four years ago.

"Let me know if you need anything." Nani's concern was obvious in her voice.

Leah forced herself to smile. "I will." Then she took her note and entered her office. She immediately looked at the clock.

He was gone.

She would not break down. There was nothing to be sorry for. It had to end one way or another. She had to move on, specifically with a new job. A new place would help her forget.

Not that she could ever forget Cord Pennington.

She shook her head. She had to prepare for her interview. It might be morning in Hawaii, but it was afternoon in Colorado, and she only had one chance to make a good first impression.

She'd just finished re-reading her resume, the very resume Cord had helped her with, when there was a knock at her door. She slipped the resume into her purse. "Come in."

Wena entered, her smile bright. "You wanted to see me?"

"Yes, have a seat. Did you get the linen issue figured out?"

Wena sat. "Yes. There are three that need to be replaced. One was ripped and you'll never guess whose room it came from."

Leah kept a serious face though it was hard. "Deidre's."

Wena's eyes widened. "How did you know?"

She chuckled sadly. "When you take over, you'll learn all about the regular guests, like who likes extra pillows. Who wants early dinner reservations. Who doesn't want their room cleaned until the late afternoon. Who goes shopping every other day, and who rips at least one set of sheets a week."

"What?" Wena stared at her as if she'd sprouted lava from the top of her head.

She nodded. "It's just a matter of being here long enough."

Wena shook her head. "I'm not going to be here that long. I'm only here for the summer until I can start at the Halekahi Resort on the Big Island."

Leah blinked. "Big Island?"

"Yes. That's where I did my internship. They hired me on, but I don't start until fall, so I asked Auntie for a summer job. I figured I could make some money while learning more about hotel management." She winked. "Doesn't hurt to ask family for a favor."

She was such an idiot! Now what should she do? She'd sent resumes, had phone interviews lined up.

"So, what did you want to talk to me about?" Wena jolted her from her thoughts.

"Oh, I wanted to know if you'd like to sit in on selling a bride-to-be this afternoon?"

"Absolutely! Do we get to taste cake?"

She chuckled. "Only the leftovers and that's if our potential customer doesn't want to take it home with her."

"What time?"

She glanced at the time on her computer. Cord would be in the airport by now, maybe even through security. "Two."

"Great. Thank you." Wena rose. "Did you need anything else?"

She shook her head.

"Then I'll see you this afternoon." Within seconds, Wena was out the door and the office quiet once again.

Leah couldn't pull her gaze away from the time. It was as if someone had tipped her life upside down then shouted "just kidding" and tipped it upright again, except so much was damaged in the transition.

Yesterday morning she was in love and planning to move to a new place for a new job closer to him. Now he was gone, taking her heart with him, and she was back to being the manager of the Puanani.

Absently, she glanced at her purse. She should call and cancel the interview. She should go to the airport and kiss Cord goodbye. There was a lot she should do.

But she didn't do any of it.

Chapter Fourteen

Scottsdale, Arizona

Cord handed the keys of his pick-up to the valet, ignoring the man's obvious disapproval of the mud-spattered fenders. He wasn't in the mood to deal with unwarranted arrogance. He was here to get answers.

Striding through the glass doors of the Scottsdale Gardens Resort, he went straight to the front desk.

A petite blonde woman smiled at him. "Welcome to the Scottsdale Gardens Resort where your satisfaction is our only goal. I'm Sheena. Are you checking in?"

He'd bet making a bunch of money was another goal of the resort. He smiled in return and tipped his hat. "I would like to speak to the manager."

"Of course, sir. One moment, sir." She didn't bat an eyelash, just walked around a corner and disappeared. Within seconds she was back. "Ms. Canon will be right out."

"Thank you." He stepped to the side of the counter, pleased that this young woman didn't look down her nose at him.

Sheena went back to her computer, swiping room keys and typing.

An older woman came from the back. He guessed she was older from the reading glasses hanging on a chain around her neck. As she approached in her tan suit, he could see that she did have a number of smile lines covered in heavy make-up.

"Hello, I'm Audrey Canon, the manager."

It was time to play the family ace. After avoiding it most of his life, it was odd to be using it. "Hello Audrey, I'm Cordell Pennington from Ironwood."

At the mention of the town named after his family's ranch, the woman's eyes lit up. "How can I be of assistance Mr. Pennington?"

"I'm here to inquire about a former employee of yours, Miss Leah Pennington."

A gasp at the counter had them both looking at Sheena, who quickly went back to swiping room keys.

Ms. Canon swallowed hard before she faced him again. "As you said, she's a former employee, so I'm not sure how I can help you."

"I plan to hire her but heard there are rumors that started from when she worked here. I came to find out if they were true."

The woman glanced at Sheena who was not only listening now but watching. At Ms. Canon's scowl, Sheena went back to what she was doing. "I'm sorry, Mr. Pennington, but all I am allowed to confirm is that she worked here and what dates. If you like, I'd be happy to print that up for you."

"I would appreciate that." He didn't need it, but now he wanted to talk to Sheena because she obviously knew something.

Ms. Canon nodded then turned and headed to the back. As soon as she was out of sight, Sheena motioned him over.

"I'm not supposed to say anything, but I was here. Leah hired me. Not only did she do nothing wrong, but they fired the two men who accused her. They were recorded in the staff room laughing about how they had finally got her fired."

Both satisfaction and anger stirred in his gut. "And they asked Leah to come back?"

She shook her head. "No. They didn't find out until months later, and she was in Hawaii by then. They didn't know that was where she went and I certainly wasn't going to tell them after the way she was treated."

Just because she told him what he wanted to hear, didn't make her a reliable source. "Is what they did to Leah the reason the two men were fired?"

She shook her head. "No. The staff room isn't usually bugged, but the manager at the time had complaints from the cleaning staff that there were dirty rooms to clean that weren't on their list. Those two losers were letting friends use rooms. They weren't even smart enough to cover their tracks. I'm glad or we would have never found out what they did to Leah."

He studied her. She was not much younger than Leah, yet she was still working the front desk? "Are you the front desk manager now?"

Her face fell. "No. I don't kiss up and pretend things are okay when they aren't. Please don't tell Mrs. Canon I told you." She glanced behind her before looking back at him.

He smiled. "Not a chance. Do you have a card?"

She pulled a hotel business card from behind the desk. "Just this one."

"Would you mind if I gave Leah your contact information? I think she would enjoy talking with you again."

Sheena's pretty hazel eyes lit up. "I'd love that." She wrote on the card and handed it to him. "That's my email address. Tell her I'd love to talk to her and catch up. Is she back in Arizona?"

He shook his head, pocketing the card. "Not yet. But she will be." That was if Ulu and Phil's plan worked. Having them both there with Leah and reporting to him made him feel like there was still a chance…even if there wasn't. "Thank you."

She nodded, and he strolled back to the end of the counter, not wanting to give Ms. Canon any reason to review the video that he was sure was being filmed by a multitude of cameras right now.

The hotel manager came out a few minutes later and handed him an envelope. "There you are. You know, you could have simply called." She looked at him suspiciously.

"I had planned to, but I was in town meeting my brother Greyson for lunch. You know, family business."

"Of course." She nodded deferentially.

He hated that. Money had nothing to do with character. "Thank you for the information." He gave her a sincere smile and held up the envelope before walking out.

Now to find the Middle Eastern restaurant his brother wanted to meet him at, and to figure out how to restore Leah's reputation. He had no idea how much time he had before she accepted a job too far away for him to reach her. The last communication he had from Ulu was that she'd applied for a job in London. How that man found out, he didn't want to know.

The Middle Eastern restaurant was on the east side of Phoenix in a nondescript building between an auto repair place and a pharmacy. He was early, so he checked his messages. There was no report on Leah, so he read the older ones.

The one that mentioned both Phil and Ulu had discovered Leah with red-rimmed eyes. The one where Phil stated he'd purposefully run into her three times to mention how much he missed his friend Cord and that he may stop by on his way home if she wanted to take a vacation.

His gut twisted at the misery he'd inflicted on her. If it wasn't for Ulu and Phil thinking with their heads and not like him with his heart, he'd be just as miserable. They planned to keep him in the forefront of her mind while keeping tabs on her job prospects, while he used his family name, wealth and connections to get Leah a job opportunity in Arizona.

Phil said he should just pay to have someone give her a job, but he knew her better than that. He just wanted someone to give her an interview. He knew she could land a job if her reputation was restored, and it looked like now he just might have a chance at that. And if all their planning didn't work?

He was prepared to leave the ranch. He didn't want to. He loved Ironwood, but he'd discovered in the last couple days that he loved Leah more. He hadn't told his dad yet. He was hoping he wouldn't have to. That would be the hardest conversation of his life.

Cord stepped out of his truck just as Grey pulled into a parking space two cars up. As his brother strode toward him in his black suit, Cord grinned. His older brother looked like a hit man…or a pall bearer. Even his hair was black.

Their black-haired father joked that Grey was his only biological child since the rest of them took after their mom, but he liked to think he was the perfect mix.

They hugged and Grey pulled back. "I didn't expect to see you until Sunday. Must be important for you to drive all the way up here to the big city."

He chuckled. "Believe me, I wouldn't be here if it wasn't." He grimaced. He'd rather chase down an errant bull than fight the traffic in Phoenix.

Grey squeezed his shoulder. "Well, you're in for a culinary treat. This little place has the best tabouli in the city."

Since he had no idea what that was, he didn't respond. Following his brother inside, he wasn't surprised that the entire staff behind the counter greeted Grey by name. He glanced up at the hand-written boards that served as the menu. The only word he recognized was "lamb."

"Everyone, this is my brother, Cord."

The staff responded with welcomes and promises of a lunch fit for paradise.

"What do you want?" Grey looked at him expectantly.

"Whatever you suggest. Why don't you order for me? Just make sure whatever it is, there's a lot of it. I'll grab a seat." He left his meal order to his brother's discretion and took a seat in the corner at a wobbly table with metal chairs. Not exactly the kind of place he expected his suave brother to eat at, but he felt comfortable.

Greyson joined him. "They'll bring it over when it's ready. So, what's up?"

He liked that his brother didn't keep his sophisticated ways around him. "Remember how I asked you to look into Leah Pennington's reputation?"

"Yes. Did you bring her back with you?"

His stomach growled more from stress than hunger. "No.

But I did go to her former place of employment to discover what happened."

Grey's eyes rounded. "Already? You haven't been back forty-eight hours yet. Do you even know what time it is?"

He waved him off. "Yeah, it's time for me to get my head on straight."

Before he could say anything else, their food arrived among many smiles and Grey getting clapped on the back at least five times. The action made him think of Leah's aversion to touch and he took a deep breath to loosen up his insides.

Grey pointed. "Start with that. It's a gyro. You'll want to add that tzatziki sauce to it. Trust me on this."

He ignored his food. "I found out the whole sexual harassment accusation was made up to get rid of her. The assholes who claimed it have since been fired for other reasons, but the resort recorded them admitting to it."

Grey's mouth was full, but he quickly swallowed. "How the hell did you get that kind of information out of them?"

"One of their employees that Leah hired told me when the manager said she couldn't confirm anything except that Leah worked there and the dates."

Grey nodded. "Would this girl tell others?"

"I don't think so. If she did, she made it clear she'd lose her job."

This time Grey waved his statement away. "That's not a problem, we just get her another one, but we may not need her. If this is true, I can probably get our lawyer to politely request copies of the tape. I'm assuming you want this woman's name cleared. Otherwise, it would be the desk clerk's word against the two men and those aren't good odds."

As Grey took another bite of what looked like an overflowing pita sandwich, Cord felt his stomach loosen. "Yes, I want her name cleared before I ask her to be my wife."

His brother sputtered, spitting out part of his meal. "What?"

"She's the one I'm going to marry. There's only two things standing in my way. The first I'm hoping you can help me with."

"Christ, Cord, really?"

He nodded, unable to help the shit-eating grin that split his face. "Really."

"Wow." Grey looked shell-shocked at first, then a slow smile changed his face. "I'm happy for you. The ranch needs another woman now that Hailey will be moving away. Mom will love it. What do you need me to do?"

For the first time in the last three days, he dared to hope. "I need you to get a resort to offer her the job of manager."

"I'll need her resume and contact information for that."

He pulled the folded-up paper out of his shirt pocket. "Here it is. I just retyped it with our changes."

Once again Grey looked at him in surprise.

He shrugged. "I was helping her with it. Her job as manager of the Puanani on Momi in the Hawaiian Islands is almost done."

Grey stopped eating for a moment and perused Leah's work history.

Cord couldn't watch his brother's face and eat his food, so he focused on the food. He'd never been big on lamb but the gyro and kabobs were excellent. He had no idea what the stuffed pita on his plate had inside, but he was more willing to give it a go.

"This is good." His brother's comment had him wiping his mouth with the paper napkin.

"Is it possible to find her something here? I'd be happy if it's in Arizona. Anywhere in Arizona."

Grey shook his head. "This will be an uphill battle. First, we need to get the rumor mill in the hospitality sector to learn about her false accusation. Then we need to find a resort who's even looking for a manager. This will take a while."

Cord's stomach tightened. "I don't think I have much time. She's already applied for positions and posted on job boards."

"Then just tell her to hold off accepting anything until we can see what we can do here."

Shit. He looked down at his food again, not even mildly interested in it.

"Cord, what aren't you telling me? Wait a minute. You said two things were standing in your way. What's the second thing?"

"Me."

Leah ended the call and slouched in her chair. The interview had gone well, but her heart wasn't in it. Denmark seemed so far away and so cold. Though she'd taken her resume off the job boards, the positions she'd applied for still had her in the queue.

She'd planned on withdrawing her name, but after getting nine requests for phone interviews, she decided to at least see them through. It was just easier than making the effort to back out and look like she was indecisive…which she was.

It had been four years that she'd worked at the Puanani,

so it was time for a bigger challenge, preferably a hotel with a full-time banquet manager. Besides, a new reason had cropped up for leaving. Every part of the Puanani reminded her of Cord, except the pool. What had once been her sanctuary from Arizona now felt like torture.

Even seeing Phil on a daily basis caused her heart to ache because he was Cord's friend. What surprised her about him was she'd found him and Ulu having breakfast together in the restaurant more than once. She knew for a fact that Phil was interested in a woman from Florida name Annalise, so the only thing she could think of was that he was giving Ulu relationship advice.

She set her phone on her desk. At least she didn't have to make a decision now. No one had offered her a position yet, and she still had her job, and if she wanted to keep it, she'd better get to work. Turning on her computer, she looked at her list of tasks for the day. Payroll would be first. Many of the employees—

The ringing of her phone interrupted her thought. She quickly grabbed it. "Hello?"

"Hello, is this Leah Pennington?"

"Yes, it is."

"This is Susan Reynolds, I'm the Human Resources Director for Vista del Sol Resorts and Spas."

Her stomach knotted. Why would an Arizona hotel be calling her?

"Our owners have instructed me to offer you a position as manager of our smaller property in Marana. Before I send over the formal job offer, I just needed to ask if you would be willing to relocate?"

A job? In Arizona? She hadn't even interviewed. She hadn't even applied!

"Ms. Pennington?"

"Yes, I'm here." She stared at her computer screen as if it could help her somehow. "I'm sorry, I'm confused. You're offering me a position?"

"Yes."

"But I didn't apply for one with your company."

"Oh, I know. However, I found your resume on the hospitality job board. The owners of our company asked me to review your qualifications and you're exactly what they're looking for. Our resort in Marana is small and in the middle of the desert as our clientele are generally those looking for an exclusive, discreet place to vacation."

She was well aware of the Vista del Sol company. She'd even had to study their business model in college. "I'm very flattered." She rolled her eyes. Not the best response.

"Are you willing to relocate, Ms. Pennington?"

Back to Arizona? In a heartbeat! "I am." But what about her reputation? Would they let her go if they hadn't heard about her problem and then found out later? That would be worse. She had to say something. "I'm very interested in this position."

"Good, I'll email you the terms and then you can call me back with any questions."

She swallowed hard before speaking. "Ms. Reynolds, I think you should know that the reason I'm surprised is that I was under the impression no one would hire me in Arizona."

The woman's tone of voice changed. "I understand. I personally had heard the rumor about your dismissal from the

Scottsdale Gardens, but I've also heard that you were set up by two male employees who have since been fired. Of course, both of those are rumors. If you wouldn't mind, I would appreciate it if you were honest with me. I don't want to do anything that would harm the image of our company."

Set up? Two men? Relief, excitement, anger burned through her faster than a road runner dodging a car. "I assure you, Ms. Reynolds, I would never do anything to harm the reputation of the company I worked for." And she'd make sure of that.

"Good. Then take a look at the offer and lodgings. We have a small casita on property as it's not close to anywhere, so you wouldn't have to find a place to live right away. We had it built for the manager to use as necessary because sometimes you may need to stay overnight with a late event."

She still couldn't believe this was happening. "Thank you."

"My pleasure. Just give me a call tomorrow with any questions. Have a good day."

She said goodbye and ended the call. Stunned, she didn't move, trying to digest what just happened. Then a surge of happiness flooded her and she smiled. She was going home!

Jumping up, she squealed. It was too amazing to be real. To make sure, she pinched herself. "Ouch." Okay, it was real. Sitting back down, she opened her email. The offer probably wouldn't come right away.

Still, with baited breath, she watched as her mailbox opened. Eleven messages had come in. She scanned the senders, but nothing from Vista del Sol. Of course not. They just hung up. The woman would have to have had the email ready to send for it to—

A new message came in.

She sucked in her breath as she clicked it open. There it was in black and white. She scanned the short email then opened the first document. It was an actual offer and at a salary higher than what she was making now. Too excited to read anymore, she forwarded the email to her personal one at home to read through after work, if she could calm down by then.

She laughed, too happy to hold it in and stood. She needed to tell someone, but who first?

She froze. She wanted to tell Cord. If not for Cord, her resume wouldn't have been noticed. If not for him… Did he have something to do with this? She shook her head. No, they were done. She'd made that clear.

Her heart squeezed. Now that she would be back in Arizona, she wanted to see him again.

If she'd known this was a possibility, would she have acted as she had? Would she have been as upset?

Yes, she would have been just as upset that he'd not told her about his family, but would she have acted differently, knowing she might see him again?

Her conscience was harsh. She definitely would have. She'd mixed her angst about him leaving with her hurt over his lie.

What would he think about her being in Marana? It wasn't far from his family's ranch. But would he care? She sighed, a cloud suddenly forming over her at her missed chance at love.

She needed to get a hold of herself. She'd just landed a great position at the best company in Arizona and she was going home. She'd have to tell her mom and her friends.

And her friends here. As much as she was excited to be going, there was a lot she'd miss about Momi and the Puanani. And the very first thing she needed to do, right now, was give Auntie notice. The email said they wanted her to start next month, so Auntie deserved all that time to find a new manager. Unless…. She grinned. She knew the perfect person, Nani.

Straightening her shoulders, she walked to her door and opened it. Today would begin a new chapter in her life. She would focus on that and ignore the ache in her heart until she figured out what to do about it.

As she passed the reception desk, Ulu was checking in a family of four. When he noticed her, she smiled. "I'm running over to the big house for a minute. I'll be right back."

He nodded before returning his attention to the new guests, gushing over the little girl's plastic tiara.

Tears formed in her eyes. Ulu was so great with children. Here on Momi, things were much more relaxed than at home, and she would miss it more than she realized.

When she got to the end of the path that split between the honeymoon suite and Auntie's, she stopped to gather herself together, though she was pretty sure she'd start crying in earnest when she told her boss she'd be leaving.

She studied the honeymoon suite as she tried to calm herself. That was where she and Cord made love. Now that she was leaving, instead of it being a source of sorrow, the happy memories she had of it made her smile. If it hadn't been for him, she may have never touched another human being for another ten years…or more.

Feeling more in control of her emotions, she continued to Auntie's.

Cord sat in his truck, air conditioner running, keeping one eye on the resort entrance and one eye on the clock. He'd waited over a month for this moment. He would have been here four days ago, but his mother had told him to wait a week to let Leah settle in. He'd finally refused to wait another day.

Now, he was nervous. What if she was still angry at him? What if she was now mad at him for interfering? Did she guess he'd used his family name to get her the position? If she didn't know, would she be mad if he told her? Make that *when* he told her. No more hiding.

It was almost six. She'd be officially off the clock in five minutes. Not able to wait another moment, he turned off the truck and grabbed the bouquet of lavender orchids. He wanted her to remember their happier times in Momi. For him, lavender was her color with so many of her clothes containing it.

Striding for the entrance, he was relieved to see through the tinted glass doors that the lobby was empty. Stepping inside, he was hit once again with cool air conditioning.

"Welcome to Vista del Sol. We're so pleased you've come."

He smiled nervously at the young woman at the counter. "I'm here to see Leah Pennington. Is she available?"

She eyed his flowers and smiled warmly. "She should be off work now, but I'm sure she'll be happy to help you. One moment."

He waited, his hands sweating as he stood in the middle of the stone and glass lobby, holding the orchids and trying not to crush them.

The woman put down the phone. "She'll be right out."

He swallowed hard, but couldn't get his throat to work, so he nodded.

The sound of high heels on the title floor warned him she was about to appear, but nothing could have prepared him for the sight of her. She wore a lavender suit that hugged her curves perfectly. She'd cut her hair a few inches so it no longer touched her shoulders and there was no flower resting behind her ear like when she worked at the Puanani.

When her gaze fell on him, he smiled hopefully.

She stopped, her eyes widening. "Cord?" Her voice was barely a whisper.

He'd practiced his speech at least a hundred times, but it flew out of his head. "I couldn't go another second without seeing you."

"Oh." Her word came out anguished and his heart lurched.

The next moment she ran to him, throwing her arms around his neck. "I missed you, too."

As he grasped her to him, he kissed her, letting everything he wanted to say out in his kiss. She felt so good against him, he never wanted to let her go.

But she broke away from the kiss and stared up at him. "I can't believe you're here. How did you know where to find me?"

And suddenly the relief he felt at her welcome dried up his throat, forcing him to swallow in order to speak. "If I tell you, will you promise not to get mad."

She pulled her arms from around his neck. "What did you do?"

Since she wasn't frowning yet, he hoped that was a good

sign. "I discovered that you'd been set up at your old job and had my brother help get the word out about it."

She cracked a small smile. "Thank you for that."

Relieved, he continued. "I knew you were looking for a new position, and I wanted you to get one nearby, so I kind of bribed the owners of Vista del Sol into taking a look at your resume."

"You what?"

He held up his hand. "Just to look at it. I didn't tell them to hire you. They did that on their own."

She crossed her arms over her chest. "And what did you bribe them with?"

He grimaced. "I'm not sure if you've seen the events scheduled for next year, but my parents will be celebrating their thirty-fifth wedding anniversary here."

She dropped her arms and stared at him. "Those are *your* parents?"

He shrugged. "Yeah. My siblings and I were planning a party, so I figured why not here, especially because you might be able to benefit from it."

She still seemed a bit in shock. That could be because they had booked every room and suite in the place. They had to, to keep the gawkers away. Something she needed to understand.

"Leah, I'm sorry I didn't tell you about my family. I've been hiding it for so long that it became a habit. I'm not embarrassed by them. In fact, I'm very proud to be a Pennington and since Momi, I'm learning to embrace that fact."

"I think I understand, now. Just like it became a habit for me to avoid touching. I think I forgave you the minute you stepped on the plane to come back to Arizona, but I didn't think it mattered because I could never return here."

He grinned. "Yet here you are."

She smiled. "I am, and very happy. Thank you for making this possible."

"Then you aren't angry with me."

She cocked her head as if thinking about it. "No. I'm not. I would have never done anything about it and lived the rest of my life thinking I'd been in the wrong. I'm grateful to you."

His heart sighed as the warmth of happiness flooded him. "Good. Then…" He knelt down before her, not even attempting to try to remember what he'd planned to say.

Her hands covered her mouth as she looked at him.

He took one of them and held it, noticing she didn't even flinch. "Leah Pennington, would you be my wife?"

She blinked twice before a smile lit her face. "Oh, yes."

He reached inside the pocket of his shirt and produced the four-karat diamond ring with one large stone surrounded by smaller ones that ran from it down onto the band. Slipping the ring onto her left hand, he rose.

Leah was smiling and crying as he stood. He pulled her back to him and kissed her gently, sealing his promise to her.

When he lifted his lips from hers, she smirked. "So, I guess now I'm going to be one of *those* Penningtons."

He laughed as he nodded. "Yes, you are, but just think—you won't have to change your name."

She rolled her eyes.

At the sound of a cork popping, they both looked over to the desk to find the clerk had produced a bottle of champagne.

Leah laughed. "Put that on *his* tab."

He kept hold of her hand as they walked over. It may have taken him a while, but he had finally found *the one*, and he would never let her go.

Epilogue

"Leah, you go get Cord. He's on the porch. I'll finish loading the dishwasher." Cord's mother shooed her away.

She was fine with that. After the usual Sunday dinner, she was nervous about the family meeting. There was only one person who could make her feel more relaxed and that was her fiancé.

She opened the front door to find Cord leaning against a post, his father in one of the rocking chairs. As she stepped out, James Pennington tapped out his pipe. "That's enough of that or I'll catch heck from your mother." He rose. "Besides, I want to grab a beer for this presentation." He winked at her before strolling by and into the house.

"You look like a deer in headlights." Cord opened his free arm, and she stepped into his embrace.

"I feel like one. I've never been so nervous."

"Why?" His brow furrowed with his confusion. "It's only my family. You deal with much more intimidating people at work."

"I know, but I'm not this invested there. And I love that you came up with this idea while at Pono Ranch. That makes this project special to me. I really want them to like it."

"It's *our* idea." He squeezed her against his side. "And if they don't like it, we'll just ask them how we can change it so they do. This isn't a one-shot deal."

She nodded, not completely convinced.

"Tell me who you think will be the hardest to convince."

That was a good question. "It's between your dad, Hailey and Greyson."

Cord laughed. "You definitely need to spend more time with my family. The hardest one to convince will be Wesley."

"Wesley? But he's hardly ever here. And he's so laid back."

Cord shook his head. "You definitely need to spend more time with them. Wesley is the quickest to turn on a dime. He can go from laughing to throwing a punch faster than an indie driver can get up to a hundred miles per hour."

She shrugged. "I guess I haven't seen him do that. Do you think he will tonight?"

"Definitely."

Great, now she was even more nervous.

"You have nothing to worry about. We're all family. Greyson will review the numbers and tell us where we're wrong, then figure it out himself. Hailey will have grand schemes of decorating and marketing before we even break ground, and we won't have to lift a finger. Dad will hem and haw about safety issues and mom will negotiate everything."

She cocked her head and looked at him. "So, if someone else was proposing a change to the ranch, what would you do?"

He pulled her into his embrace. "I'd tell them no. Then pretend to come around after they convinced me."

"You would not."

"Okay, I wouldn't pretend, but I'd be very practical and that's what this idea is—practical."

From rote, she quoted him. "Because diversification means long-term sustainability."

He grinned and kissed her on the nose. "Exactly. See, we'll make a Pennington of you yet."

"Excuse me, but I am already a Pennington. And don't you dare say it."

He laughed, but he didn't say *the* Penningtons.

She grimaced. "You didn't tell me what Wesley will do."

He sighed. "Because you never know with him. I do know he resists all change to the ranch. He was the biggest hurdle I had to get over when we leased the land for the tower."

She frowned. "But if he's not here that much, why would he care?"

"I'm not sure. I think he just doesn't want to see Ironwood change. He's the one who's gone the most, yet he's the one who probably appreciates this place the most because he's not here."

In an odd sort of way that did make sense. "And what about Dillon?"

"He's a wild card since this is his first family meeting, but I think he has a pretty level head on his shoulders. I guess we'll find out soon." He turned his head toward the front door.

She looked over to see it opening and Hailey stuck her head out. "Okay you two, you can do that later. You have a meeting to run."

Cord nodded. "We'll be right there."

Hailey looked at him and then at her and then back at Cord. "You so owe me."

He shook his head. "No way, sis. My debt is paid. That I reaped the reward is all my doing."

"It was worth a try." Hailey winked at her. "I'm very excited about The Puanani. Not sure any other place will be able to knock it from my top spot." She gave an appreciative nod then headed back inside.

Leah smirked at Cord. "Do you know where she's sending Wesley?"

He frowned. "No. Do you?"

"Yes, but I'm supposed to keep it a secret."

He frowned. "I thought we promised, no secrets between us."

She rolled her eyes. "Fine, but don't say anything. Promise?"

"I do promise, especially if it has to do with Hailey."

She sobered at that thought. Hailey may have forgiven Cord, but he hadn't quite forgiven himself yet. "She's sending him to St. Croix."

"What? Why didn't she send me there? I know people. I could have found out the local side of things."

She pulled out of his arms. "For starters, Hailey said that would have been too easy for you. And secondly, are you saying you're sorry you were sent to Momi?"

His eyes widened and he quickly pulled her to him. "Not even a little bit. In fact, I won't tell my brother anything. Well, maybe I'll give him the name of one person that could help him, just to be nice."

She smiled again. That sounded like the Cord she loved. "Should we go in now?"

He turned back to the view off the front porch. The sun was just setting beyond the mesa, sending out streaks of orange and red, the pinks and purples still to come. "In a minute."

She stayed within his arms, watching the color change, loving that she was finally back home, even if it was a new home. She'd never expected this, and it wouldn't have happened if the cowboy whose arms held her hadn't walked into her resort on Momi, clueless about weddings and unhappy he had to take a vacation.

She enjoyed the moment with him, completely at *maluhia* —peace.

Cord dipped his head and gave her an everlasting kiss before dropping his arms and taking her hand. "What do you say we go inside and tell them the next best improvement to Ironwood Ranch?"

"Next best?" She held back as he reached for the door. "I thought you said this was the best."

His gaze softened. "No. You're the best improvement to this ranch. The best improvement to my life."

She placed her hand on his chest. "Aloha, Cowboy."

His lip quirked up on one side. "Aloha?"

She smiled. "Remember, aloha means grace and love."

"I forgot. I like that." He gazed at her, his love for her shining in his eyes, then he opened the door. "Time to put our stamp on this place, my bride-to-be."

As she walked by, he lowered his head and whispered. "Then tonight we can celebrate."

Her heart warmed. Her life was finally on the perfect track. Holding Cord's hand, she walked into her first family meeting excited, instead of nervous, to tell them all about her and Cord's plans for a dude ranch.

Read on for an excerpt of Wedding at Poker Flat (Poker Flat #5) Releasing 2018

Chapter One

Kendra Lowe absently reached for her ringing phone. "Yes." Her mind was on the profit and loss statement on her computer screen. Closing Poker Flat for five days for the wedding would hurt their bottom line.

"Sorry to bother you, boss, but I have a woman up here at the garage claiming to be your mother."

"What?" She glanced at the time. It was almost two in the morning.

"I didn't know I'd need a security clearance just to see my own daughter. Remind her she invited me to her wedding." Her mother's voice came through Mac's phone loud and clear.

"Did you catch that?" Her security guard's tone held quite a bit of sarcasm, and she couldn't blame her.

"Yes, I did. Bring her down. I'll meet you."

"You've got it." Mac ended the call.

She looked at the small calendar on her desk. The wedding was still a week away. What the hell was she supposed to do with her mother?

Quickly, she hit the keyboard and pulled up the reservations. "Well, damn." Scanning the list of rooms on the resort one more time, she closed it out and rose. Out of habit, she jammed the brown cowboy hat on her head and strode out of her office and into the great room, past the large stone fireplace, and toward the floor to ceiling glass double doors of the log and stucco main building.

Solar ground lights lit the desert pathways outside as well as the circular dirt area for golf carts when guests came in for meals or events. The area directly outside was empty, everyone in their casitas or at each other's depending upon their preferences.

Hopefully, none of them would go out for a midnight stroll and drop into the main building like one pair had last night. The last thing she needed was for her mother to stare in horror at a pair of naked guests.

She leaned on one leg and watched the dull yellow lights of a golf cart crest the other side of the ravine and slowly wind down the switchback path that led to a tiny stream at the bottom. It would be a while before they crossed the bridge at the bottom and made it up to the main building.

She pulled out her phone. She hated waking Wade up in the middle of his night, but there was no way around it.

"What's wrong." His deep voice on the other end settled her nerves far better than any drink could.

Just another reason why she loved him. "Sorry I had to wake you, but my mother just arrived."

"Now? Today?"

"Those were my thoughts exactly, but it's really her. Mac's bringing her to the main building. She's going to have to sleep on our couch tonight."

The momentary silence was telling. "No casita available?"

It wasn't really a question. "No." She didn't want her mother in their space either. It wasn't that she didn't love the woman. She just didn't have a lot of respect for her. She had no backbone. Oh, she talked a good game, but when push came to shove, she always caved.

A heavy sigh sounded over the phone. "I guess there's no help for it. Don't get me wrong, I'm looking forward to meeting her."

She smirked. That was so Wade. "I know you are." He was the one who insisted she invite her mother. Actually, he'd insisted she invite her parents but she drew the line after that parent. "Too bad we couldn't put her in the massage room, but I'm sure there are early morning appointments."

"And that wouldn't be very comfortable for her."

"What about Jorge's office? That has a nice big comfy couch in there. Far bigger than ours." The lights across the ravine had disappeared, which meant her mother was on her way up. "Do you know if any trail rides are scheduled tomorrow morning?"

"Hold on, let me check." The sound of her fiancé pulling out the chair in their home office came across. "I thought the plane ticket you sent was for next week."

"It was." Which is why she was more than just a little confused. "I don't think it's even arrived yet." What was she going to do with her mother for a week? Poker Flat was a nudist resort and last she knew, her mother wasn't a nudist. Actually, she sincerely hoped that was the case. That was a sight she really didn't want to—

"We're in luck. No rides tomorrow at all. Looks like the horses have the day off. I'll get dressed and run our extra set of sheets and a blanket over there. If you can grab a pillow from the linen room, she should be set for the night."

And that was another reason she loved him. He was one

step ahead of her half the time. "I will. Thank you." She headed back down the hall to the laundry area.

"You know you'll owe me one."

She laughed, knowing exactly what he had in mind. "And I'll be happy to 'pay' up." She grabbed their last new pillow all wrapped in plastic and turned out the light. "I'm looking forward to it. The sooner the better." As she entered the lobby again, a glow of lights appeared near the ridge. "I have to go. She's here."

"Remember." Wade's voice held amusement.

Her heart warmed. "I know. You're all-in. See you soon, Cowboy." She ended the call and put her phone in the back pocket of her jeans before taking a deep breath.

As the golf cart pulled in front of the main doors, she strode forward, her cowboy boots loud in the empty building. Pushing one large glass door open, she smiled. Truth be told, she was excited to see her mother again. It has been a few years.

"There she is. The queen." Donna Lowe grabbed the side of the golf cart and unfolded herself from the seat with a grunt. "That was a long ass freakin' ride."

Ignoring the usual complaint, Kendra stepped forward. "Hi, mom."

Her mother, who was more than a few inches shorter than her, finally focused on her and gave her a brief hug, her rose perfume filling the air. When she stepped back she squinted. "Did you get taller?"

"No, I'm the same height I was when I saw you last." Her mother's normally white hair was dyed a dark brown now, but it was still short. The button-down shirt she wore to cover her own large chest was wrinkled, but still a step up from her usual clothing. The striped leggings she wore made her skinny legs look even smaller. With her waist as big as her chest, people who didn't know her might think she would topple over, like humpty-dumpty.

Her mother wiped her hands on her shirt as if they were sweaty. "I'm shrinking. That's what it is." She turned to Mac, who was seriously tall. "You're gonna bring my sweeties and the rest of my bags now, right?"

Mac shook her head. "Not until Kendra tells us where you're staying. Like I said, the resort is full." Mac moved her gaze to her. "Right, boss?"

She nodded. "We are, but I'm sure mom is tired, so we can put her in Jorge's office for tonight. In the morning, Lacey can work her magic I'm sure."

"Office? What, you expect me to sleep on a desk or something?" Her mother frowned, clearly expecting the worse. "Why can't I stay with you?"

"I'm afraid all I have is a small couch and Jorge's office has a big comfy one. Wade has already gone over there and made it up for you."

Her mother crossed her arms over her ample bosom. "The groom. I want to meet this man. I didn't inspect your last fiancé before that marriage and look how that worked out."

Her chest squeezed at the reminder of what an idiot she'd been. "Very true. I'm sure Wade will answer any questions you have tomorrow. I think we should get you settled in."

"To an office. Nice way to treat your mother."

Kendra ignored her mother's mumbled words. She had no doubt her mom would be thrilled with the accommodations once she saw them. "Mac, why didn't you just bring her bags down on the cart?" She'd noticed there was only one bag on the back.

Mac glanced at her mother. "Because we're going to need the wagon to get them all down here."

"What?" She looked at her mom. "What did you bring? The kitchen sink?"

Her mother's lips formed a slow, smug smile. "I would have if I could have cut the pipes."

Airlines charged per bag. Her mother didn't have that kind of money. In fact, she couldn't have received the airline ticket yet, since it had just been mailed two days ago. "Mom, how did you get here?" Even if she took the bus, a cab ride to Poker Flat would have been hundreds of dollars from the Phoenix station.

Her mother shrugged. "I drove."

She widened her eyes. "Drove? You and Fred bought a second car?" Could the man who produced her have gotten his act together after all these years?

Her mother laughed. "Not even close. I took the car, everything I could fit in it and all the money in our account. I've left your father. I'm going to live here while the divorce goes through. Aren't you happy?"

In complete shock, it took her a moment to notice the vibration in her back pocket. Turning away from her mother's triumphant smile, she answered the phone. "Yes?" Her voice came out in a whisper.

"Kendra, what's wrong?" Wade's voice on the other end had her heart clicking into a more normal rhythm. Only he had the sixth sense when it came to her emotions.

Taking a few steps away from her mom, she kept her voice

low. "Mom just informed me she's divorcing Fred and plans to live here until it goes through."

Wade's low whistle on the other end reassured her he understood exactly how impossible the situation was. "That's a big pile of shit to deal with at this early hour in the morning. Just bring her over here, and we'll hash it all out later."

"Right."

"That's awfully rude." Her mother's voice carried as it always did. "It's the middle of the fucking night and she has to take a phone call?"

She took a deep breath. "We'll be right there." Ending the call, she spun around and strode toward her mom. "Okay, let's get you to bed."

"Who was that? Don't they know it's the middle of the night? I've been driving for hours just to see you and you take a call? What's wrong with this generation?"

She ignored her mom's complaining, something she'd learned to do at an early age. "Mac, I'll take it from here. You can grab another golf cart."

"Will do." Her crazy-fit female security guard wasted no time jumping onto another golf cart and beating a hasty exit. Kendra didn't blame her.

Finally, she turned back to her mom. "If you'd like to climb back in, I'll take you over to the stable manager's office. It's a whole separate building and has everything you'll need including a full bathroom."

Her mother stepped up into the passenger side of the cart still grumbling. "Now you're putting me in a stable. What do I look like, Mary Magdalen? I'm not pregnant. I'm not fat either. Things just shifted. It's called post menopause and it will happen to you, too. Just wait. Hey, what about my stuff? Is that amazon going to bring them?"

She turned the cart on and pressed the pedal. "Not tonight. I want to get you a real room, so you can have your own space. There are no trail rides scheduled tomorrow, but I'm sure Jorge and Crystal will need to use the office at some point."

Her mother grabbed a hold of the side of the cart as they went over a rock. "So now I'm an inconvenience?"

"Of course not. We just weren't expecting you until next week. Every guest room is booked right now. It's winter and high season for tourists." She glanced at her mom. "I wanted to make as much money as possible so I can afford to feed all our wedding guests." That her mother would get.

"That's my girl. You take after me, you know. Your father couldn't keep a nickel in his pocket if it was stuck in there with chewed gum. But me—" Her mother's smile became devious. "I know how to stretch a penny and save. What your father doesn't know won't hurt him."

Her stomach lurched. She didn't want to know, but her gut told her she would soon be learning all the torrid details soon. She was torn about her mother's announcement. Half of her was damn proud of her. Fred had always treated her mother like crap. She'd even stopped calling him dad at the age of nine because she couldn't stand the thought that they were related in any way.

But the other half of her worried about the repercussions of her mother's decision, both in what might happen for her mom and how it would affect her and Wade. Fred wouldn't take his housekeeper and cook skipping out on him laying down.

She drove the golf cart up the slight incline toward the

barn and office. Despite knowing she'd probably regret it, she had to ask. "Why did you finally leave Fred. He didn't hurt you, did he?" The thought of him hitting her mother had her hands squeezing the steering wheel.

"Of course not! If he dared lay a hand on me, I'd beat his scrawny ass from here to kingdom come."

She relaxed. Fred was an unfaithful asshole and a drunk, but he'd never done anything physically abusive. He didn't have to, his mouth did it all for him.

"Then why did you leave him now?"

Her mother grinned. "When you called and said you owned a resort and were getting married, I figured you had finally settled down."

Okay, that might be true, but what did that have to do with leaving Fred? "I don't understand."

"It's simple. Sally left the park after her husband died and moved in with her son and daughter-in-law. Betty's daughter renovated her garage into a mother-in-law apartment so Betty could leave that falling apart trailer she was living in. And now I can move here to be with my daughter."

Kendra was back to squeezing the steering wheel as she pulled to a stop in front of the stable manager's office next to the golf cart already parked there, her shock and fear so complete she wasn't sure she could move.

Luckily, Wade opened the door and strode out, a smile on his face as he walked toward her mother's side of the golf cart. "You must be Donna. I'd know you were Kendra's mother even in a crowded fair. You are obviously where she got her good looks."

Her mother looked at her and rolled her eyes before

turning back to Wade. "Well now, if that ain't a crock of shit I don't know what is?" She waved him toward her. "And you just keep piling it on honey."

Wade chuckled as he tipped his hat. "I'll do my best, ma'am."

Her mother looked over at her again. "Is he for real?"

She managed a weak nod.

"Well, damn me to hell and back. I'm gonna like it here." Her mother turned toward Wade, who offered her his hand to help her out. "Oh, yeah, I'm gonna like it here a lot."

For a peek at Hailey and Dillon's story, read on for an excerpt of Dillon's Dare.

Chapter One

"What the hell?" Dillon Hatcher stepped out of the barn at Last Chance Ranch to find a hot air balloon sinking fast just beyond the house.

"What is it?" His grandmother joined him, wiping her brow with the back of her gloved hand. "Well, I'll be a burro's butt. Are they supposed to come down that quickly?"

At her question, the fear in his gut was confirmed. "Shit, no." Running for the corral where Eclipse was trying to impress Macy, he whistled. The black stallion turned at his call and broke into a run. Dillon swung the gate wide, and as the horse came to a halt before him, he grabbed his mane, jumped on his back, and kicked him toward the soon-to-crash balloon.

Galloping through the desert, as opposed to the new dirt road put in for Cole and Lacey's house, made it a shorter ride, but he still wasn't going to get there before touchdown. "Come on, boy."

Unfortunately, his position gave him the perfect view of the catastrophe about to unfold. Two people stood in the basket, one working on something while the other was clearly yelling. He hoped his grandmother had called 911.

"Holy shit." The balloon dropped fast, closer to the prickly pear cacti covering the area. Just as the basket was about to meet its shadow on the ground, it jerked upward about twelve feet.

His heart in his throat, he squeezed his thighs to get Eclipse to slow down and jumped to the ground.

The balloon floated slowly down to Earth, somehow finding an empty spot between the plant life.

Running up, he grabbed the rope lying on the ground, not sure he'd be able to keep the balloon from moving, but it had to be worth a try.

Laughter, light and happy, came from the basket, causing him to move his gaze to the occupants. The contrast between them couldn't have been greater. A dark-haired man scowled and shook his head at the woman with golden blonde hair, who was clearly thrilled by the experience. Somewhere in the back of his head he was thinking that she should be screaming or crying at the operator of the balloon.

"Hector, that was awesome!" She threw her hands up before giving Hector a squeeze he clearly didn't appreciate.

"You almost destroyed my balloon."

She pulled back, keeping her hand on his arm. "You know if that happened, I'd take care of it. How am I supposed to learn? I have to do it myself. I have to make my own mistakes and learn from them. And look, I did! Here we are safe and sound."

From the man's shaking head, Dillon was pretty sure he wasn't convinced. That's when the man saw him and nodded in his direction.

The blonde turned around and he froze, irritation sizzling up his spine. "You."

"Dillon Hatcher, right?" She hopped up on the edge of

the basket and jumped down onto the desert floor. "I didn't expect you to be out here."

"Hailey Pennington, are you crazy?" He stared at the woman his mother had been trying to get his brother and now him to marry. Or rather, one of the women she wanted them to marry.

Hailey paused, cocking her head to the side. "I don't think so. You are Dillon, right?"

He barely controlled the low growl wanting to come out and threw his free hand up toward the balloon. "I mean the balloon. What the hell were you doing driving that thing, or flying or whatever you call it?"

She grinned. "Oh, I was learning how to fly it. It's an amazing feeling." Her green eyes lit with the thrill of her adventure. "Have you ever been in one?"

His stomach lurched at the thought. "If man was intended to fly, he would have been given wings. I keep my feet firmly planted on mother Earth."

"Well, it's exhilarating to reach beyond our limitations. You should try it some time." She spun toward the balloon. "You can go, Hector. I'll just catch a ride back to my car."

Hector looked him over as if deciding if he was safe to be in Hailey's company then scowled.

He let the man off the hook. "Go ahead, Hector. I'm sure someone at the ranch house can give Ms. Pennington a ride. It's probably safer than letting her back in your balloon."

Hector's lip quirked up before he nodded.

Hailey turned back to him, giving him a brilliant smile. "That's very gracious of you."

"This way." He handed the rope to Hector and turned on

his heel toward Eclipse. As much as he wanted to jump on his horse's back and return to the house without Hailey Pennington, his mother had raised him right, despite her machinations to marry him off, and he'd walk her back. Besides, he'd catch hell from his grandmother if he left Hailey out here.

He stepped up to Eclipse and patted the stallion on his neck. "Come on boy, we're heading back."

"Is this your horse?" Hailey walked to Eclipse's other side and started to pet him, cooing as if he were a baby. "You handsome boy. I bet you make all the fillies giddy."

Dillon rolled his eyes and clicked his tongue. Eclipse turned toward him and moved forward toward the ranch. "Yes, he's my horse."

Hailey let Eclipse walk by her then fell into step next to him. "He has no saddle or bridle. You must have been in a hurry."

He ground his teeth as anger surged anew at the almost mishap. "It *did* look as if you were going to crash. I wouldn't be surprised if Gram called 911."

"Oh, Annette is here? That's wonderful."

At her obviously happy mood, he grew more irritated. "Which begs the question, why are you here? You're a long way from Ironwood or was the balloon crash just a coincidence." He let his sarcasm be obvious.

She gave him a disgruntled look. "That's a nice welcome for a guest. As a matter of fact, I've been taking lessons up here for a little privacy. Too many people know me closer to Tucson, and since I'm in the market for a rescue horse, I thought I'd kill two birds with one stone, so to speak."

And almost kill herself while she was at it. Still, a twinge of guilt crept into his conscience for assuming the worst, which was that his mother had sent her to stalk him. If Hailey was really at Last Chance to buy a horse, he needed to retrieve his manners. His brother, Cole, was always looking for kind owners for his rescue horses.

He had no idea if Hailey was kind to her animals, but he did know the Ironwood Ranch had a luxurious stable for its working horses. "Cole will be pleased to hear that. He's at the fire station today, but I'm sure Trace would be happy to show you the horses that are ready to leave or almost ready to leave."

"That would be great. I think what Cole has done here at your grandparents' ranch is wonderful."

"Yeah." It *was* wonderful, and it never would have happened if his mother hadn't refused to allow Cole to do it at Morning Creek. Despite missing his home, he was happy with his decision to move to his brother's and grandparents' horse rescue ranch. His mother had to learn that he wasn't her puppet.

"Did you get Eclipse from here?" She sounded so impressed, it made him want to say yes.

"No, I bought him." Much to his mother's displeasure, which had been exactly what he wanted, though it hadn't been his primary motivation for purchasing the Frisian stallion.

"He's beautiful."

He glanced over at her. She was admiring his horse who had his ass to them. For some reason, that lightened his mood. "Your family has a lot of horses. Why do you need another?" Shit, that sounded accusatory, though he hadn't meant it to be.

She moved her gaze from his horse to him. "I know, but I thought it would be a nice thing to do to give a rescued horse a home for the rest of his or her life."

Though she appeared sincere, his bullshit meter woke up. "Did my mother send you out here?"

Her head jerked back as if he'd slapped her and her brows lowered. "No, why would your mom have anything to do with my decision to buy a horse from Cole?"

Now he'd gone and stepped in it. He shook his head. "No reason." Though he didn't look at her, he could feel her gaze on him.

"Dillon, why are you here at Last Chance? Last I saw you, you were living at Morning Creek breeding American Quarter horses."

Yup, he'd stepped in it and now he was up to his waist in shit. "Hanging out with my cousins." That was true…in a sense.

"It's your mother, isn't it?"

He snapped his head around to look at her. At the sympathy in her eyes, he dropped his gaze.

Hailey sighed. "I can't imagine what it must be like to have Beverly as your mom. She's been less than subtle about getting me or one of my friends interested in you and Cole. At Cole's wedding, she must have been getting desperate because she even introduced me to Trace."

At the sound of Hailey's chuckle, he glanced at her. Her cheeks were pink with the sun or the heat, he wasn't sure.

"I thought Whisper was going to lose it and hit your mother a good one to the jaw."

He wouldn't put it past his cousin's girlfriend. She didn't exactly act like most people in social situations. "I'm sorry my mother has been so obvious about her wishes."

She waved away his apology. "Oh, don't be. She's not the

first and she won't be the last to try to bring a Pennington into her family. When you're part of the oldest family in Arizona, you get used to it."

He'd never thought about it from her perspective. While Morning Creek Ranch was a thriving Quarter horse operation, Ironwood Ranch was the largest cattle ranch in the state. "And the wealthiest." Shit, that was rude.

Hailey laughed. "Yes, that, too. My poor middle brother, Cord, really takes issue with it and hides on the ranch most of the time, but the rest of us are fine with it."

He couldn't help looking over at her. She was so comfortable in her own skin. He liked that.

She turned her head toward him. "How long have you been hiding out here?"

He shrugged. "A couple months."

"Ah, that explains the long hair. The last time I saw you, I think it was at Cole's wedding, you had it very short."

He rubbed one side of his face with his hand, partly from habit, partly from the realization he also hadn't shaved in a couple days. He probably looked like he'd been out on the range for a week. "I think Last Chance is just as good a place as Morning Creek." Even if he did miss his work at home. Had Salud foaled yet?

Hailey shook her head. "Beverly must have really—ack!"

Luckily, he was looking at her when she tripped and started to fall. He grabbed her arms, just before she hit the ground.

Pulling her back up, he was unprepared for her to fall against him, and his body immediately responded to her soft breasts as they pressed against his chest.

Just as quickly, she tried to step back. "Ow."

Once again, she lost her balance.

He helped her stay upright, careful to hold her away from him.

"Shit. Excuse my language. I think I twisted my ankle."

He looked toward the ranch house. They were still a ways off. He clicked his tongue and Eclipse stopped. "Here, you can ride on Eclipse."

"Hold on, let me see if I can walk it out. It might just be sore." She held onto his arm and hobbled forward a couple steps before conceding. "I think you're right. Damn, I'm supposed to go out with my friends tonight."

"To the movies?" If that was the case, she could get a pair of crutches and hobble in.

She shook her head. "No, dancing."

He helped her over to Eclipse. "Grab his mane and step into my hands with your good foot."

She did as he asked, and he lifted her up high enough for her to swing her leg over. That she did it with ease wasn't lost on him.

He walked around to the other side. "Your ankle could be swelling. Let's get you to the house and get it packed in ice."

She grinned down at him. "Yes, doctor."

He ignored her comment, instead patting Eclipse to get him walking again.

"He's a large one. I thought you bred American Quarter horses."

He didn't look at her. "We do."

"Um, this big guy is no Quarter horse."

"As I said, I bought him. I wasn't planning to breed him. Just ride him."

At the sound of Hailey's laughter, he finally looked up. Her chin tilted up, and her cheeks were rosy as her lips lifted in a wide smile. Was she always so happy? Then again, she was a Pennington, so there wasn't much to cause her trouble. "Did I say something funny?"

She shook her head. "I guess not. It just struck me as funny. Here I was thinking you had some grand plan to start a new breed or something and you simply bought him to ride. I like that."

He looked forward again, avoiding the cacti as they came closer to the house. His grand plan had been to buy a reliable horse and piss off his mother, and he'd succeeded. Unfortunately, it hadn't stopped her from trying to marry him off. If she even thought he was talking to Hailey right now, the wedding invitations would be in the mail.

The last thing he had any intention of doing was marrying someone his mother had chosen. One of the great things about living at Last Chance was that the local women had no idea he was connected to Morning Creek, so he'd been having fun dating everyone from a cocktail waitress at the Black Mustang to Dr. Jenna's closest neighbor.

He only had two criteria for the women he saw. They couldn't be someone his mother picked out and they couldn't be wealthy. Anyone else was possible relationship material, and if they liked his long hair even better.

Hailey admired Dillon as he strode through the desert in his tight blue jeans and sleeveless button-down shirt. Every step he took was sure and confident. She'd liked that about him the first time they'd met at his home when Beverly was trying to interest her in Cole.

He'd come in from outside while they were in the kitchen, his face covered in sweat as he'd walked in. Taking off his hat, he nodded to her as his mother gave a half-hearted introduction. Then he'd pulled a cooler out of a lower cabinet, filled it with bottled water from the fridge and lifted it into one strong arm as he grabbed up his hat with the other.

"It was nice to meet you, Miss Pennington." Were his final words before striding out the door.

She couldn't help looking at his ass as he exited. Even then, she'd thought him much more attractive than his brother. It was one reason why she'd always accepted Beverly's invitations. Her hope was that she might see Dillon again. It happened less often than she'd wished.

Despite her best efforts to forget about him, when she'd come to his brother's New Year's Eve party only to discover it was a surprise wedding, she'd finally accepted that she had a crush on Dillon, who just happened to look hot in his tuxedo since he was the best man…in so many ways.

At first, she thought fate was on her side as Beverly went out of her way after that to throw the two of them together as often as possible, but the more his mother pushed, the less he'd participated.

She wasn't sure, but she had a feeling the final straw was the Bachelor Auction for a children's charity. She'd seen that Dillon was on the roster of men to be auctioned off, presumably to take the lucky lady, who was willing to bid the highest for charity, on a date of her choice. There was no way she'd let anyone else have him if he'd volunteered, but if his mother had somehow forced him, she had planned to bid the highest and let him off the hook. His mother was more of a hinderance than a help in this instance.

Her excitement had grown as she caught a glimpse of him getting out of his truck in a black shirt covered in rhinestones. On any other man it would have looked feminine, but Dillon filled it out perfectly and that stride of his just made her sigh.

Yet when they called his name to come out on stage, her heart beating so hard she could barely breathe, he never appeared. The announcer covered it up, joking that men were a dime a dozen that night and moved on to the next bachelor. Since no matter what Beverly had conjured up, Dillon had always been polite, she had a feeling something big must have occurred between them.

It had taken her a while to figure out where he might have gone. When she finally did, she'd hatched her own plan. Maybe without Beverly, they could get to know each other like normal people. "So, bring me up to speed on how everyone is. I haven't been here since the wedding, though I heard that Beverly told your grandmother about Whisper's parents. I knew I knew her from somewhere."

"Yeah, that didn't go over so well. Things got hairy there for a while, but her and Trace are living in a couple trailers up on the north ridge."

"A couple trailers? You mean they aren't together?"

He shook his head but didn't look up at her. "Oh, they're together. Whisper and Trace in the new one and Old Billy and Uncle Joey in the other."

"I don't think I met those two men."

He chuckled, something she'd yet to hear him do. "Those

two were meant to be friends. Uncle Joey can't talk due to a stroke, but he understands everything, and Billy never shuts up. It's a perfect pair."

That sounded precious. "I would love to meet them."

He looked up at her at that. "You would?"

She smiled. "Of course, they sound interesting."

He looked forward again shaking his head, but he didn't comment.

They were almost to the house, which meant soon she would have to share him with everyone else. "What about your cousin Logan?" Beverly had tried to get her interested in him as well, but the man barely spoke two words to her, which was just fine with her. "He didn't seem very happy at the wedding."

"He's happy now. He and Charlotte moved in with Dr. Jenna, the vet who checks out the horses here at Last Chance."

"That's great to hear. I mean, about Logan and that the vet checks out the horses. I have a feeling I'm not going to be able to look at any today though. I really hope this ankle isn't a sprain. I've had one of those and they take forever to heal."

Dillon led the horse right up to the front porch. "Don't worry. If you have to come back, the same horses will probably still be here along with some new ones." He shook his head. "I don't understand it."

"Understand what?"

He looked at her then. "I don't understand how people can be so inhumane to these outstanding animals." His blue eyes blazed with anger under his dark brows, proving him to be a man of strong emotions, which she'd always suspected.

"I don't either. I've always felt their punishment should be equal to what they inflict."

He nodded curtly before reaching his arms up. "Let's get you down from there and into the house."

More than happy to slip into his arms, she placed both her hands on his shoulders, glad he'd come to the side with her good ankle, though she fervently wished they were both good.

He grasped her waist and pulled her toward him until her leg cleared the horse's back. He was a big man, so his strength didn't surprise her, but it did cause the faeries in her stomach to dance around. As she landed on her good foot, she made sure to keep her other from touching the ground. She couldn't afford to have it ruin all her plans.

Dillon kept her at arms-length, not really where she wanted to be.

"Can you walk?" He appeared concerned.

That had to be a good thing. "I don't know. Let me have your arm, just in case."

He let go of her waist and held out his arm. She was more than happy to grasp his bare forearm, the muscle beneath her hand like a rock. Their warmer than usual November had its advantages after all, like Dillon wearing a sleeveless shirt that revealed his masculine arms.

Taking a step on her sore ankle, she felt a sharp twinge and quickly compensated with her other foot. "Crap. It figures I could land a hot air balloon safely but can't seem to walk through the desert without injuring myself."

Dillon shook his head. "No use complaining about it now. Let's get you up these stairs."

She was pretty sure her ankle wasn't sprained, but the thought of testing it on the steps had her pulling back. "I guess I could hop up?"

He gave a heavy sigh. "No. You'd probably break your neck." Peeling her hand from his arm, he scooped her up and strode up the three steps.

She'd barely had time to enjoy the thrill of being in his arms before he set her down on the wrap-around porch. Luckily, he kept one arm around her back because sore ankle or not, she was sure she'd lose her balance after that excitement.

"Gram, we have a guest," Dillon yelled into the house, the screen door the only obstacle to his voice.

In no time, footsteps sounded on the hardwood floors. "Is it the idiot who almost crash-landed?"

Hailey felt her cheeks heat, but at Dillon's mortified look, she sucked it up. "Yes, it's the idiot who almost crashed in your backyard, though I need to emphasize the *almost*."

The screen door opened, and Annette Benson stood in the doorway.

"Hello, Mrs. Benson."

"Hailey Pennington. What are you doing here?"

She chuckled. "Crash-landing in your backyard."

Annette waved her comment aside. "But as you said, you didn't. Come in."

Dillon held out his arm again. "If you could hold the door Gram, I can help her in."

Annette's brows lowered in concern before she stepped out, keeping the door open. "What happened?"

She grasped Dillon's forearm again and used it to hobble into the farmhouse kitchen. It was a lot like the one at Ironwood, with a few more windows which made it a lot brighter. She waited as he pulled a chair out for her then sat, grateful to be off her foot.

Annette bustled in after them. "Dillon, pull out another chair and grab a couch pillow from the family room, so she can put her foot up." Annette turned to her. "I'm assuming you hurt your foot in the landing?"

She shook her head. "No. I brought that baby down with barely a bump, but I couldn't seem to put one foot in front of the other without tripping on the ground."

"*You* brought the balloon down?"

At Annette's surprise, she grinned. "I did. Made a couple mistakes at first but figured it out in time. It was the walking that did me in." She pouted before she grinned.

"But why here?" Annette pulled a pitcher from the refrigerator and took out two glasses.

She was about to answer when Dillon came back in and set up the chair next to her with a pillow.

"Try that." He stood back and let her put her foot on the chair.

"Dillon, you need to take off her boot so we can see if it's swollen. Actually, I think we should ice it down anyway."

"Really, Mrs. Benson I don't—"

"Don't even try." Dillon shook his head. "It will go a lot better for you to just do as she says." He sat on another chair and gently pulled the boot off and studied her sock.

Shit. She'd never thought he'd be looking at her socks when she'd dressed herself that morning.

"Hailey." His voice was deep, but there was a hint of humor in it. "Why do you have on purple socks with black bats on them?"

"Dillon."

At Annette's scolding tone, he smirked. "It doesn't look swollen."

As he sat back, she peered down at her ankle. Thank her lucky stars because she needed her foot if she was going to catch his attention. "No, it doesn't. I'm so glad."

He met her gaze. "But I think your dance plans for tonight are still off."

That was fine with her.

"Dance plans?" Annette bustled over with a dishtowel full of ice. "Absolutely not. You're not going anywhere, young woman."

Huh? She widened her eyes and snapped her gaze to Dillon, who just shrugged.

"You're going to stay right here." Annette carefully placed the knotted dishtowel on her ankle. "Until you can walk again, it's our responsibility to see you are well since it was our land that tripped you up."

Also by Lexi Post

Contemporary Cowboy Romance

Cowboys Never Fold
(Poker Flat Series: Book 1)
Cowboy's Match
(Poker Flat Series: Book 2)
Cowboy's Best Shot
(Poker Flat Series: Book 3)
Cowboy's Break
(Poker Flat Series: Book 4)
Wedding at Poker Flat
(Poker Flat Series: Book 5) *Coming 2018*

Christmas with Angel
(Poker Flat Series Book 2.5/Last Chance Series: Book 1)
Trace's Trouble
(Last Chance Series: Book 2)
Fletcher's Flame
(Last Chance Series: Book 3)

Logan's Luck
(Last Chance Series: Book 4)
Dillon's Dare
(Last Chance Series: Book 5)
Riley's Rescue
(Last Chance Series: Book 6) *Coming 2019*

Aloha Cowboy (Island Cowboy #1)

Military Romance

When Love Chimes
(Broken Valor Series: Book 1)
Poisoned Honor
(Broken Valor Series: Book 2)

Paranormal Romance

Masque
Passion's Poison
Passion of Sleepy Hollow
Heart of Frankenstein

Pleasures of Christmas Past
(A Christmas Carol Series: Book 1)
Desires of Christmas Present
(A Christmas Carol Series: Book 2)
Temptations of Christmas Future
(A Christmas Carol Series: Book 3)

One of A Kind Christmas
(A Christmas Carol Series: Book 4)*Coming 2018*

On Highland Time
(Time Weavers, Inc. Book 1)

Sci-fi Romance

Cruise into Eden
(The Eden Series: Book 1)
Unexpected Eden
(The Eden Series: Book 2)
Eden Discovered
(The Eden Series: Book 3)
Eden Revealed
(The Eden Series: Book 4)
Avenging Eden
(The Eden Series: Book 5)
Beast of Eden
(Eden Series: Book 6) *Coming 2019*

About Lexi Post

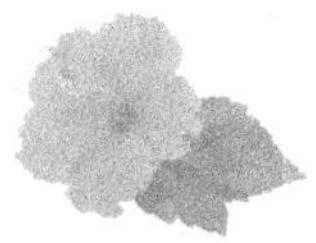

Lexi Post is a New York Times and USA Today bestselling author of romance inspired by the classics. She spent years in higher education taking and teaching courses about the classical literature she loved. From Edgar Allan Poe's short story "The Masque of the Red Death" to Tolstoy's *War and Peace*, she's read, studied, and taught wonderful classics.

But Lexi's first love is romance novels. In an effort to marry her two first loves, she started writing romance inspired by the classics and found she loved it. From hot paranormals to sizzling cowboys to hunks from out of this world, Lexi provides a sensuous experience with a "whole lotta story."

Lexi is living her own happily ever after with her husband and her cat in Florida. She makes her own ice cream every weekend, loves bright colors, and you will never see her without a hat.

www.lexipostbooks.com